# Christmas Bliss

# Mary Kay Andrews

## *Christmas Bliss*

ST. MARTIN'S PRESS
New York

CHRISTMAS BLISS. Copyright © 2013 by Whodunnit, Inc. All rights reserved. Printed in the United States of America. For information, address St. Martin's Press, 175 Fifth Avenue, New York, N.Y. 10010.

www.stmartins.com

*Design by Kathryn Parise*

THE LIBRARY OF CONGRESS CATALOGING-IN-PUBLICATION DATA IS AVAILABLE UPON REQUEST.

ISBN 978-1-250-01972-1 (hardcover)
ISBN 978-1-250-01973-8 (e-book)

St. Martin's Press books may be purchased for educational, business, or promotional use. For information on bulk purchases, please contact Macmillan Corporate and Premium Sales Department at 1-800-221-7945, extension 5442, or write specialmarkets@macmillan.com.

First Edition: October 2013

10  9  8  7  6  5  4  3  2  1

*For Stuart Krichevsky,*
*who saw something I couldn't,*
*and made me believe I could*

# Acknowledgments

✦

Deepest thanks go to Savannah attorney Carl Pedigo, and U.S. Coast Guard Petty Officer Mark Barney, Miami, District 7 Public Affairs office, for legal and technical advice. Any errors or misstatements in this book are my own and not theirs. Extra thanks to the SKLA team— Stuart Krichevsky, Shana Cohen, and Ross Harris—not just for their usual stalwart expertise and support, but this time around for help with New York landmarks and logistics. With each new book I am reminded of how lucky I am to have the amazing Jennifer Enderlin as my editor. Thanks also to everybody at St. Martin's Press who make my books happen—including, but not limited to, Sally Richardson and Matthew Shear, Jeanne-Marie Hudson, Anne Marie Talberg, and art director Michael Storrings, whose covers just get better and better. Meg Walker of Tandem Literary is my secret marketing weapon and a dear friend and colleague. And thanks and love to my family—Tom, Katie, Andy, and Mark, who make every day together as sweet as Christmas morning.

# Christmas Bliss

✦

# Chapter 1

✦

*'Twas the week before Christmas*

Jean Eloise Foley!"

Marian Foley tugged hard at the fabric of the ivory lace dress. "How am I going to fix this dress if you can't stand still for five minutes?"

I squirmed and looked over my shoulder and down at my mama, who was glaring up at me. I was standing on a none-too-sturdy wooden kitchen stool, and in high heels yet.

The volume on the red plastic radio that had stood on my parents' green Formica countertop for as long as I can remember was turned down, but I could still hear strains of Brenda Lee singing "Jingle Bell Rock" and the telltale ching-ching of the cell phone on the counter next to the radio.

"Mama," I pleaded. "That has to be Daniel, texting me. Can't we just stop for a minute so I can grab my phone?"

"Don't you move," Mama managed to say, despite the fact that her lips were clamped tight around a clutch of dressmaker's pins. "Not an inch. We have to get this dress fitted and pinned today. No more excuses. We're already weeks behind schedule, and if I don't get started cutting this dress down this afternoon, you'll be getting married in your slip."

"Wouldn't Daniel just love that." I looked longingly at my phone, which sat only a few feet away. "I'm dying to hear how it went at Cucina Carlotta last night. There were rumors the food critic from the *New York Times* might sneak in."

"I don't care if the pope himself ate there," Mama said. "Daniel Stipanek can just wait his turn. Anyway, didn't he call you last night?"

"No," I admitted. "He's been so crazy busy with work, he hasn't had a minute to talk. So we've been texting."

"Ridiculous," Mama said with a sniff. "I don't know why you all can't just pick up a phone and communicate like normal people. I still don't understand all this texting foolishness."

"He's been up there for three weeks, and he's still working nearly eighteen-hour days. He warned me it would be like this. New York isn't like Savannah. He says the pace is twice as fast as it is here, and the kitchen is twice as big as his kitchen here at Guale. Cucina seats eighty people—that's a lot! He's spending most of his waking hours in the middle of a kitchen surrounded by the staff. He doesn't want people listening in on our private conversation. Anyway, it's only for one more week. Then he'll be home, the wedding is Christmas Eve, and then life is back to normal, until we can get around to the honeymoon in Paris."

"What makes you think he won't want to stay up there in New York after the wedding? Savannah is going to seem like Hicksville to him now," Mama warned. "The next thing I know, you'll be telling me you're moving up there for good."

"Daniel doesn't want to work for somebody else—even if Carlotta Donatello does own the hottest, hippest restaurant in New York right now. I keep telling you, he's only a guest chef. It's some sort of gimmick. Mrs. Donatello has invited six different chefs from all over the country to come in, design menus from their own region, and run the kitchen for a month at a time. It's a huge honor that she asked Daniel to be the only Southern chef. And it's great publicity for Guale."

"If you say so," Mama said, but her face showed she was clearly dubious of any enterprise that threatened to send her only child off to the wilds of what she considered the frozen wastelands of the North.

"I do. Now, if you'd just hand me my phone," I coaxed, "I can find out how it went last night."

Instead, Mama cinched in another two inches of lace on the right s de seam of the dress.

"Owww!" I howled. "That was my hip you just pinned."

Jethro, my black Lab mix who was lounging nearby under the dinette table, raised his muzzle, and gave a short, sharp warning bark.

"Hush," Mama said, giving Jethro a withering stare. "You too, Weezie. Quit squirming and stalling, and quit being such a baby."

She gave a long, martyred sigh. "Honestly, I don't know why you can't just go out to the mall and buy a nice new dress like every other girl in the country. This old thing is way too big and way too long on you. You're swimming in it. There's no easy way to shorten this skirt with all this scalloped lace at the hem. I'm going to have to completely remove the skirt from the waist and cut it off there. Same thing with the sleeves. They were three-quarters on me, but look, on you, they hang down almost to your wrists."

She bunched the fabric on the opposite side of the dress and pinned, and that time, I swear, she drew blood.

"Damn, Sam!"

"Sorry," Mama muttered. "I told you to stand still."

"I *am* standing still. I know it's a lot of work, but I've always dreamed of getting married in Meemaw's dress. I could spend ten thousand dollars and not find a dress as perfect as this one. Or one that means as much to me."

"Then why didn't you wear it the first time?" Mama shot back.

I winced. Mama has never recovered from the demise of what was supposed to be my fairy-tale marriage to Talmadge Evans III, the scion of an old, socially prominent Savannah family. That marriage had an unhappy ending after Tal cheated with Caroline DeSantos, a dark-haired vixen who'd worked at his architecture firm. Caroline had ended badly too, murdered by a romantic rival.

"I was only twenty and dumb as dirt back then," I said. "Tal's mother brainwashed me with all that crap about how every Evans bride for five generations had worn that stupid gown of theirs. Their gown, their church, their friends. This time around, the wedding is all Daniel and me."

Marian took a step back and considered her handiwork. "I still don't think it's right, you wearing a white dress for a second wedding."

I fluffed the billowy tulle skirt. "It's not white anymore. It's closer to buttercream. Anyway, if Daniel had his way, we'd get married in flip-flops and shorts on the beach out at Tybee. He's being a good sport to put up with even the tiny little ceremony we're having at my house on Charlton. But he knows how much it means to me to wear the dress you and Meemaw wore."

"Hmpph," Marian said. "Now you're just being silly and sentimental."

Marian Foley didn't do sentimental. She lived in the here and now. She liked her furniture and clothing new and store-bought, her coffee strong and black, and a nice, orderly life. But I've always been the exact opposite, a dreamer and a schemer who made my living selling antiques, which she thought of as peddling other people's castoffs.

I smoothed my hands over the gown's creamy lace-over-satin bodice. As I was growing up, my grandmother had often told me stories about taking the train up to Atlanta from Savannah, to buy the fabric and lace for her wedding dress at Rich's Department Store. The gown was a confection straight out of the 1950s, with an off-the-shoulder bateau neckline and a tight-fitted ruched waist that billowed out at the hips into a ballet-length skirt consisting of reembroidered lace over layers of tulle.

"Go ahead and hop down and take it off," Mama directed. "I want to get started on it this afternoon."

She was helping me unfasten the row of tiny satin-covered buttons when the kitchen door opened and my daddy, balding and still in his pajama bottoms and house slippers, walked slowly into the kitchen, sniffing the air expectantly.

He planted a kiss on the top of my head.

"Marian, when's lunch?" he asked plaintively. "I'm getting pretty hungry."

"Joe, honey, you know you just had lunch an hour ago," Mama said, rolling her eyes. "Remember? You had a grilled cheese sandwich and some tomato soup and some Christmas cookies Weezie brought you."

Daddy rubbed the graying stubble on his chin. "I already ate?"

"Sure did," I said. "You even ate the other half of my sandwich."

"Oh, well, all right then," he said. He looked me up and down and beamed his usual loving smile. "Shug, you look real pretty in that dress. Are you going to a party?"

Mama's face paled and two bright pink circles bloomed on her cheeks. "You know Weezie's getting married in a week. This was my wedding dress. Weezie's going to wear it when she marries Daniel on Christmas Eve. Remember? We've been talking about it for months now."

Daddy bristled. "I know that, Marian. Think I don't know my own daughter is getting married? She's marrying that boy at the restaurant. Some name that starts with a D. You don't have to treat me like a child, Marian."

"I'm sorry," Mama said.

"His name is Daniel," I reminded him. "Daniel Stipanek."

"Damned right," Daddy muttered. He turned and shuffled out of the kitchen, his worn leather shoes sliding on the checkered linoleum.

I waited until he was completely out of earshot. "Mama, how long has Daddy been like this?"

"Like what?" Marian frowned down at the gown. "I believe I'm just going to hand-baste these side seams and then fit it on you again before I do any cutting."

"Like that," I said, gesturing toward the door where my father had just exited. "Mama, you can't pretend you don't notice. Daddy didn't remember he'd eaten lunch. He didn't know why I was wearing your wedding dress, or even Daniel's name."

"He's fine. Just a little forgetful, that's all. You'll forget things too, when you're nearly eighty."

She lifted the dress over my head and laid it across the back of a kitchen chair.

"I think it's more than that," I said gently. "He hasn't shaved today. That's not like him. Used to be, sometimes he'd shave twice in one day, especially if company was coming over. And he's still wearing his pajama bottoms and slippers."

"Would you please just drop it?" Mama's voice was shrill. "It's Saturday. He likes to sleep in. Forty years with the post office and now that he's retired, he can do as he pleases. Do you have to make a federal case about it?"

"No," I said, knowing the subject was closed. "You're right, he's probably fine." I picked up my phone and read the text message.

"Is it from Daniel?" Mama asked. "Does he say how it went last night?"

"It's from Julio, one of Daniel's chefs at the restaurant. Just reminding me that I'm doing a tasting of the food for the reception this afternoon." I was trying not to let her see how disappointed I was that the text wasn't from Daniel himself. "Guess I better get over there."

"Go on then," Mama said. She picked up the dress and began threading a needle.

"Look," I said, sitting down on the chair beside hers. "You're right. It's not fair to put this much work on you. I'll hire somebody to alter the dress."

"No!" Mama cried. Her eyes were suddenly red-rimmed. She clutched the gown with both hands. "I *want* to do this. For you. I don't want a stranger cutting up your grandmother's dress."

"All right." I gave a short whistle and Jethro crawled out from beneath the table and trotted over toward the kitchen door. I gave my mother a quick hug. "I'll talk to you later. Tell Daddy bye for me."

"Don't forget to tell those folks at the restaurant to save a place on the buffet for my fruitcake," Mama called after me. "You know how everybody always anticipates it this time of year."

Anticipates it? Dreaded it, was more like it. Mama's fruitcake was notorious in Savannah. Heavier than a concrete block, drier than sawdust, and studded with weird candied fruits in colors not found in nature, it showed up on the doorsteps of family and friends every year at Christmas, wrapped in tinfoil and tied up with one of the recycled bows Mama had been saving my whole life. I could have repaved my patio with the blocks of fruitcake she's presented me with over the years. Instead, every year, I politely thanked her for the fruitcake and then promptly pitched it in the trash, unopened. Even Jethro knew better than to try that fruitcake.

The Saturday lunch rush at Guale had subsided. Julio stood by the table nearest to the kitchen door, in his spotless white chef's smock, a pale blue linen kerchief knotted smartly around his neck. He gestured proudly at the dishes arrayed around the tabletop. "I hope you're hungry."

My eyes widened. There were at least a dozen platters and bowls. "Good heavens. I thought Daniel said we were just doing appetizers for the reception."

Julio shrugged. "We are the best restaurant in Savannah. In the Southeast. Your guests expect a lot more than some bowl of boiled shrimp and some cheese cubes. Daniel's instructions were clear. 'Dazzle 'em,' he told me."

"All right. I guess I see your point." I picked up a fork. "Tell me what I'm tasting."

"Start with the hot things," Julio said. "We just took the mini crab cakes out of the oven. And that's a new remoulade I came up with."

I dutifully nibbled and nodded my approval. He went on ticking off the various dishes. "Beef tenderloin on brioche with horseradish cream. Chicken satay. Salmon tartar in cornmeal cups, baby lamb chops with cherry-balsamic reduction, pork tenderloin with cranberry-fig compote . . ."

Julio handed me a plate and began to heap it with more morsels. "Sweet potato puffs. Deviled eggs with caviar, Boursin-stuffed snow pea pods, mini grits and greens tarts . . ."

"No more," I groaned after only a few bites. "Seriously, Julio. It all looks and tastes divine, but I can't eat one more crumb."

His cheerful face fell. "But you haven't even tried the desserts yet. My chess-pie tartlets, the Maker's Mark bread pudding . . ."

"Don't forget Marian Foley's fruitcake," I added, grimacing.

"What's that?"

"Never mind. If we're done here, I'm just going to check Daniel's office to see if there's any mail that needs immediate attention, and then I've got another appointment."

He followed me through the swinging doors to the kitchen, and I was about to walk into Daniel's converted broom closet of an office when something on the staff bulletin board caught my eye.

I stopped. It was a computer printout of a newspaper clipping, blown-up larger for easy reading, and tacked to the board amid photographs of the staff, recent restaurant reviews, and thank-you cards from happy patrons.

The clipping was from the *New York Post*'s Page Six gossip column. And the thing that caught my eye was a photograph of a willowy dark-haired beauty in a spangly cocktail dress with a plunging neckline. Said beauty had her arms wrapped across the chest of a certain hunky chef, resplendent in a black tuxedo. The beauty was staring at the chef with what I interpreted as naked lust. Like she'd just found a gift under the Christmas tree that she was dying to unwrap. The chef? To his credit, Daniel Stipanek just looked startled. Or tired.

But he didn't look nearly as startled as I probably did at that moment.

The photo had been circled with a thick red marker, and somebody had scrawled on the clipping "The Boss Out on the Town." I stood closer so I could read the photo caption.

*Cucina Carlotta owner Carlotta Donatello's latest dish isn't Italian—he's Daniel Stipanek, the Savannah-born guest chef at Donatello's hot new Downtown eatery, for whom the heiress-about-town threw a celebrity-studded bash this week.*

I stood and stared at the photograph. This was Daniel's new boss? When he'd announced the guest-chef gig, I'd been elated for him, picturing Carlotta Donatello in my mind as a short, dumpy Italian *nonna* type, with a white bun, faint mustache, thick-lensed eyeglasses, and sensible black lace-up shoes. I'd pictured a senior citizen in a flour-dusted apron, wielding a wooden spoon.

The actual Carlotta Donatello was nobody's *nonna*. She was probably in her mid-thirties, with a long lustrous mane of hair and huge, long-lashed doe eyes which, in the photograph, were fixed longingly on my fiancé. Also? She had a generous helping of cleavage pressed right against Daniel's chest.

I felt my face begin to burn.

Julio noticed me noticing, of course. He reached out and ripped the clipping from the bulletin board, wadding it up in his hand. "Pay no attention," he said. "Ella put this up. She's from New York and she's always reading those newspapers online."

"Umm-hmm," I said. "Interesting."

He made clumsy small talk while I sorted through the mail, but I wasn't paying attention. I couldn't get that image of Carlotta Donatello out of my mind—the sexy cocktail dress, the pose—with her arms wrapped around Daniel. Daniel! In a tuxedo. As far as I knew, he'd never owned a tuxedo in his life. And a party? He'd never said a word to me about a party. In fact, I hadn't actually talked to Daniel in two days. And now I knew why. He'd been a busy chef-about-town.

My stomach roiled. Maybe it was all that rich food I'd just sampled. Or maybe it was the indigestible idea of my future husband locked in the sinewy embrace of a rich, glamorous "heiress-about-town."

# Chapter 2

✦

I was still fuming when I left the restaurant, but there was really no time to sulk. My prewedding to-do list was set in stone.

I was expecting a call from BeBe Loudermilk, my best friend and maid of honor, at any minute. It was BeBe who'd set me up with Daniel in the first place, right after she'd hired him as chef at Guale. For a hard-core matchmaker like BeBe, our upcoming wedding was the ultimate validation and demanded updates on every aspect of the ceremony.

But in the meantime, I needed to check in at Babalu, the upscale gift shop Manny Alvarez and Cookie Parker run on the other side of Troup Square from my own antique shop.

I was on a strict timetable. Or so I told myself until I spotted a hot pink poster tacked to an oak tree at the corner of Habersham and 45th, in Ardsley Park, one of my favorite Savannah neighborhoods for junking. The magic words—estate sale—jumped out at me like a twenty-foot neon billboard, even though they were actually only scrawled in Magic Marker on an eleven-by-fourteen sheet of poster board.

I was almost through the intersection when I glimpsed the sign and the arrow pointing right. No time for a turn signal. I made a hard right onto East 45th and was rewarded with an angry blast of a horn from the car right behind me.

Developed as Savannah's first suburban neighborhood around the turn of the twentieth century, Ardsley Park homes ranged from impressive brick Georgian Revival mansions to chunky Craftsman bungalows to tidy 1940s and 1950s brick cottages. It's primo antique territory. And this was an estate sale—not a yard sale or a moving sale—which meant dead people's stuff—my favorite kind of acquisition for my antique shop.

"Sorry," I muttered, cruising slowly down the street in search of another sign directing me to the house where the sale was being held. Two blocks down, I spotted another pink "Estate Sale" sign planted in an overgrown yard.

As soon as I pulled up to the house, my junk antennae went into overdrive and I knew the antique planets were in alliance. The house was a solidly built Colonial revival, but it had seen better days. The yard was weedy and overgrown, the windows cloudy with grime. A battered cardboard box rested at the curb, and spilling out of it were the sadly bent and tangled wire arms of a disassembled vintage aluminum Christmas tree.

This was a good sign; in the junk game, neglect and decay usually signal treasure within.

Jethro, an experienced junk sniffer who had himself been plucked from a curbside pile of debris, thumped his tail on the leather truck seat. I patted his head in approval. "Good boy. Stay here, buddy."

I got out of the truck and made a beeline for that aluminum Christmas tree. But when I picked up one of the branches, the brittle foil leaves disintegrated into glittering shards. Sad. I have an irrational affection for cheesy midcentury holiday décor, and aluminum trees are always at the top of my want list. But this one had obviously fallen victim to time and temperature—stored in a blazing hot Savannah attic over the decades.

I put the tree branch back in the box and studied the homemade sign. It was hurriedly written in black marker, and directed sale-goers to proceed around the corner to the lane running in back of the house. Homemade was good—it meant the sale was not being run by a pro. Furthermore, I hadn't seen any ads for the sale in Craigslist or the *Savannah Morning News* or the *PennySaver*, which hopefully meant that my competition, other dealers, hadn't already swooped in and scarfed up all the good stuff. And best of all, the sale had started only an hour earlier. Who starts an estate sale at three on Saturday afternoons? Amateurs, that's who!

I got back in the truck and drove around to the lane, where I spotted another excellent sign—an enormous pile of stuff stacked beside the trash cans. Old cardboard cartons, broken chairs, mounds of clothing still in yellowing plastic dry cleaner's bags, the skeletons of broken aluminum lawn chairs, and yes—the best sign of all, a cast-off walker and a potty chair.

Like a seasoned anthropologist, I quickly read this particular dig. From the age and water-soaked condition of the boxes, I could tell that somebody had excavated a leaky basement, attic, or garage and they were disposing of anything that looked old or worthless, including clothing. My nose was already twitching in happy anticipation. The folding lawn chairs were exactly like the kind of sixties-era chairs my parents still had in their garage.

Best of all was the presence of the walker and the potty chair. And let's not forget that ruined aluminum Christmas tree. This homeowner had likely been elderly, which meant their belongings were as vintage as the house. Jethro and I had stumbled across the holy grail, a true, grandma estate sale.

He must have sensed my excitement, because his tail was thumping the leather passenger seat like a snare drum, and he was pawing at the door. "Good boy, Ro-Ro," I said, giving him a chin scratch. "You stay here and be on the lookout for other dealers."

I picked my way carefully over a crumbling concrete walkway that lead through an overgrown thicket of privet and headed for the door of a ramshackle screened porch that looked like it had been tacked onto the back of the house some time in the seventies.

An attractive woman dressed in a black Nike tracksuit and spotless pale pink Lanvin sneakers sat at a card table just inside the doorway. In her forties, with short dark hair and a deep tan, she was talking on her cell phone. The pear-shaped diamond on her left hand looked like at least three carats, and the diamond earrings twinkling from her ears were a good two carats apiece. If this was what she wore for tennis, I wondered what kind of jewelry she had for grocery shopping?

"Go ahead on in," she said, in a refined accent that bespoke a lifetime of sorority chapter meetings and cocktails on the veranda. She held the phone away from her face. "There's stuff in every room, and prices are negotiable. I've got to get this dump emptied out by the end of the day. The contractor's coming in Monday to start gutting it out." She wrinkled her elegant nose. "You'll have to excuse the mess. Bless her heart, my great-aunt Edith really wasn't able to keep up with housekeeping these past few years."

I stepped into the house and into the 1960s. The kitchen was smallish, lined with rusting metal cabinets painted the same pale pink as the walls and the linoleum floor. Great-aunt Edith had a thing for pink. All the drawers and cupboard doors were ajar. I lifted a plate from a stack in the cupboard near the sink. It was a hugely popular pattern from the sixties, Franciscan's Apple Blossom, featuring, of course, pink apple blossoms. There were ten plates in the stack, but each one was chipped. Pass.

Nothing else in the kitchen caught my fancy, so I pushed through a swinging door into the dining room, hoping for better hunting.

Sun shone weakly through the now-naked windows. The floors were bare, and my footsteps echoed in the high-ceilinged room. A dusty crystal chandelier was centered over the dining room table, but only one lightbulb was working.

The dining room furniture was the predictable repro Empire, in predictable Grand Rapids mahogany. An array of dishes, crystal, and silver were spread across the table, which was covered with a heavy damask tablecloth. I snagged a pair of ornately decorated silverplated candlesticks with a masking-tape price tag of $5. In a sterling-loving town like Savannah, I probably couldn't turn much of a profit on this pair, but I liked them, and that was enough.

Great-aunt Edith's "good" china was nice enough, with delicate pink roses and swirling gold edging, but I rarely buy or sell what I think of as fussy "tea party" porcelain and crystal, only because it just doesn't float my boat.

My eyes alighted on a large, yellowing cardboard box with familiar green graphics on the sides, and I felt the familiar thrill of discovery. The ruined Christmas tree at the curb had raised my hopes for this sale—maybe, just maybe, I'd find some vintage ornaments.

The vintage gods were with me. The box was an old Shiny-Brite ornament box, with twelve corrugated compartments for glass ornaments. But it was heaped with probably three dozen ornaments, all tossed casually into the fragile cardboard carton.

I marveled at their beautiful pastel colors and intricate designs as I carefully lifted each ornament for inspection. They were figural ornaments, grinning snowmen, Santa Clauses, angels, and reindeer. There were ovoid and teardrop-shaped mercury glass indents in my favorite shades of dusty pink, turquoise, seafoam, and faded gold, and an entire orchestra of miniature gold glass instruments.

The ornaments had obviously been long used and well loved. Some were missing the small metal cap that would have accommodated a hook to hang on the tree, a couple of the silver and gold ones had tarnished finish, and at least one reindeer was missing its antlers. But I didn't care. It was an enchanting collection. The masking-tape tag read "Antique Ornaments. Very Rare. $40."

One of the dining room chairs held a tall stack of neatly starched and ironed table linens. I rifled through the stack and set aside a dozen damask banquet-sized napkins, another dozen linen cocktail napkins with perky red and yellow embroidered roosters on the corners, and an adorable set of embroidered "day of the week" dish towels, each with a different vintage forties-era design.

Miss Edith's niece obviously knew nothing about vintage linens. She'd marked the bundle of dinner napkins at $2 and the cocktail napkins at $1, probably because they were yellowed and rust-spotted with age. But I knew a good soaking in OxiClean and some determined spot-cleaning would leave the beautiful old fabric as snowy as the day they'd been sold. And then they'd be worth ten times the price that I'd pay for them. Not that I intended to sell them. I have such a soft spot for old linens that my best friend BeBe calls me a linen slut.

As for the kitchen towels, I'd sold a similar set on eBay two months earlier, for $40. The masking-tape price on this set was $1. Score!

I was loading the linens into my tote bag when I noticed, for the first time, that everything was monogrammed with a large, elaborate *S*.

I sighed happily. I'd never changed my name to Tal's during that marriage, which was a source of endless disappointment to Tal's mother and mine. And now that I was marrying Daniel Stipanek, in my middle-thirties, I intended to keep my maiden name. But I was tradition-loving enough to appreciate the idea of setting a table for a dinner party with linens emblazoned with my new husband's initial.

The mahogany china cabinet taking up the far wall of the dining room was loaded with dozens and dozens of collectible Boehm porcelain birds, but I deliberately avoided them, as well as the stacks of Bradford Exchange plates and Precious Moments figurines, all of them coated in dust.

Instead, I opened one of the cabinet's shallow drawers, more from idle curiosity than anything else. Nestled inside the top drawer's felt-lined compartments was a large cache of flatware. The silver was blackened with decades of tarnish, decorated with a pattern of baroque curlicues and flourishes, and engraved with a large $S$ on each piece. I picked up a fork and weighed it in my hand, turned it over and grinned. This was sterling silver. Heavy, gorgeous old sterling. I counted all the pieces. There were eleven place settings, complete down to old-fashioned pieces like demitasse spoons, fruit knives, and fish forks.

I opened the second drawer and found it equally crammed with matching serving pieces, like ice tongs, a carving set, and slotted spoons.

None of it was priced. I felt my heart thumping in my chest. Just as I was counting out all the serving pieces, I felt the cell phone I'd tucked in the pocket of my jacket buzz with an incoming text. Finally—Daniel must have finished up with the lunch crowd and snatched a moment of privacy.

I pulled out the phone and sighed. The text was from Cookie. Again.

## WHERE ARE U? THE TULIPS ARE WILTING!

I dumped all the silver from the second drawer into the top drawer, hefted my tote onto my shoulder and sped back to the porch to the cashier statement.

Diamond Lil was still on her cell phone, chatting away. She put the phone down and looked at the drawer in my arms. "The dining room suite is two thousand dollars. It's solid mahogany and the table has three leaves. It's a great buy, but you'll have to bring somebody to help you load. It's ungodly heavy."

"I'm actually only interested in this flatware," I said. "How much?"

"Where'd you find this stuff? I've never seen it before, and I've been through this house with a fine-toothed comb."

"It was in the china cabinet. Look, I'm sorry to bother you, but I've had a family emergency and I need to leave right now." I set the drawer on her card table and gestured at my tote bag. "I've got a bunch of napkins and some candlesticks here, and that comes to fourteen dollars. What would you want for all the flatware? There are eleven place settings and nine or ten serving pieces."

"God. Aunt Edith had stuff stashed everywhere. And I guess you can tell her taste wasn't really all that great. She was a schoolteacher for thirty-five years, so I guess she bought what she could afford on what they paid teachers at Blessed Sacrament."

"She taught at Blessed Sacrament? That's where I went to school."

Lil's eyes flickered over my underwhelming attire—the tattered jeans and the vintage Kool and The Gang concert T-shirt worn with unlaced red Chuck Ts. "Hmm. My sisters and I went to Savannah Country Day."

"What was your aunt's name?"

"Edith Shanahan. I think she mostly taught sixth grade."

"Mrs. Shanahan taught me sixth grade!" I cried. "She was your aunt? She was so wonderful! She took our class on field trips to the Telfair Museum and camping on Cumberland Island, and she wrote and produced our class musical. We all adored your aunt."

"Yeah, she was kinda cool, I guess," Lil said. She looked down at the silver, picked up a spoon, then put it back down again. "It's nice silver," she said, suddenly warming up to her late aunt's questionable taste.

"It really is," I said, holding my breath. I didn't want to offer a price, because if I offered too little I might offend her. Too much and I'd tip her off that the silver was actually worth something.

She picked up a pocket calculator and began punching in numbers. "Let's see. Five pieces in a place setting, times eleven, that's fifty-five. And you said there are like, what? Twelve serving pieces?"

"Something like that."

"We'll round it up to seventy pieces, shall we?"

"Okay."

"Hmm. Well, it has been kind of slow, and I've never seen this pattern before. Edith probably got it with her S&H Green Stamps or something." Her nose wrinkled at the thought. "I couldn't possibly take less than one-fifty. And I'll have to ask you for cash."

"Of course," I said sweetly, fishing three fifties and a twenty from my junking cash stash and placing it on the card table.

"Almost forgot," I said, handing her two more twenties. "I've got the vintage Christmas ornaments too. Forty dollars, right?"

"Right."

Her cell phone rang and she picked it up and began chatting, at the same time sliding the bills into a metal cash box—without offering me the six dollars in change I should have had coming.

She also didn't offer to help me get the silver out of the drawer, so I grabbed an empty cardboard box beside the card table and dumped all the silver inside. Lil shot me an annoyed look for all the racket I made, but I put the empty silver drawer back on the table and high-tailed it out of there. I was humming "Have Yourself a Merry Little Christmas" under my breath as I trotted toward the truck.

Under normal circumstances, I might have felt a strong pang of re-pressed Catholic guilt over scoring such a huge bargain on the sterling flatware. But not today. Diamond Lil might not have thought much of her late aunt Edith—or her middle-class taste—but I was thrilled to have bought something with a connection to my beloved teacher.

# Chapter 3

✦

I heard the music just as I was rounding Troup Square. Tubas! Half a dozen of them, blooping and bleating something that bore only the faintest resemblance to . . . "Silver Bells"?

Sure enough, there, clustered on the sidewalk in front of Babalu were a squadron of tuba players, adorned in smart matching navy wool band uniforms, their elephantine brass instruments raised heavenward. Dozens of people stood around watching, some of them singing along.

Jethro's ears pricked up and he leaned across my lap to scout out the cause of the cacophony.

"Those boys!" I said, smiling fondly.

I hadn't always viewed "the boys"—aka Manny and Cookie, my across-the-square neighbors—with affection.

Manny Alvarez was a retired landscape designer from Delray Beach,

Florida, and Cooksey "Cookie" Parker had been a Broadway chorus boy in his youth, before working in retail in New York. When they'd first opened their upscale gift and interiors shop a year or so ago, I'd viewed them as interlopers, out to steal my best merchandise lines and snake away my valued customers.

Babalu was just across the square from Maisie's Daisy, the antique shop that I operate out of the carriage shop behind my townhouse. I'd started my junking career as a picker—somebody who sources antique and vintage items at estate sales, junk shops, and yes, even a few Dumpsters—and it had taken me years to get up the gumption—and the funds—to open my own shop.

The boys' over-the-top shop displays grated on my nerves. And let's face it, I was more than a little jealous of their success, and they were more than a little eager to show a small-town Southern girl how it was done in the big city. Our relationship became even more strained after I won first prize in the downtown historic district's holiday decorating contest with my Blue Christmas display window, beating out Babalu's Winter Wonderland tableau.

Eventually, however, we'd become fast friends—and in-laws, sort of, after Jethro fathered a litter of puppies with their dog Ruthie. This year, what with the wedding planning, I'd let my Christmas decorating slide a little, which meant that Manny and Cookie had easily won first place.

The brick storefront of Babalu had been magically transformed into a gingerbread palace, with faux icing swirls and swoops outlining all their building's architectural details. Giant faux candy canes, red and green gum balls, and chocolate drops bordered the shop window, and two enormous potted Fraser fir trees on either side of the front door were festooned with every kind of candy imaginable.

The tuba players finished their rendition of "Silver Bells" and launched into an oompified version of "Santa Claus Is Coming to Town," and as we walked inside the shop, a costumed gingerbread boy handed me a cellophane-wrapped cookie—a miniature version of the shop. When Jethro looked up expectantly, the gingerbread boy reached in a basket on the counter and tossed him a dog treat, which Jethro caught in midair.

Although Babalu was thronged with customers, Cookie swooped in and enveloped me in a bear hug as soon as we stepped foot (and paw) in the shop.

He was dressed in camel-colored wool slacks, a fisherman knit sweater with a Burberry plaid scarf looped around his neck, and Gucci loafers.

"Weezie, you bad girl!" he chided. "Manny is in back, in an absolute dither over the flowers. You were supposed to be here hours ago."

He scooted me through the aisles of the shop and through a swinging door to the stockroom, which now resembled a florist's warehouse.

Flowers and plants lined every available surface of the room. There were towering buckets of pink lilies, freesias, hollyhocks, stocks and orchids. I counted four full-sized potted pink dogwood trees in full bloom, and buckets and buckets of tightly closed pink tulips.

In the middle of everything, Manny Alvarez stood, wearing a white lab coat, with a pair of garden clippers in one hand and a huge roll of pink silk ribbon in the other.

"Oh my," I whispered.

Manny beamed. "Isn't it glorious? Can you believe all this fabulousness will transform your townhouse in one week?"

I blinked. "All of it? Manny, it's beautiful—but we're having a wedding, not a coronation. Where do you intend to place all this stuff?"

He waved his hand airily. "Everywhere. The dogwoods will go in those gorgeous urns on either side of your front stoop—I'll have them all decked out in tiny white lights, of course."

"Of course," I echoed.

"Then I'm doing banks of arrangements on your mantel, on that table in your entry hall, your coffee table, and every other flat surface in the parlor. Interspersed with thousands of little white lights and the palest pink wax taper candles. Which reminds me—you need to dig out all those sterling candlesticks of yours. The dining room is going to be my pièce de résistance."

"Oh?"

"Tell her about the altar," Cookie urged.

"Shhh!" Manny said. "It's supposed to be a surprise." He turned to me. "You don't mind a surprise on your wedding day, right?"

"As long as it's a good surprise," I said cautiously. "But nothing too outlandish, right?"

"Everything will be in perfectly good taste," Manny said.

I looked around at the avalanche of flower overflowing from every corner of the workroom.

"I like it," I said hesitating. "I really do. But it's not very, uh, Christmasy, is it?"

"What? You were expecting some of those hideous foil-wrapped poinsettias like they sell at Kroger? Maybe a ginormous wreath of holly?" He laughed and looked at his partner for reassurance.

"Ugh, poinsettias. So five years ago," Cookie said. He gestured around the room. "This, darling Weezie, is going to make your wedding the social event of the Savannah season."

I felt a small twinge of . . . something. "But Daniel and I don't really want an event. We just want a lovely, warm, intimate family wedding. You do know we're only having forty people, right?"

Manny sighed dramatically. "You're breaking my heart, Eloise. Only forty people to enjoy this masterpiece I'm creating for my favorite couple?"

"I did warn you from the beginning. Nothing too excessive."

"Who's being excessive?" Manny asked. "This is simplicity itself. In Miami? This would be considered absolutely spartan."

"Well . . ." I started. "How much is all this costing, anyway? I told you, my budget is tiny. Minuscule. We're saving our money for the trip to Paris in the spring."

"Do not worry your pretty head about cost," Cookie put in. "This is our gift to you two."

"I can't accept something this extravagant as a gift! All these flowers must have cost thousands and thousands. The blooming dogwood trees—where do you even find dogwoods in bloom in December, anyway?"

"Trade secret," Manny said coyly. "Anyway, I buy smart and I buy wholesale. And the dogwood trees are only rented. Christmas morning they'll be on a truck to St. Simon's Island for some Coca-Cola heiress's open house."

"It's really too much," I fussed. "I know you two boys mean well, but honestly, I feel terrible. When you got married in New York in the fall, my present was just a silly little cake knife."

"An antique sterling cake knife," Cookie corrected.

"In our pattern," Manny added.

"And we'll never forget that amazing garden party you gave for us when we got back to town," Cookie said. "Look, sweetie, neither of us ever had a sister. Manny's people are dead, and mine are practically fossils. You're family now, as far as we're concerned. So we are giving you these flowers as a wedding gift, whether you like it or not. All right?"

"All right," I said meekly. "But nothing else. And if we could just scale back the teensiest little bit, I'd feel a lot better."

"Scale back?" Manny shrugged and turned to Cookie. "What ees thees *scale back* the *chica* says?" he said, in his best affected Cuban accent.

"Never mind," I surrendered. "It's lovely. All of it." I glanced at my watch. "But I've really got to scoot."

"Ooh, I meant to ask. How was Daniel's first night at Cucina Carlotta?" Cookie asked. "Was it a smash hit? We want to hear every little detail."

I felt that ugly twinge of jealousy stabbing my gut. "I don't actually know," I admitted. "We haven't talked yet. But I'm sure he'll call later."

"Give him our love," Manny said. "And tell him not to get any big ideas about stealing you away to the Big Apple."

"I will, and he won't," I promised.

# Chapter 4

✦

# BeBe

A bell chimed from the front office, alerting me that we had a guest, which surprised me a little. It was after three on a Saturday afternoon. Winter is our off-season on Tybee Island, and the Breeze Inn, our small, twelve-room tourist court, charming though it is, doesn't usually get much walk-in traffic the week before Christmas. We were full up, though, with regulars who return to the island every year for the holidays.

I'd been doing paperwork on the dining room table, but I made my way to the office, and our little dog Jeeves followed right at my heels.

The woman didn't look like our typical guest. She was older, probably in her early seventies, with white hair cut in a severe bob and serious, no-nonsense eyeglasses. She wore a gray wool skirt that touched below the knee, and a somewhat pilled and frayed navy blue sweater.

Definitely not a vacationer, I decided. Anyway, she looked vaguely familiar.

"Hi," I said brightly. "Can I help you?"

She was still looking around the reception area. Now she seemed to be studying the framed magazine articles from *Southern Living* and *Savannah Magazine* touting our cool, retro motel vibe.

"Ma'am?"

The stranger looked up now. She looked down at Jeeves. "What a sweet little dog. Is he a Westie?"

"That's right," I said. "Jeeves is the Breeze Inn mascot. If you're looking for a room, I'm afraid we won't have anything until the day after Christmas."

Her eyes were watchful. "Er, no. Actually, I'm looking for Mrs. Richard Hodges."

"Who?"

"Mrs. Richard Hodges," she repeated a little louder, in case my hearing was off.

It took me a moment to regain my composure. "Mrs. Hodges? I'm sorry. She's dead. She's been dead for ages. Twenty years at least."

"Surely not," the old lady said. "What a shame. She was so young too."

"Not really. I never actually met Corinne, but I think she must have been in her late sixties when she passed away."

The old lady's lips twitched slightly. For the first time I noticed she carried a file folder under her arm. She opened it now, read from something in the file, then looked up at me. "Corinne? No, you misunderstand. I'm looking for BeBe Loudermilk Hodges—married to Richard Hodges?"

I felt like I'd been punched in the belly. The mere mention of my second husband's name does that to me. I'd been married to the snake for only a little over a year, and it seemed like a lifetime ago, but that had been enough.

I steadied myself by grabbing hold of the edge of the bamboo reception desk. When I felt calm, I took a deep breath. And then another.

"Why are you looking for this woman, may I ask?"

"It's personal," the old lady said. She was still searching my face. "A legal matter."

A legal matter. That shouldn't have come as a surprise, not where Richard was concerned.

She was studying the framed *Southern Living* article again. The lead photograph was of me, standing in the doorway of our own living area, which featured a vintage rattan pretzel sofa slipcovered in a barkcloth fabric with huge pink hibiscus blossoms and fern branches. *"Owner BeBe Loudermilk traded the life of downtown businesswoman for funky Tybee Island hotelier,"* the photo caption read.

"You're Mrs. Richard Hodges," the old lady said. "Aren't you?"

I returned her steady gaze. "Not anymore. Actually, I never even took the rat's name for the twenty-seven seconds we were married. I'm still BeBe Loudermilk. So if you're looking for Richard because he owes you money or skipped out on bond, you're out of luck. I haven't seen him for nearly six years. We're divorced, you know."

Her watery blue eyes blinked rapidly. "Oh no, dear. I don't think so."

* * *

The baby kicked me so hard in the ribs, I could have sworn it knew where all this was headed.

"What did you just say?" I whispered.

"I said you're not divorced from Richard Hodges." She held up that file folder again. "That's actually why I'm here."

Suddenly I felt very light-headed. The old lady's face grew blurry and her voice seemed to be coming from a long way away, just a faint echo. I felt myself swaying and my spine seemed to collapse in on itself, like a Slinky.

The next thing I knew, I was sitting on the floor, my back against the reception desk, and the old lady was squatting next to me, patting my hand. She held a wet cloth up to my forehead, and she was holding a cell phone in her hand. Jeeves was sitting on his haunches, whimpering softly.

"Is there somebody I should call?" the woman asked. "I'm afraid I didn't handle that very well, especially with you, er, in your present condition. Should I get an ambulance or something?"

"No ambulance. I'm all right," I insisted. "Let's get back to what you were telling me before I passed out. Something about Richard?"

"Wouldn't you be more comfortable sitting down in a chair or something?"

"Probably. But it could take a while for me to get back on my feet again."

She held out her hand. "Come on. I'll help."

I laughed despite myself. "That's sweet. But you probably don't weigh ninety pounds soaking wet. I don't see how you're going to haul me up off this floor."

"You'd be surprised," she said, a glint in her eye. "I'm stronger than I look. Do you mind if I ask when the baby is due?"

"Not for another month," I said. "I know, I look like I could drop this kid any second, but my doctor assures me the due date is January 15."

She stretched out both arms to me. "Grab hold of my elbows. Bend your knees, now. We'll take it nice and slow."

We did take it nice and slow, and she was surprisingly strong for her age. Five minutes later, I was seated on that same rattan sofa in our living room, and she was handing me a cup of tea.

"Thank you," I said, taking a sip. "I don't think I caught your name."

"I'm Inez Roebottom," she said. "Are you feeling any better? I do apologize for nearly sending you into an early labor."

"I'll be fine. No contractions. Could we get back to what you were saying before I did my big swoon? Because this can't be right. Richard and I were divorced right before he went to prison."

"Only you weren't divorced," Inez said gently. "That's what I was trying to explain." She brandished the file folder again. "Your husband, Richard Hodges, did have an initial consultation with a lawyer about a divorce. But he never followed through. No divorce decree was ever filed with the court."

"That can't be," I said heatedly. "Richard swore to me that he'd gotten the divorce. He said he owed it to me, after everything he'd put me through. He got the divorce right before he went to prison."

Inez was still shaking her head. "Men," she said sadly.

"What's your involvement in all of this?" I demanded. "How do you know whether or not I'm divorced? Are you a lawyer?"

"I worked for the lawyer Richard Hodges hired to start the divorce proceedings. Howard Roebottom."

"Your husband?"

"My son. Late son," she corrected herself. "Howard passed away eight months ago."

"I'm so sorry," I mumbled.

"It was very sudden. Heart attack. His father died three years ago, from the very same thing," Inez said. "My husband Warren started the firm, and Howard went to work for him right after he got out of law school. I ran the office. For thirty years. Now, I'm just trying to finish closing the office down. Howard had a carton of old, inactive files on a bookcase in the conference room. I was going through them when I found this." She handed the file folder to me.

I opened it and stared down at the single sheet of paper. I'd left my reading glasses in the other room. The black letters seemed to swim before my eyes and I started feeling woozy again.

"What does any of this mean?" I asked. "You say there was never a divorce decree filed with the court?"

"I'm afraid not. It happens sometimes. People get angry, decide they want a divorce, see a lawyer, then they cool off and nothing ever comes of it. But in this case, it appears that your husband—"

"Ex-husband," I said firmly.

"Have it your way," Inez said. "Richard Hodges came to see my son about getting a divorce. He paid a retainer fee by check, and it appears Howard started the proceedings. But then..." Her voice trailed off.

I already knew where this was heading. "The check bounced, didn't it?"

"It did. Of course, around that time, your husband's trial was getting a lot of publicity. It was on television and in the newspapers. I remember being so surprised. He seemed like such a nice young man. Beautiful manners, always dressed in expensive clothes. But the things he did, I remember being shocked. And I don't shock easily."

She didn't have to tell me. My cheeks still burned with the remembered shame of that time.

Richard came from a respected Savannah family. When I met him I was twenty-eight, and I'd been single for several years, following a very brief teenaged marriage to my older brother's best friend Sandy Thayer. Richard was a successful stockbroker, on his way up the career ladder, or so it appeared.

As it turned out, everything about Richard was a lie, but I didn't know any of that until too late. I didn't know he had a secret double life that included swindling his elderly clients by emptying their trust accounts. It wasn't until I went poking around on his home computer that I discovered the rest of it; the revolting computer porn and the thousands of dollars he'd drained from our joint checking account to pay for phone sex.

After I confronted him with what I'd found, Richard broke down in tears, admitted everything, and begged me to forgive him. As I was walking out the door, he promised to make it up to me by giving me a quick, painless divorce.

The lying scum-sucking bastard.

I was still clinging to straws. "But just because Richard didn't follow up with your son, that doesn't mean he didn't see another lawyer. He probably did. I mean, maybe he got his criminal attorney to do the divorce. Sort of a package deal."

"Maybe," she shrugged. "Did you ever receive your divorce papers? The final decree? It should have been mailed to you."

I searched my memory, but the months after Richard went off to prison were a long-ago blur. "Now that you mention it, I guess I didn't ever get a final decree. But maybe it got lost in the mail."

"Did you move after you split with him?" she asked.

"No," I whispered. I felt the baby kicking again. I pressed the palms of my hands atop my belly and closed my eyes.

"I'm sorry to bring you such unwelcome news," Inez said. "So, you really haven't had any contact with Richard in all these years? Not even a letter from prison?"

"I got a letter. Just one. I burned it. And then I went about rebuilding what was left of my life after he wrecked it. Richard Hodges is dead to me. Or he was right up until half an hour ago when you walked into my life."

"What about the father of your child?" she asked. "Does he know about any of this?"

"Harry knows I was married before," I said. And then I felt the blood drain from my face as it hit me. "Oh my God. If what you say is really true . . . I got remarried, after Richard went to prison. To Sandy Thayer."

"Sandy Thayer? I'm confused. Didn't you say that was your first husband's name?"

"It was. I married Sandy again. Another big mistake. Sweet man, but we . . . Oh dear God. If I was still married to Richard, when I married Sandy, that would mean I committed bigamy?"

"Maybe." She gave me a weak smile. "You said your baby's father is named Harry? What happened to Sandy? I thought your husband's name was Sandy. How does Harry fit into all this?"

"The second time around, I only stayed married to Sandy for eighteen months, then I filed for divorce. We were better as friends than we were as husband and wife. Harry and I have been together two years."

She raised an eyebrow. "But you and Harry aren't married?"

"No. And with my history, I have no intention of getting married ever again."

"I suppose if you don't intend to remarry, it's probably immaterial whether or not you're still married to Richard Hodges."

"Are you kidding?" I cried. "I can't still be married to that man. Even the mention of his name, all these years later, makes me want to vomit."

"That might be morning sickness," she said, standing up. "Try sucking on a peppermint first thing in the morning before you get out of bed."

I managed to get to my feet again. "You're leaving? You can't just walk in here and drop a bombshell in my lap and then just walk away,

Inez. What should I do? I've got to get this settled. Right now. If Harry finds out..."

She shrugged. "I'm not a lawyer, dear. I'm just an old busybody. But if you're asking my advice, I'd say you should probably talk to a lawyer. Maybe you're right. Maybe Richard Hodges did follow up and get a divorce decree. But for your own peace of mind, you should probably find out."

I walked her out to the reception area and Jeeves followed. The sun was going down, and a gray pall was cast across the now-darkening room. The red "No Vacancy" sign blinked off and on in the window. Without thinking, I switched on the small Christmas tree that I'd so carefully placed in the corner two weeks earlier. Tiny white lights twinkled among the strings of oyster shells, starfish, and bleached-out sand dollars I'd hung there.

Her hand was on the doorknob.

"Inez? Why did you come here today? You don't even know me. Why'd you go to all the trouble of tracking me down?"

"I was wondering that myself, the whole time I was driving out here today," Inez said. "I shredded all the other files. But it's not true that we're strangers. Warren and I used to dine at your restaurant all the time."

"That's how I know you! From Guale. You liked table three. He always ordered the seared tuna. You liked the pecan-crusted chicken."

"You were very kind to us, especially with that bothersome walker of Warren's. We missed seeing you at the hostess stand after you sold the restaurant to your chef. I almost did shred that file of yours. But then I saw your name and I remembered you from the restaurant. It's not a very nice Christmas gift. But I do think it's better to know, don't you?"

"I do. Thank you."

"Merry Christmas, BeBe Loudermilk." The doorbell chimed again as she walked out. I watched her car, a modest midsized beige Acura, pull out of the parking lot. Without thinking, I hid the file folder.

I looked over at Jeeves and put a finger to my lips. "Not a word."

# Chapter 5

✦

# Weezie

I was just getting ready to take the lemon pound cake layers out of the oven when I heard my cell phone dinging to notify me of an incoming text.

Jethro stood directly under my feet as I placed the three layers on a wire rack to cool, hoping an errant crumb would fall his way.

I gave him a stern look. "No counter surfing. You understand?"

His tail thumped twice and he crouched down in his waiting position.

The text was from BeBe and it was in all caps.

NEED U @TYBEE. ASAP!

I sighed and looked around for my car keys. BeBe has an annoying habit of having emergencies when I'm right in the middle of something crucial—like baking test versions of my own wedding cake. But she *is* my best friend. She'd bailed me out of jail, wiped away my tears after my divorce, loaned me money, and most important (and annoying) she'd shoved me right into the arms of the waiting and willing Daniel at the lowest point of my life.

I owed her, doggone it.

ON MY WAY, I texted back.

My pulse was racing as I urged Ol' Blue to its top speed of fifty miles an hour, wondering about BeBe's urgent message. I tried to call her a couple of times, but my calls went directly to voice mail.

Luckily, since it was Sunday morning, most of the good citizens of Savannah seemed to be either slumbering or worshipping. Still, the trip to BeBe's seemed to take forever. Not because of the distance. From the downtown historic district to Tybee Island is maybe fifteen miles. But culturally, politically, and socially, Tybee and the sometimes snooty, snotty downtown couldn't be farther apart. Downtown is chablis and caviar. Tybee is Pabst Blue Ribbon and boiled peanuts.

I pulled into the lot at the Breeze Inn, but every slot was full, and the "No Vacancy" sign was lit up—even now, in the dead of winter.

BeBe's new Mercedes was parked in front of the manager's unit, and since there wasn't an empty parking slot, I was forced to park at the construction site next door.

I blew through the front door of the manager's quaint whitewashed log cabin cottage without knocking, leaving the fir wreath swinging from its hook.

Although the Christmas tree was lit, the front office was deserted.

"Babe?" I noticed the door to their living quarters was ajar, so I pushed on through. The silence felt ominous, and I felt a prickle from the back of my neck.

The cozy living room, with its whitewashed pine walls, vintage rattan sofas and chairs, and shell-encrusted fireplace, was empty. Jeeves, a white West Highland terrier with a personality of a dog twice his size, rose up from his perch on a chair by a sunny window and gave me an inquiring look, but I didn't even pause to pat his head.

"Babe?" I was starting to feel panicky.

"Back here," she called finally. "In the bedroom."

"Are you okay?" I covered the distance of the tiny hallway in three strides. One look into the unit's only bedroom told me that something was definitely amiss.

The room looked like a tornado had just blasted through. Clothes were strewn on every surface—floor, bed, chair, nightstands, and dressing table. Shoes were tossed atop the clothes, and in the middle of the mess sat BeBe Loudermilk, on a flowered chintz slipper chair, dressed only in an oversized T-shirt and what looked like men's cotton drawstring pajama bottoms.

"Do I look okay?" she demanded, running her fingers through an unruly tangle of blonde curls. She thrust her feet out in front of her. "Look at these!"

BeBe's size five feet were encased in a pair of fluffy white slippers with floppy pink-lined ears.

I bent down to get a good look. "Bedroom slippers?"

"Bunny slippers," she groaned. "The only shoes I can get on my big, fat, swollen, two-years-preggers feet."

I flopped down onto the bed. "This is your idea of an emergency? Swollen feet? Really? You scared the bejeezus out of me! I know Harry's on a fishing trip. I was terrified you were going into premature labor and I'd have to deliver the baby myself."

"No such luck," BeBe said glumly. "When I went to the doctor last week he said this kid of mine already weighs probably seven pounds. Seven pounds, Weezie! And I still have four weeks to go till my due date. What if I gain another ten pounds? What if this baby weighs nine or ten—or God forbid, eleven pounds? Did I tell you Harry casually admitted last week that he weighed over ten pounds when he was born? That's almost twice what I weighed at birth."

She placed both hands on top of her swollen belly and glared downwards. "Slow down in there, Squirt. You hear me? Your mama can't be rolling no ten-pound baby."

I cupped my hands into a megaphone and addressed the baby myself. "Squirt Sorrentino. Ignore your silly mama. You just keep on growing. Aunt Weezie's gonna be right here when you get out."

"Whoopedy-shit," BeBe said. "I'm gonna be the one doing the hard labor while you get to stand around out in the waiting room looking all cute and smiley in your 'I'm the godmother' T-shirt."

"That reminds me." I reached into my tote bag and brought out a small tissue-wrapped bundle. "I picked up a little push present for you at an estate sale in Ardsley Park yesterday."

"What is it?" She regarded the bundle suspiciously, even as she took it from me. "Some kind of antique scalpel? A pair of forceps?"

She tore at the paper, then smiled as the gleam of silver emerged from the tissue.

"It's a sterling Tiffany baby rattle," I said, taking the dumbbell-shaped ornament and jingling it back and forth to demonstrate. "It was at the bottom of a drawer full of sterling flatware I picked up at the same sale. I didn't even notice it until I started polishing everything last night."

She traced the ornately etched letter *S* on the stem of the rattle with a knowing touch. "This is hand-engraving. How did you have the time to get it monogrammed so quickly?"

"I didn't. All the silver was monogrammed with that same big old *S* on every piece. Eleven place settings. Plus serving pieces. Not to mention a bunch of gorgeous damask banquet napkins, also monogrammed. Guess how much?"

She pursed her lips and considered. Like any proper Southern postdebutante, she knew a thing or two about sterling silver. "What pattern?"

"Francis First," I said, sounding as smug as I felt.

"That's nice," she said, staring down at her swollen ankles.

"Nice?" I repeated. "Nice is an iced tea spoon for fifty bucks. I just scored eleven place settings of gorgeous sterling silver that is probably worth at least a hundred bucks for each piece, for a hundred and fifty bucks. Total."

"A place setting?"

"For all of it—a hundred fifty for eleven place settings, plus. But I'm going to keep it as a wedding present to myself. The *S* just seals the deal."

"*S*?" She had a blank look on her face.

"For Stipanek, of course. BeBe, are you sure you're feeling okay? You're acting so spacey." I turned around and put my hands on my hips, like a disapproving room monitor. "What happened in here?"

"I had a severe wardrobe malfunction. I can't show up for my baby shower at Merijoy Rucker's looking like Who-Shot-Sally. Especially since Merijoy herself is pregnant again, and damn her, she looks like an absolute goddess." She gestured around the disheveled room. "This is every piece of clothing I own, including all the cute maternity things I bought at that new boutique up in Atlanta, and none of it fits anymore. Face it. I'm an elephant. I look like shit on a stick."

"Merijoy's knocked up again? I didn't know that. What is this, her ninth or tenth kid?"

"Sixth. She's six months pregnant. Swear to God, Weezie, I saw her at Publix last week and she was wearing jeans. With a belt! And in the meantime, here I am, schlepping around in my ugly maternity top by Omar the tent-maker and Harry's old sweatpants. I wanted to kill myself. I still might if I can't find something to wear to this shower."

"Quit being such a drama queen," I said, looking around the room. "You are not that big. There must be two dozen outfits here. Surely one of them fits."

"No," she said mulishly. "I look awful in everything. I'm fat as a pig. I'm gross. I don't know why on earth I ever let Harry talk me into having a baby." She picked up her cell phone and tossed it to me. "You're just going to have to call Merijoy and tell her I can't make it to the shower. Tell her I'm dilated or something."

"Nuh-uh." I tossed the phone back, but it fell to her feet.

She just stared down at it. "I can't bend over to get that, you know. I haven't seen my toes in weeks. Months, even."

"Too bad, but I'm not doing your dirty work. Call her yourself." I dropped the phone in what was left of her lap.

"Come on," she cajoled. "You're a way better liar than me."

"Nobody's a better liar than you. Anyway, you can't skip out on your own baby shower. It's just not done. What about your grandmother? And don't you have some other family coming into town for this shindig?"

"My aunts and all my girl cousins are driving down from Charleston and Fripp Island," she said gloomily. "And the only reason they're coming is to see just how fat and gone to seed I am."

"You are *so* not fat. You're almost eight months pregnant. You look terrific. I bet you haven't even gained twenty pounds."

"Try twenty-seven pounds. And eight ounces." She thrust her rounded belly forward, to emphasize her point.

I picked up a coral silk floral print A-line dress with a sweetheart neckline, and draped it over her abdomen. "Why can't you wear this? The color is great on you."

"All those flowers?" She shuddered. "I'd look like my grandmother's sofa."

I picked through the pile of garments on her bed. Finally I handed her a chocolate-colored jersey knit wrap dress with three-quarter sleeves and pale blue banding at the hem and cuffs.

"Here. Wear this. It's adorable." I peeked at the price tag still hanging from the sleeve. "Holy geez! Three hundred fifty dollars? Are you kidding me?"

BeBe sighed heavily, but she unknotted the drawstring on her pajamas and let them slide to the floor, and pulled the shirt over her head. It was the first time I'd seen her undressed since she'd started to show.

"Stop staring," she ordered, unzipping the dress. "I already feel like a freak."

"You're not a freak," I said. "But I had no idea being pregnant made the blood vessels in your stomach look so blue. Or that you had an outie belly button."

"I didn't until I got knocked up. Isn't this gross? I have to put a Band-Aid over it if I want to wear anything the least bit stretchy."

"It's not gross at all. It's kind of cool, I think. Especially the boobs. You used to just barely be an A-cup, right? Now you're what, a C?"

"You sound just like Harry," BeBe said, sliding the dress over her head. "He seems to think my body is some fascinating new amusement park. You'd think he'd be turned off, but not old Harry." She rolled her eyes meaningfully, then turned back to the mirror, to appraise her appearance.

"It fits all right, I guess, but doesn't it make me look like a Hershey's Kiss?"

"No it does not. Stop running yourself down. You look great. The dress is chic and flattering. Being pregnant totally suits you. Your hair and skin look great."

"If you tell me I'm glowing I'm going to barf," she warned.

I handed her a wastebasket. "Be my guest. I'll tell you something else, BeBe Loudermilk. Even if you don't want to hear it. Harry Sorrentino is the best thing that ever happened to you. He is the real deal. He's smart and kind and sexy as hell. And he's an honest-to-goodness grown-up adult—which we both know are an endangered species as far as men are concerned. Also? He happens to adore you. So you need to stop all this bitchin' and moaning about being pregnant and do the right thing for your child and for yourself and Harry. You need to marry your baby daddy, BeBe."

She got a funny look on her face. Then she slumped down, buried her head in her hands, and began to sob.

"I can't," she said, her shoulders shaking with emotion.

"Sure you can," I said, stroking her back in an attempt to comfort her. "It's easy. You get a marriage license and a ring, and find yourself a justice of the peace and bingo—instant respectability."

That made her cry even harder.

"Okay, I didn't mean to insinuate you're not already respectable," I said, backpedaling as fast as I could.

She sat up and dabbed at her eyes with the hem of one of her discarded dresses. "You don't understand," she said, sniffling louder. "I mean I really can't marry Harry. Even if I wanted to."

"Why not?"

A fresh round of tears welled up in her eyes. "Because . . . because I just found out I'm probably still married."

She was as serious as a heart attack. "Married? To who? I mean, whom?"

"To Richard!" she cried. "Oh my God, Weezie. It's my worst nightmare come true."


When she had calmed down a little, she told me the whole ugly story.

"You have to promise not to tell a soul," she cautioned.

I gave her a look.

"I know you wouldn't, but still, if Harry finds out about this, it'll just kill him."

"You're not going to tell him?"

"That the mother of his unborn child is apparently still married to a sex freak and convicted criminal, who, I pray to God, is still locked up in prison? That I'm probably a bigamist, because I married Sandy Thayer while I was still married to Richard? Are you nuts?"

"Harry knows your backstory, and he obviously doesn't care," Weezie said. "Think how hurt he'd be if he found out you'd been keeping this a secret. I just don't want you to mess this up, BeBe."

# Chapter 6

✦

## BeBe

I didn't want me to mess this up either. It had taken me years, but I'd finally managed to find Mr. Right. And I didn't intend to let anything or anybody spoil my hard-won happiness.

Of course, our relationship got off to a pretty bumpy start.

A little over two years ago, I woke up one morning and discovered that a charming snake in the grass named Reddy Millbanks III had managed to cheat me out of literally everything except the clothes on my back.

I'd met Reddy on the rebound from yet another doomed romance— at the Telfair Ball, of all places, an annual charity benefit attended by the cream of Savannah society. How could I know he'd weaseled his way into that party the same way he later weaseled his way into my bed and my bank accounts?

When the dust settled from that fiasco, I was homeless and forced to move into the manager's unit of the broken-down tourist court on Tybee Island that Reddy had bought with my money—and without my knowledge—with the intention of selling it off quickly to make another fast buck.

Imagine my surprise to find said manager's unit already occupied by an irascible charter fishing boat captain named Harry Sorrentino. Imagine my further surprise to find myself quickly falling in love with Harry—and his little dog Jeeves. The baby had been a surprise too. At thirty-seven, I'd figured I wouldn't ever have children. But when I discovered I was pregnant and hesitantly shared the news, his reaction was one I never could have predicted.

He'd wept! And then he asked me to marry him. But I'd resisted, and considering this unwelcome latest development, it was a good thing I had.

Now, in the meantime, I still had to make an appearance at that dreaded baby shower. Weezie was determined to make that happen.

She held up a pair of brown suede pumps. "Here. Put these on."

"Can't," I said, sticking out my bare legs so she could see the pitiful condition of my puffy ankles and feet.

"All these gorgeous shoes. Can't you wear any of them?"

"Nope." I pointed at a pair of plain black flats by the closet doors. "Those nun's shoes are the only ones that fit. Unless you count flip-flops. And I'll be damned if I'm going to wear flip-flops in December."

Weezie handed me the shoes and I managed to wedge my feet into the flats.

"You look nice," she said, ever the loyal best friend.

"Liar."

"What does your grandmama have to say about your refusal to get married?"

I rolled my eyes. "About what you'd expect. She's scandalized, disappointed. She says the least I can do is lie to people and say we're engaged. And of course, she says my mama is rolling over in her grave."

"Which she probably is," Weezie pointed out. "We'll get my uncle James to straighten out this mess. And after he does, I still think you need to marry Harry."

"You can talk till you're blue in the face, but you won't change my mind. Marriage is fine for some people—I think it's absolutely right for you and Daniel—but Harry and I don't need a piece of paper to prove our commitment to each other."

"Whatever." Weezie knew it was pointless to keep arguing. She gave me a critical once-over. "Okay, so we're good here, right? You've got a cute outfit and some, uh, semi-cute shoes. Now, slap on some makeup and your big girl jewelry and let's hit the road. Merijoy gave me strict instructions that I was to get you to her house half an hour early."

"Do I have to?"

"Don't make me come over there and whomp you upside the head with an eye-shadow brush," she said, handing me my cosmetic bag.

I sat down at my dressing table and did as I was told, smoothing foundation over my face, followed by a quick sweep of eyeliner, mascara, and coral lip gloss, while Weezie roamed around the room, putting it back just the way she designed it all those months ago after Harry and I formally moved in together.

I glanced over my shoulder at her. "Speaking of weddings, how are the plans coming along? Did your mama get your dress fixed? How did the tasting go at the restaurant?"

"Mama's working on the dress. It'll be fine. It's Daddy I'm worried about."

"How so?"

"He's just not himself. He forgets things—and not just little things. I asked Mama about it, and she about bit my head off. She's in denial."

"That's a tough one," I agreed. "What about the food for the reception? Has Julio got something fabulous planned?"

She nodded. "Wait'll you see. It's gonna be amazing. Julio and Daniel have outdone themselves. Tiny little crab cakes and lobster bisque and on and on."

"Which reminds me. Wasn't Friday night the big night at Cucina Carlotta? How did it go? Is Daniel the toast of the town?"

Weezie's usually cheerful face clouded over. She bit the side of her lip and wrinkled her nose.

"What? He burned the biscuits? Overcooked the shrimp?"

"You know better than that," Weezie scoffed. "It went great, from what I can tell. He says the restaurant has been totally slammed."

"You don't look too happy about it," I pointed out. "What's going on, Weez?"

"It's probably nothing."

"Tell me," I ordered. "I've known you long enough to know when something's wrong."

She busied herself straightening my room, putting shoes back in boxes, hanging clothes in the closet. "I'm being silly. I know I am, but I can't help the way I feel."

"What is it you're being silly about? Something with Daniel?" A hideous thought occurred to me. "Oh my God. Tell me you're not having second thoughts. Just because marriage isn't right for me, that doesn't mean it isn't right for you. You and Daniel are perfect together. I knew you would be, the first time I laid eyes on him."

"It's not that," Weezie said. "It's the dumbest thing. When I was at Guale yesterday, one of the waitresses had tacked up a photo of Daniel and Mrs. Donatello—Carlotta, on the bulletin board."

"What kind of photo?"

"It was from one of those New York tabloids—taken at this swanky party Carlotta threw in his honor."

"And?"

Weezie was standing in front of the closet, her back to me. I heard a muttered stream of words, only a few of which I could make out. But the words and phrases "bombshell," "cleavage," "dinner jacket," and "shit-eating-grin" seemed fairly distinct.

I managed to heave myself up from my perch. I gently placed my hands on my best friend's shoulders and turned her around to face me. Her eyes were red. She sniffed loudly.

"So. I gather the photo was of Daniel and some tramp named Carlotta and her boobs. He was wearing a dinner jacket and a stupid smile.

And this is making you insane with jealousy. Is that about the gist of it?"

She nodded and gulped. "I *told* you it was crazy. I'm ashamed of myself. But I can't stop thinking about it. I thought he was going up there to work for some big fat Italian lady with a white bun and fallen arches. You know, some sweet old *nonna* type. And Daniel never said anything to let me think otherwise. Then I see this picture of her— swear to God, BeBe, she looks like a young Sophia Loren, and she's got herself wrapped around Daniel . . . pasted to him!

"And the thing that gets me? The worst part? He was wearing a dinner jacket. Daniel Stipanek—in a dinner jacket!"

I patted her shoulder. "You're right. The dinner jacket thing is unforgivable. The man is totally not to be trusted and you should definitely cancel the wedding."

She gave me a baleful look. "He didn't call me for two days. Not even a text. And he never mentioned the party she gave him or the fact that his boss looks like a supermodel."

"So you're saying you don't trust him?"

"No! I trust him completely. Utterly. It's that woman I don't trust."

"Have you discussed this with him?"

She nodded. "He finally called last night. And he did say he hasn't had a spare minute. He claims he didn't mention the party because he didn't think it was important. Because he hates big crowds."

"Which he does," I pointed out. "What does he say about this Carlotta hag?"

Weezie shrugged. "You know how Daniel is. He claims he doesn't have any idea how old she is or that she was planning that party. And he says he's lonely. And he misses me."

"All of this sounds exactly like the Daniel I know," I told her. "When I owned Guale and he was single and available—every gorgeous woman in Savannah made a run at him. And he never even noticed them. Daniel's no player, Weezie. He's in love with you."

"The rational me knows all that," Weezie said miserably. "The rational me knows he'll be home in a week, and we'll get married and it'll all be good. But the crazy-pants Bridezilla me cannot get rid of the image of that woman with her boobs all pushed up in Daniel's grille."

Her eyes were starting to tear up again.

"I thought I was the one with raging hormones." I gave her shoulder a final pat. "You know what I think?"

"What?"

"I think the only way you're going to get through this next week with your sanity intact is to go up there."

She looked startled. "New York? Are you crazy? I'm getting married in a week. It's Christmas. My busiest time of the year at the shop. I can't just drop everything and go to New York."

"Okay. It was just a thought." I grabbed my pocketbook and my keys and headed for the front door. As soon as I walked into the living room, Jeeves hopped down from his chair and trotted over to the door. With effort, I managed to lean over far enough to scratch his chin.

"Sorry, sport. This is a baby shower. It's strictly chicks. No boys, no dogs allowed." I tossed him a treat from the jar by the door, and he caught it in midair, then trotted back to his chair to savor.

Weezie followed me out the door and stood by while I locked up.

"Anyway, I don't need to go to New York," she continued. "Yes, he's lonely. And I've never been there, and even Daniel, who hates Christmas, says it's pretty cool to be in New York during the holidays, but there's no way I could go. I'm getting married next Sunday."

"You're absolutely right," I agreed. "Besides, I need you to take a look at the new kitchen cabinets and give me your opinion on the paint color. I'm thinking maybe it's too dark."

Weezie turned and pointed in the direction of our latest construction project. "How's the house coming?"

Living in the charming but cramped manager's unit at the Breeze Inn was always supposed to be a temporary solution to our housing situation, but with the baby coming, Harry had the bright idea to buy a dilapidated old 1920s-era wood-frame house located on the north end of the island and have it moved to a vacant lot beside the motel. That was six months ago.

The house, which had once been the commissary for Fort Screven, a decommissioned World War I army post on Tybee, had been partially disassembled, jacked up, and loaded onto a flatbed tractor-trailer for the mile-and-a-half trip down Butler Avenue to our property on the south end of the island. The plan was for the commissary to be reassembled on a new raised foundation, and transformed into a period-perfect three-bedroom, three-bath nest for our new family. But plans have a tendency to go awry. Especially on Tybee, where everybody and everything runs on island time.

"You know how it goes out here. Always something. First the

electrician's helper got put in jail for DUI. Then the Sheetrock guy's truck got repossessed, so we had to start all over with a new guy, but then the new guy's wife kicked him out and sold all his tools on Craigslist, so now Harry's been staying up all hours of the night trying to get it done. In the meantime, all the new windows are on back order, and my new Viking stove is sitting in a warehouse somewhere in Jacksonville, but my appliance guy can't find the paperwork to prove we paid for it."

I let out a long, exasperated sigh. "And, oh yeah. I just found out I might still be married to Richard Hodges."

"Sorry I asked," Weezie said. "But look on the bright side. You've still got six weeks until your due date. You and I have done our job. We bought the crib and the changing table; the drapes and slipcovers are done. Your rugs were delivered this week. The house is going to be amazing. Especially the nursery. I can't wait to paint Squirt's nursery."

"Really? It'll all get done? I won't have to bring my baby home to sleep in a dresser drawer in an eight-hundred-square-foot apartment? "

"Really. I promise. Totally ah-freakin'-may-zing."

"And we'll figure out how to make sure I'm divorced?"

"James will."

I gave her a hug and held up my pinkie. "Swear?"

She laughed and wrapped her pinkie around mine. "Pinkie swear."

# Chapter 7

✦

# BeBe

When we pulled up in front of the Ruckers' sprawling Colonial Revival mansion in Ardsley Park I spotted a huge bouquet of bright pink balloons tied to the mailbox and waving in the breeze. I leaned forward in my seat to get a better look. "Are those what I think they are?"

"Babies. Yes. You are correct. Those are giant pink naked baby-shaped balloons." Weezie glared at me. "Cute, right? No more Ms. Cranky-pants. If I know Merijoy she's gone to a lot of trouble to put together a fun and tasteful baby shower in your honor. You'll get a ton of useful loot for the baby. This was a very sweet and thoughtful gesture on her part. So you need to put on your best party manners and be a gracious and grateful honoree. Right?"

"Right," I mumbled. "Gracious. Grateful."

A hideous thought occurred to me. "What if somebody knows? About Richard?"

"Who would know?" she scoffed. "Hardly anybody even remembers you were married to him."

"It's Savannah," I said darkly. "Nobody here forgets anything. Especially the bad stuff. There are people in this town who still remember the day Sherman and his Union troops rolled into town back in 1864."

It was still daylight, but I could see the glowing icicle lights dripping from the eaves of the house. The enormous cast-iron urns on either side of the front door held large topiary boxwoods crisscrossed with more lit Christmas lights, and large pots of white poinsettias lined either side of the steps leading up to the covered porch. Wreaths hung from every window of the house, and the wreath on the front door was decked out with pink and blue pacifiers, miniature baby bottles, and plastic rattles.

Merijoy herself opened the front door just as I went to ring the doorbell. She was dressed in a form-fitting dark green sheath. Of course my eyes went directly to her abdomen. No noticeable bump. Well, maybe a small I-just-ate-a-cheeseburger one.

"BeBe!" She folded me into a hug, which was awkward, because my enormous baby bump looked like it could totally beat up her nonexistent one. "Don't you look precious!"

"Thanks," I said, graciously and gratefully. "You look wonderful. You're seven months along? How is that possible?"

"Oh, honey," she drawled, slapping her backside. "That's just how I'm built. I always carry my babies high and tight up front. You should see the rear view. I look like a water buffalo!" She turned around and wriggled her very tiny hiney, to prove it to us.

"As if," I said under my breath, earning myself a jab in the ribs from Weezie.

"And here's our bride too," Merijoy said, ushering us into her house. She beamed at Weezie. "Are you getting nervous yet?"

"Not at all," Weezie assured her.

While Merijoy gushed about weddings, Christmas, and the imminent birth of her sixth child—a boy, she confided—I glanced around the living room. A towering fir seemed to fill one corner of the room, its angel tree-topper touching the two-story-high cathedral ceiling. The thing was plastered with hundreds and hundreds of gilded and glittered angels, all of them lit by miles and miles of tiny white lights.

"Wow, what a tree. Is it real?"

"Oh yes," Merijoy said. "Randy Rucker won't allow a fake tree in his house. So we actually have six trees—the others are in the dining room, the kitchen, the great room, his office, and the children's playroom. All of them have different themes. And I spend most of my waking hours vacuuming up pine needles."

Merijoy plucked a cellophane box from a console table behind a green velvet sofa, opened it, and took out the largest orchid I have ever seen. "This is for you," she said.

It was approximately the size of a dinner plate.

"Oh, wow, thanks," I said feebly. "A corsage. I don't think I've had a corsage since I went to the KA pledge party at Ole Miss."

The doorbell rang just then, and she left me to fasten my own corsage.

Pinned atop my now D-cup boob and trailing pink and blue ribbons, I felt as though I were wearing a potted plant on my chest. I glanced over at Weezie. "How'm I doing?"

Before she could answer, I was suddenly engulfed in a tidal wave of female relatives; my grandmother, my great-aunt Helen from Beaufort, Aunt Bizzy from Charleston, and the clot of cousins I've always referred to as "the Marys"—Mary Margaret, Jeanne Marie, and Mary Elizabeth.

With affectionate squeals and shrieks and pats and hugs and kisses, they circled around me, exclaiming over their joy at seeing me, their approval of my dress—Aunt Bizzy referred to me as "cute as a bug," something nobody has said of me since I was eight—and questions. Endless questions.

"Is it a boy or a girl?"

"Don't know," I said breezily.

"But which would you prefer?" somebody asked.

"A healthy baby," I responded.

"Have you picked out names yet?"

"Not really. We want to wait to see who the baby is before we commit to something as important—and permanent—as a name."

"I always think family names are the most suitable," Aunt Bizzy opined. "And you know, none of the cousins has ever named a child after your grandparents. Wouldn't that be a lovely tribute to them?" She gave me a meaningful wink.

I adore my grandparents—whose names are Spencer and Lorena. Nice enough names, I suppose, but not ones I would ever choose for my own child. I was about to remind Aunt Bizzy that *she* hadn't bothered to name any of *her* five children after her own parents, but thank God, Grandmama overheard.

"Good heavens! I've always hated the name Lorena, and I'm not keen on Spencer either, which is why we didn't foist them off on any of our own children."

She gave me a stern look. "BeBe, I absolutely forbid you to name a child after either of us."

"If you insist," I said gratefully.

"Don't ask her about when she's getting married," Grandmama said when there was finally a temporary lull in the conversation. She was seated in a leather armchair in front of the fireplace, her silver-knobbed cane resting against her legs, which were clad in her customary dark orange surgical stockings.

Five sets of eyes stared at me. I smiled sweetly. And said absolutely nothing.

Fortunately, more waves of women soon landed in the room, another two dozen or so—and they barely made a dent in the Ruckers' expansive living room, with its jewel-toned Oriental rugs, velvet sofas, and paisley armchairs and leather wing chairs.

I circled the room and made polite conversation.

"Do you have a birth plan yet?" asked Stephanie Gardner. Stephanie was a Georgia Tech–educated engineer, and she and her husband, Jeff, also an engineer, lived two doors down from my town house downtown. I liked Stephanie, but her brilliance and efficiency always made me feel inadequate. In fact, she was so efficient, she'd managed to have twins three years ago and six weeks later ran a marathon.

"Do I need a birth plan? Nobody told me."

"Of course! When I had Addison and James, I had a whole spreadsheet printed out and packed in my hospital bag. Jeff had a copy, and my mom and mother-in-law had theirs, and I made sure to e-mail copies to my obstetrician and his partners."

"I don't think I have one of those," I admitted. "I sort of just thought when the time came I'd go to the hospital and, you know, have a baby."

"Oh, BeBe, you're so cute and funny," she said, rapping my arm playfully.

I turned away slightly and bumped into Karen Turner, a former classmate from Savannah Country Day.

"Oh, a Christmas baby," she cooed, placing both hands on my belly. I backed away a little. Baby or no, I've never gotten used to people, even well-meaning semi-friends, randomly fondling my abdomen.

"Uh, actually, no. I'm not due for another six weeks."

Her eyes widened. "Really? Ugh. Another six weeks? I remember when I was pregnant with Creighton, those last six weeks were torture. I couldn't sleep, because he kicked nonstop, plus I had to get up every ten minutes to pee. The back pain was agony! And then I got gestational diabetes, which meant blood testing and insulin injections. Plus, I had this really heinous constant heartburn, and then my hands were so swollen Wendell had to take me to the emergency room and get my wedding ring sawed off."

She gazed meaningfully down at my ringless left hand.

What do you say to something like that? I blanked, which Karen took as a signal to overshare with one last tidbit of her maternity miseries.

She leaned in and lowered her voice. "I guess Merijoy probably told you about my episiotomy disaster, right?"

*Episiotomy disaster?* If ever there were two words no pregnant woman ever wants to hear uttered together, it was those words. I looked around for Weezie, frantically searching the room, hoping she would rescue me. But she was clear across the room, laughing and chatting with our hostess, without a care in the world.

"I'm still not right," Karen was saying.

I felt dizzy. I put both hands on the back of a nearby chair to steady myself, but the room seemed to suddenly go a little fuzzy around the edges. I took a couple of deep cleansing breaths, the kind I'd read about on somebody's mommy blog.

"Are you all right?" Karen asked.

"Could you excuse me?" I managed. "I have to go powder my nose."

I ran-walked to the powder room, making it just in the nick of time. Afterward, I ran cold water on one of Merijoy's monogrammed linen hand towels and dabbed my face and neck with it. I leaned against the locked bathroom door and checked the time on my cell phone. Only twenty minutes had passed since I'd arrived. Twenty minutes!

More deep breaths.

Finally, after ten minutes of stalling, I sidled back into the living room and concentrated on making myself invisible—no easy task when you're the size of a Winnebago and the party is in your honor.

Thankfully, nobody else had the nerve to inquire about my plans—birth or marriage. And I managed to steer well away from Karen Turner for the rest of the afternoon.

Finally, mercifully, Merijoy herded us all into the dining room, where we exclaimed over her snowman-themed Christmas tree and loaded our hand-painted luncheon plates with the obligatory Southern lady party food; tiny, delicious little crustless sandwiches made with shrimp paste or egg salad or pimento cheese, deviled eggs, a pecan-speckled cheese ball surrounded by strawberry preserves, and of course cheese straws. In Savannah, there's a law that says you cannot get engaged, married, christened, or buried without a nicely polished silver tray of cheese straws.

When I'd eaten my fill of cheese-related products, plus four or five Christmas cookies, I allowed myself to be steered back to the living room, where I sank gratefully into one of the armchairs by the sofa, hoping nobody would notice as I removed my shoes.

"How're you doing?" Weezie asked, grabbing the chair beside mine. "I saw Karen Turner bending your ear earlier. And then I noticed you mysteriously disappeared. For a minute there, I was afraid you'd left. And then I remembered I drove. So, is everything okay?"

"Everything is just peachy. Stephanie Gardner pointed out that I don't have a birth plan. And then Karen attempted to regale me with a hilarious account of her botched episiotomy, after which I had to race to the bathroom to barf. Good times!"

Weezie winced. "Sorry. But cheer up. All you have to do now is open some presents and look gracious and grateful. Twenty, thirty more minutes tops, we'll be out of here."

Unfortunately, our hostess hadn't gotten the memo about Weezie's timetable. Merijoy stood in front of the fireplace and clapped her hands to silence the chattering crowd.

"Okay, y'all," she announced. "You know what time it is, right?"

"Game time?" squealed one of the Marys. "Ooh, I love silly shower games."

I didn't dare look over at Weezie.

We scooted our chairs into a semicircle. Merijoy's eyes gleamed with excitement as she brought out a large cardboard box. She reached in and brought out what looked suspiciously like a stack of disposable diapers.

"Now, girls, everybody take a diaper, but don't unfold it yet. No peeking!"

I stared dumbly down at the diaper in my lap.

"When I say 'Go!' everybody open your diaper. There's a little surprise in there. You can touch it and smell it—but you can't taste it. Write down what you think it is on your little notepad, and then pass it along to the next person. Keep it moving! When I say stop, the first person who has all the correct answers wins a prize. No cheating, now!"

"Yay!" chirped Mary Elizabeth, at twenty-three the youngest of the Marys. "I love the doody in the diaper game!"

Seeing my expression, Weezie leaned over and whispered in my ear. "Don't worry. It's just some melted candy. You know, like a Butterfinger or a Tootsie Roll."

"That's the sickest thing I've ever heard of," I whispered back.

"Go!" Merijoy ordered. Immediately the room erupted in a chorus of shrieks and giggles.

I reluctantly unfastened the tapes of my diaper and gazed down at the contents, which appeared to be some kind of brown lump encrusted with peanuts.

"Snicker," Weezie whispered. I rolled my eyes but dutifully wrote it down. As soon as I'd finished, Weezie handed me a diaper that had been handed to her. I glanced, shrugged, and scribbled something illegible. Another diaper, then another and another were handed around. Each time I passed it along without looking. Fortunately, the other women were so immersed in the hilarity of the game nobody noticed my lack of participation.

"Stop!" Merijoy called, and she was greeted with groans and more giggles. When the notes were tallied, it was no surprise that Mary Elizabeth was the big winner—correctly guessing twelve different kinds of mashed-up or melted candies.

Merijoy's next game was just as sick and twisted as her first. She quickly produced another large cardboard box—full of baby bottles.

"Y'all are gonna love this one," she exclaimed. "Everybody gets a bottle, okay? They're all filled with something different." She nodded in my direction. "Don't worry, BeBe, I'll make sure yours doesn't have anything alcoholic in it."

"Yippee," I said weakly.

"When I holler go, everybody has to suck their bottle down. All of it! Whoever finishes first, wins. Isn't that hilarious?"

"I don't think I'll participate in this one, dear," Grandmama said when Merijoy handed her one of the bottles.

"I'm going to opt out too," I whispered. "I'm just the slightest bit queasy right now. In fact, I'm just going to run along to the bathroom."

"Oh, pooh! You're no fun," Merijoy said, but she went all around the circle, passing out bottles.

Weezie sniffed hers. "Cranberry juice. And vodka, I think."

"Make sure you don't drink all that," I said, getting to my feet. "You're driving us home—and I've got a baby on board, in case you've forgotten."

"As if," she said.

"Go, Bizzy, go," the women were chanting as I waddled out of the powder room and into the living room. My aunt Bizzy, the same serene former president of the Charleston Junior League, was leaned backwards in her chair, sucking so hard on her baby bottle that it looked like she'd turn her cheeks inside out.

"Go, go, go," my cousins chanted, their own bottles forgotten. The other women in the circle were still delicately sipping and sucking on their own concoctions.

Finally Bizzy held her empty bottle up for inspection. "Done," she called breathlessly.

"What was it?" Jeanne Marie asked. "Mine was apple juice."

"Not sure," Bizzy said, her voice thick and a little woozy. "Something chocolatey."

"Ooh, you got the Baileys Irish Cream," Merijoy exclaimed. "You win!"

Next, Merijoy went around the circle handing out balls of string and pairs of children's blunt-tipped scissors.

I glanced uneasily at Weezie, who seemed to be a font of knowledge when it came to disturbing trends in baby shower games. "I'm afraid to ask," I whispered.

"Uh-oh," she said, shaking her head and laughing. "You're for sure not gonna like this one."

Merijoy stopped when she got to me. "Come on, BeBe, I need you to stand up," she ordered. I just barely managed to squeeze my feet back into my shoes before she gave me her hand, and with effort, managed to haul me out of the armchair.

"Stand here in front of the fireplace," she instructed. I did as I was told. Merijoy Rucker somehow has that effect on people. Even me. She rarely raises her voice, but she always gets her way.

"Turn around. Slowly."

I did a slow spin, my cheeks burning.

"Good. You can sit down now."

"Now, girls. You've all got your string and your scissors. I want you to figure out the distance around BeBe's waist, and cut your string to that length." She waggled her finger at my cousins. "And no fair measuring your own waist or anybody else's. You're just supposed to eyeball BeBe. Got it?"

I smiled brightly. This was fun, right? Fun, fun, fun. So why was I so miserable?

I turned to Weezie, but she wasn't there. She was walking rapidly in the direction of the dining room, her cell phone pressed to her ear.

I felt a hand on my elbow and turned to see that Grandmama had taken Weezie's vacated chair.

"It's just a game, sugar," she said, her voice low and soothing. "I know you don't like the way you look right now, but no woman really feels attractive when she's as far along as you are. Why, when I was pregnant with your daddy, the last month, I refused to leave the house."

She took my hand in hers and squeezed it. Her skin was cool and dry to the touch, and I could feel the ropy outline of her veins under my own fingertips, and it made me miss my own mother so keenly it nearly took my breath away.

"I wouldn't even sleep in the same room with your granddaddy, because I didn't want him to see me in my nightgown," she continued.

"Really?" My voice was wobbly. Damned hormones.

"Really. And for what it's worth, I think you look lovely. You might not think so, but pregnancy suits you. Your skin and hair are so soft and shiny, you're just beautiful."

"That's what Harry keeps telling me," I whispered.

"I like that Harry," she said, smiling. "I do wish you would marry him, but I promised your granddaddy I wasn't going to pester you about this today. So I won't. I'll just say we're very, very happy to see you so happy these days."

I leaned over and kissed her papery cheek, then took my finger and rubbed at the lipstick smudge I'd left.


Somehow I managed to get through the rest of the fun and games. I opened what seemed like an endless array of gifts, smiling and exclaiming at the usefulness of everything.

"It's all so sweet," I said when Merijoy's rug was covered in what seemed like a foot of crumpled paper and ribbon. Weezie was busily loading my gifts into a gleaming European stroller, and Merijoy was bundling the rest of them into an antique wicker cradle that had been her gift to me.

"Thank you, everybody," I said, gazing around at the circle of women. These were my people—friends and near friends, relatives and neighbors. An imperfect circle, but mine nonetheless. And it struck me that Weezie was right. These women were here because they were happy for me and wanted to celebrate the birth of my baby. Maybe it was the hormones, or maybe it was the shadow of Richard looming large in my subconscious, but suddenly I was feeling all weepy and grateful, maybe even just a tad gracious.

# Chapter 8

✦

After we'd finally managed to wedge all my loot into the backseat and trunk of my car, I was only too happy to accept Weezie's offer to drive me home. My lower back was aching and I was exhausted. I laid my head back and closed my eyes for what seemed like a matter of seconds, but before I knew it, we were parked in front of the Breeze Inn, and Weezie was gently shaking me awake.

"Home sweet home," she said, pointing at the blinking neon "No Vacancy" sign. I yawned widely.

"Are you all right?" she asked, peering over to check my face in the fading light. "You look kind of pale."

"Just tired," I said, stifling another yawn. I glanced around the parking lot, hoping to see Harry's truck, but it wasn't there.

"Is Harry coming back from his fishing trip tonight?" Weezie asked, realizing what I was looking for.

"Don't know. He took one of his rich snowbird clients early this morning, and he wasn't sure how far south they'd go before they started catching fish. He usually calls around six to touch base with me."

She got out of the car and hurried around to open the trunk and start unloading my gifts. It took us three trips to get it all into the apartment, where Jeeves immediately busied himself circling the packages, sniffing expectantly.

"Sorry, pal, no dog biscuits or bones in there," Weezie said, scooping the dog up into her arms and allowing him to lick her face.

"Sit down," she said, pointing at the armchair Jeeves had only recently vacated. "I'm going to fix you some hot tea. What about dinner? Are you hungry?"

"Tea would be nice, but no dinner. I think I ate my weight in those damn Christmas cookies."

"It was a really lovely party, I thought," Weezie called from the kitchen. "Except for those stupid, horrible games."

"Who even thinks that stuff up?" I demanded. "Making people chug from baby bottles? And did you see how long my cousin Mary Elizabeth's string was? She obviously thinks I'm the size of a cruise ship. Or maybe an aircraft carrier. I swear, that string was at least three yards long."

"Mary Elizabeth might want to take a peek in her own mirror before she goes thinking about how big you are," Weezie said tartly. "Cuz there's enough room on that back porch of hers to hang a swing and a glider!"

"I noticed you were on the phone for a pretty long time right about then," I said. "Or was that just a ruse so you didn't have to participate in the fun and games?"

She came into the living room and sat down on the chair across from mine. "I was talking to Daniel. He sounded so unhappy. So lonely. He's got an awful cold, and he finally admitted he's not sleeping, and there's no real food in the apartment they're putting him up in. I'm thinking . . . I'm really sorta wondering if maybe I should go up there and take care of him."

"Of course you should!" I cried. "That's what I've been telling you! You're unhappy, he's lonely. It makes no sense for you not to go."

She shook her head. "This is crazy. Buying a plane ticket so late like this—and it being the holidays? I probably can't even get a flight—and if I could, it'd probably be way too expensive. I hate to spend the money when we're going to Paris in the spring."

But I was already out of my chair, retrieving my phone. I scrolled through my contacts until I found the number I wanted, and touched the icon.

"What are you doing? BeBe—no! I'm not letting you do this."

I waved away her objections while I was on hold with the airline. "You can't stop me. I've got enough Delta frequent-flier miles to fly around the world. Twice. I'm not buying you a ticket, I'm just loaning you my miles."

The operator came on in a surprisingly short amount of time. I made the reservation, gave the operator Weezie's phone number and email address, and clicked off.

"This is nuts," Weezie started.

"Hush! Listen. You're on a direct flight to LaGuardia. You better go home right now and pack, because your plane leaves at six forty in the morning. I've got you returning at eight forty p.m. next Friday. Now. Clothes. You don't actually own a real winter coat, do you?"

"Just a sort of vintage car coat I bought at an estate sale. It's black cashmere with dolman sleeves . . ."

"Cashmere is not going to cut it in New York in December. Especially vintage cashmere, which probably has vintage moth holes to match. Am I right?"

"Maybe a few. Just around the hem . . ."

I sighed and handed her a room key. "You'll have to go unlock unit six—the little studio efficiency? I'm using that as a closet until they finish with the new house. Take my long black camel-hair coat. There are some wool scarves on a hook near the door. My slacks will all be too short on you, but help yourself to some of my sweaters."

"I can't just take off and fly to New York like this," BeBe said. "You don't understand. This is our busiest time at the shop . . ."

"Which is why you're going to call Courtney and tell her she can have all the extra hours she wants this week. You did say she was looking to make some extra money over the holidays, right? And what about those SCAD kids who've been working part-time? Why couldn't they come in to help Courtney?"

"Ellie and Alex did say they aren't going home for Christmas this year," I admitted. "But what about the wedding? Mama will want to do one more fitting for my dress, and I'm still not sure about the cake. I baked some more layers this morning, but I can't decide on the frosting. I don't even have a cake topper yet!"

"Weezie! Stop with the excuses. You told me earlier your mama fitted the dress on you yesterday. She's been sewing for you her whole life. The dress will be fine. And as for the cake, I don't get why you have to bake your own cake when Daniel has an amazing pastry chef at Guale. You can pick up a cake topper in New York. They have stores there, in case you haven't heard."

"I don't know," she repeated. "I want to go. I'm *dying* to go. But it's so . . . irresponsible to just drop everything and take off at the last minute like this." She gave me a long, searching look. "What about this thing with Richard? Plus I wouldn't feel right, taking off so close to your due date. What if the baby comes early?"

"I'll call your uncle James first thing tomorrow. As for the baby, it might *never* come," I said. "You know I want you right here when the time comes, don't you?"

"I'll be right there, with a big ol' thermos of frozen daiquiris, the minute that baby is safely delivered," Weezie pledged.

"Well, my time for sure isn't going to come in the next five days." I splayed my fingertips over my belly. "I swear it feels like I've got a bowling ball pressing down on my bladder."

"Call the airline and cancel that reservation," Weezie said. "I mean it. What with Daddy acting all squirrelly and all the wedding stuff on my mind, I've got no business even considering a trip to New York."

"You are going," I insisted. "I have weeks and weeks to go before Squirt gets here. You've got good help at the shop, and if you're worried about the wedding stuff, just turn it all over to Cookie and Manny. Your daddy? Well, if he has dementia or Alzheimer's or whatever, your mama is eventually going to have to deal with the reality of that."

She sighed. "I'm so conflicted."

"Go. Your uncle James is only five minutes away if something comes up with your daddy. I can help out in the shop if the girls need an extra hand. So why are you hanging around here when you've got so much to do before morning?"

"I guess there's no good arguing, since you put it like that." She stood up and gave me a hug. "Which unit did you say the coat is stashed in?"

Five minutes later she was back with an armful of clothes. "I just remembered—what do I do about Jethro? I can't ask Mama to take him, not with Daddy like he is. And Cookie and Manny have enough to deal with with Ruthie."

I rolled my eyes. "Okay, he can stay with me. I'll pick him up in the morning. Now get out of here before I change my mind."

Six o'clock came and went. My phone calls to Harry went directly to voice mail. I tried not to worry, telling myself the weather was perfectly normal. It had been a warm, positively balmy day in Savannah, and the temperature had dipped down into the sixties only after sunset. At seven,

I clicked on the weather radio we keep in the office, but all the forecasts were good. Seas were calm, it wasn't too windy.

I wondered how many thousands of other wives and sweethearts of fishermen all over the world were doing what I was doing tonight; pacing the floor, worrying about their mates out on the deep blue sea.

Harry Sorrentino was an experienced charter boat captain. He'd grown up fishing these waters, bought his first flats boat at the age of fourteen, and gotten his captain's license at eighteen. He'd taken charters as far north as Cape Hatteras in North Carolina and as far south as the Florida Keys. At one point in his life, he'd actually gotten a law degree, but he'd never really practiced law.

We'd met at a low point in both our lives. Two consecutive years of bad fishing and high fuel and repair costs had resulted in his ex-wife repossessing his beloved boat, the *Jitterbug*, so he'd taken the only job he could get at the time, as maintenance man and manager of the Breeze Inn. My plight wasn't any better, after Reddy took off with not just my own money but my grandparents' life savings as well, I was penniless *and* homeless.

But together, with Weezie and even Granddad along for the ride, we'd tailed Reddy all the way down to Fort Lauderdale, and managed to con a con and eventually recover most of my fortune. Along the way, Harry and I had fallen hard for each other. We've been together ever since.

And we would stay together, I promised myself, no matter what. Tomorrow I would call James Foley and enlist his help to untangle my marital mess.

Jeeves was standing expectantly by the door. I was exhausted, but dogs don't care. I snapped on his leash and we went for our evening walk. When we got back, I picked up my phone, expecting to see that Harry had called. Instead, there was a message from Otis, our plumber. I recognized his high, nasal voice even before he identified himself.

"Miz Loudermilk? This is Otis Bembry. Listen, uh, about that old beat-up kitchen sink your friend wants to put in the new house. I been studying that thing, and I just don't think I can make that work. You'd have to send off clear to Atlanta to get the right drainpipe. But don't you worry. I went over to the Home Depot and got you a brand spanking new one, nice and shiny white, and it didn't cost but ninety-eight dollars."

"No, no, no." I slapped my own forehead in frustration. Because the "new" house was actually a wood-frame cottage built around 1914, Weezie had found an original porcelain-over-cast-iron farm sink at a local architectural salvage yard. She'd designed our kitchen around the sink. Otis's cheap shiny white sink would ruin the whole effect.

The next message on the Inn's machine was also about the house.

"Hey, uh, Miz Loudermilk? Henry here. Me and the crew were supposed to be over to your place in the morning, but uh, Lamar and Junior, my helpers? They, uh, got in kind of a jam down in Jacksonville Saturday night. Junior, he's got a busted right hand, and Lamar thinks maybe he's got a couple cracked ribs. Anyway, we'll probably see you around the middle of the week. Okay?"

"Not okay," I muttered, setting the phone down. Henry was our roofer, and he was already a week late. The only real roof we had on the house right now was a big blue tarp. And the forecast for the coming week was rain and more rain.

It was no good my calling him back and threatening to fire him. I'd already fired Henry once and had to rehire him, because I couldn't find another roofer on such short notice.

Harry did most of his own mechanical work on the *Jitterbug,* but maybe something had gone wrong. He could have blown an engine or sheared off a propeller. His radio might have been disabled, or his GPS navigational system could have been knocked off. Or . . . my God! I'd read about rogue waves, three, four, five stories high, engulfing boats . . .

Between worrying about my marital status with Richard and annoyances at our contractors and my fears for what could happen to Harry, by the time I heard the crunch of tires in the Breeze Inn's parking lot, I'd managed to work myself into a full-blown panic attack.

# Chapter 9

✦

Harry strode into the apartment, grinning ear to ear. His face was windburned and his hair was stiff with salt spray. Jeeves was flinging himself at his legs, in a delirium of joy.

Me? I burst into tears.

"Hey," he said softly, stopping a few feet short of me. "What's all this about?"

"I thought you were dead!" I said accusingly. "When you didn't call at six like you usually do, I started imagining all the things that could go wrong. That the boat broke down or your nav system quit working. And then I started thinking about rogue waves and sharks and . . ."

"Damn!" he said, reaching into the pocket of his fleece-lined Windbreaker. He held up his cell phone. "Dead as a doornail. I'm so sorry, babe. We were out at the snapper banks, and the fish were biting like crazy. Snapper, grouper, sea bass, we were pulling them in so fast, I guess I lost all track of time. My client said it was the single best fishing day of his life."

His hand went back in his pocket and he brought out a wad of cash. "Look at this! A five-hundred-dollar tip. And that's not all. I've probably got a couple hundred pounds of fish out in my cooler. I'll sell 'em to the seafood wholesale house in the morning and probably end up clearing close to a thousand bucks for one day's worth of fishing. Not bad, huh?"

Tears were running down my face, and I was powerless to stop them. "The money's great, but I was so worried. What if something really had gone wrong?"

He gathered me into his arms and held me close. "Nothing's gonna go wrong. I've been doing this my whole life. I just overhauled the boat last month. She's running great. The seas are calm, the weather is perfect. My guy wanted to stay out overnight and fish again in the morning, but I told him nothing doing, I had to get home to you."

He placed his right hand on my belly. "How's the baby? Everything good? Was the shower fun? Looks like we got a lot of presents, huh?"

"The baby's fine. The shower was fine." I sniffed and took a step away from Harry. "You smell like the bottom of a bait bucket."

He cupped my chin with his hand and kissed the tip of my nose. "Sorry about that too. I'll hit the shower, than we can talk, okay?"

"I guess."

By the time Harry was out of the shower, I'd managed to compose myself. A little.

He walked out of the bedroom, barefoot, in a clean T-shirt and his oldest, most worn pair of jeans. His deeply tanned face and arms were in stark contrast to the white shirt, and his damp hair still wore comb tracks.

"Better now?" he asked, putting his arms around what was left of my waist.

I buried my nose in his shoulder, inhaling the scent of the bleached-out shirt and his soap. His hands, resting lightly on the skin of my back, felt warm and strong. And I felt safe and loved. Being in his arms made me feel safe and good, and finally, for the first time in my adult life, I knew I was exactly where I was supposed to be.

We stood like that for maybe five minutes, not talking, just leaning into each other. I sniffed again and took a half step backwards.

"Did you get something to eat?"

"Oh yeah," he said carelessly. "I stopped at the Publix on Wilmington Island on the way home. I actually sort of thought you might already be asleep."

"No way." I shook my head. "Is your phone working okay now?"

"I plugged it in and it's recharging right now. It was just the battery."

Damn it, I felt tears welling up in my eyes again. "Get a new battery, please. In fact, get a new phone. I can't stand to worry about you like this."

"My phone is fine," Harry said, his voice serious. "Come on, let's go sit down. You've got yourself all worked up over nothing."

I let him lead me to the sofa by the hand, like a naughty child. I sank uneasily into the deep cushions and he settled at the opposite end of the sofa.

"How are your feet?" he asked. "Want me to rub 'em?"

I answered by stretching out full-length. He took my right foot and began kneading the toes.

"Tell me about the baby shower," he said. "Was it fun?"

"I guess."

"What's that mean?"

"They played a little game to guess how big around my waist is."

He winced.

"And Karen Turner filled me in on just how miserable I can expect these next six weeks to be. Among other things, she mentioned her episiotomy disaster."

"Ouch."

I raised my head and looked at him. "And did you know we were supposed to have a birth plan?"

"We do have a birth plan," he said, in that rational voice of his that makes me crazy. "We have a doctor and a hospital. We've been to birthing classes. That's a plan, right?"

"Not according to Stephanie Gardner."

He just rolled his eyes. "What else?"

"Grandmama wants me to make an honest man out of you."

"I love that old lady."

"And she loves you. She told me so. But we've been over this a million times, right?"

"If you say so."

I could sense the direction this conversation was headed in, so I deliberately switched gears. "Otis called."

"The plumber? What's he want?"

"He doesn't think Weezie's sink is going to work. So he took it upon himself to buy us a 'shiny new sink' at Home Depot. For ninety-eight dollars."

"Shit." He rubbed his eyes wearily. "I'll call him in the morning and tell him to take the new sink back. Anything else?"

"Henry's two helpers are banged up from a bar fight. His message said maybe he'd see us on Wednesday. Harry, it's supposed to rain this week—and if it does, and the wind picks up, which it will, we're screwed. That tarp will blow off and the oak floors we just refinished will be ruined." I blinked back a fresh set of tears.

He kneaded my toes with his strong hands for a minute, watching my face. "BeBe?" He gently pulled me up to a sitting position and gazed into my eyes. "I'll install the sink myself. And we'll find another roofer. What else can I fix?"

"Me," I said, looking away from his searching glance. "I wish you could fix me."

"You?" He was incredulous. "You're the strongest, smartest woman I know." He gestured around the room. "You took this dump and turned it into a moneymaking machine in three months. You bought and sold real estate, ran a successful restaurant, manage your grandparents' finances. You don't need fixing, just a little rest, that's all."

"It's not that I'm tired. And it's not the hormones making me cry. It's me.

"I'm so scared," I whispered. "What if I can't do this? Be a mom? I don't know anything about babies. I never even babysat. And I can't ask my own mom because she's gone. I wish you'd met her, Harry. And I wish she could meet you. She was so good at being mom. All those kids, and I never remember her being flustered or overwhelmed. She made it look so easy. Maybe that's what made me think I could do it. I want this baby, I really, really do. But I'm terrified I'll mess it up."

"You won't mess it up," he assured me, gathering me into his arms again. "You are a loving, caring, giving woman. Anyway, there's two of us, remember?"

"You're as inexperienced as me! Like, you didn't even know we were supposed to have a birth plan. I bet you didn't even know we needed a baby wipe warmer. But apparently we do, because we got two as gifts today."

"It can't be that hard," Harry insisted. "You feed 'em, burp 'em, change 'em, and love 'em. You don't need a plan for that. And you sure as hell don't need warm baby wipes."

I clutched his hand. "See? That's why I was so panicked when you didn't call today. I can't do this without you."

"You won't have to. I'm here. And I'm not going anywhere." He looked around the room, at the blinking white lights on the Christmas tree in the corner, and then back at me.

"I've been thinking about this, BeBe. I think probably it's time I give up fishing and stay home and get a real job. Something reliable so I can be around for our kid. Not like my old man, who'd be gone weeks at a time, shrimping as far away as Mexico some seasons."

For a minute, I was too stunned to speak. Since the day we'd met, Harry had made it clear to me that being a charter boat captain was the only career he'd ever wanted. He'd tended bar, worked construction, and run a marina over the years, but as far as he was concerned, those were only temporary assignments, something to put gas in his boat and food on the table.

"You have a real job," I said finally. "I'm not asking you to give up fishing, just because we're having a child. I would never expect that. I just want you to keep your cell phone charged. That's all. Just make sure your phone works!"

"And I appreciate that," he said gravely. "But this is something I need to do. There's a guy at the marina, he's been bugging me about selling him the *Jitterbug*. It's running great, so now's the time to sell it. Maybe I'll pick up a spare charter on weekends, or something, after the baby's older, but I promise you, BeBe, from now on, you won't have to be living *The Old Man and the Sea*."

"Don't you dare," I said, my eyes flaring. "If you quit fishing, what will you do? I don't want you hanging around here all day, telling me how to do my job running the Breeze."

"I've got options," he said. "Plenty of 'em, and none of 'em involve me second-guessing you."

He stood up and yawned widely, and I did the same. He extended his hand. "Come on. If I'm gonna lay a roof tomorrow and find a job, you better take me to bed."

* * *

An hour later, with Harry spooned up behind me, his breath warm in my ear, the baby kicked so hard, it jolted me awake. A moment later, I heard rain falling softly on the inn's tin roof. It was late. Too late to wake Harry. I fell back asleep, praying our blue tarp wouldn't blow away. That we'd find another roofing crew. That Harry would give up the idiotic idea of selling the *Jitterbug*. Mostly, though, I prayed that I'd wake up and discover that I was not still married to Richard Hodges.

# Chapter 10

✦

# Weezie

Cookie Parker was standing behind the cash register, counting out the day's receipts, when I walked into Babalu. His dyed blond hair was slicked back from his receding hairline, and he was decked out in his favorite Christmas finery: a Burberry plaid bow tie, cashmere argyle sweater, and dark green corduroy slacks.

He looked up and gave me a broad smile. "You're just in time," he said, coming out from around the mahogany store counter. He went to the door and pulled down the shade and locked it. "Manny's upstairs, and he's got dinner almost ready. Boliche, black beans and yellow rice, fried plantains, and flan."

"Oh nooo," I groaned. "It sounds divine. I adore Cuban food, but I've just come from a baby shower, and I'm still stuffed from all the goodies. Besides, I don't dare gain an ounce. Mama's altering her wedding dress for me, and she'll have a cat-fit if I'm too fat to fit into it."

"You? Fat? Never happen," Cookie said. "On the other hand, Manny and I have already made our New Year's resolutions. Come January first, we're going to start running and hitting the gym. And no more Cuban food." He shrugged. "Anyway, that's what we're telling ourselves." He tugged at my hand. "If you won't eat, at least come upstairs and have a drink."

"I'll come upstairs, but only for a minute. I actually came over to ask a huge favor."

I followed Cookie through the gift shop's back room and up the staircase to their sumptuous apartment above the shop. The irresistible smell of garlic and roasting meat wafted into the hallway.

We found Cookie's partner, Manny, in the kitchen, chopping onions and humming along to the Christmas music blaring from an iPod deck. The polished mahogany table in the kitchen's bay window was set for two, with Spode Christmas tree china, heavy crystal goblets, and highly polished sterling silver flatware laid out on an antique deep red paisley cloth. A footed silver compote held a tight cluster of lush white roses. I'd had dozens of meals with these two men, and this was how they always dined—even if they were just having a breakfast of Pop-Tarts and coffee.

"Weezie!" Manny put down his knife and kissed both my cheeks. "Thank God you're here! I've made this huge feast, and there's only the two of us for dinner tonight." He reached into a glass-fronted cupboard and grabbed a third plate.

"Sorry, I can't stay," I said. "I've got to go home and pack. I'm going to New York in the morning!"

Manny put the plate back into the cupboard but brought out a wine-glass and poured me a glass of merlot.

"You're going to New York? What fun! Oh my God. Christmas in New York." Cookie got a dreamy look in his eyes. Although he was over fifty now, and closing in on three hundred pounds, Cookie loved to re-gale me with gossipy stories of life in the big city, and on the road with the touring company of *Les Misérables.*

"This trip is pretty sudden, isn't it?" Manny asked. "Has something come up?"

"Not an emergency or anything like that. It's just that Daniel's been working so hard, and he's got a terrible cold, and he's lonely, and I'm lonely . . . and after all, I've never been to New York, and I might never get another chance like this, and before I could stop her, BeBe bought me a ticket with her frequent-flier miles . . . so I guess that means I'm going to New York."

"Does he know you're coming?" Manny asked.

"I haven't told him. I've got the address of the place he's staying. I thought I'd just take a cab over there and surprise him."

"That is so romantic," Cookie said. "So, what kind of a favor do you need? A ride to the airport? We can keep an eye on the shop if you need us to, but I'm assuming the girls can handle everything while you're gone."

"Actually, I *could* use a ride to the airport, and the girls do know how to keep things running at the shop. The thing is . . . I'm going to stay until Friday. And with the wedding just a week away, I know it's really crazy and irresponsible to just take off like this, but . . ."

"Say no more," Manny said. "We'll take care of everything. You know I've already ordered all the flowers, and I'll check in with the boys over at Guale later in the week, just to make sure I have all the silver serving pieces we'll need polished and ready."

"Leave everything to us," Cookie added. "Now. Tell us what exciting plans you have while you're in the city."

I blinked. "I really haven't had time to make any plans. The main thing is to be there for Daniel. I want to see the restaurant, Cucina Carlotta, where he's guest chef, and then—I've dreamed of going to New York at Christmas since I was a little girl and watched *Miracle on 34th Street.*"

"You'll see a Broadway show, of course," Cookie said. "You absolutely must."

"I'd love that. It doesn't matter what, since I've never seen a real Broadway show. Whatever it is, I know it'll be wonderful."

"The theater's nice, but as a retailer, you really must take a stroll down Fifth Avenue to see all the fabulous Christmas windows," Manny said. "There's Saks and Tiffany and Bergdorf Goodman and Lord & Taylor . . ."

"And Chanel and Bloomingdale's and Cartier," Cookie added.

"And the FAO Schwarz toy store, so amazing at Christmas. And whatever you do, you absolutely have to go over to the Upper East Side and see the Ralph Lauren town house," Manny said.

I laughed. "Guys, I'm only going to be in the city for five days."

"I wish I were going with you," Cookie said wistfully. "Savannah's lovely, of course, and I do not miss the cold weather and the dirt and the noise . . ."

"And rude New Yorkers," Manny put in.

"They're not really rude. They're busy. Preoccupied," Cookie said.

"Rude," Manny insisted.

"Christmas in New York," Cookie said. "Enchanting. Promise you'll take lots of pictures, Weezie."

"I promise. So you really don't mind taking over the wedding planning? There's really not that much left to do, but you know how things crop up at the last minute . . ."

"Leave it to us," Manny said. "A wedding like this is nothing for Manny and Cookie."


I laughed uneasily. "But, now guys, remember, this is just supposed to be a quiet, understated wedding. Simple. Charming. Not fussy."

Manny offered me a bland, noncommittal smile.

"No snow machines," I said sternly, a reference to an over-the-top Christmas display the two of them staged in order to win the historic district decorating contest a previous year. "No children's choir from the orphanage."

Cookie looked crestfallen.

"And definitely, positively, no horse-drawn Cinderella carriages arriving to whisk us away on our honeymoon. We're not Prince William and Kate. We're Weezie and Daniel. Remember that. Simple, understated."

"What about a simple, understated pair of bagpipers greeting your guests?" Manny asked hopefully.

"Negatory."

He exchanged a worried look with Cookie. "Photo booth with period costumes for the guests?"

"Absolutely not."

"Borrr-ing!" Cookie said. "So unimaginative. You might as well just have punch and cookies at your mama's house."

We both laughed at that suggestion. They'd been to my mother's house and tasted her atrocious, if well-intentioned cooking.

"I better go," I said finally. "I've got a million things to do yet. I've got to pack and call Mama and let her know I'm leaving town . . ."

Manny and Cookie walked me downstairs and out the front door. The temperature had dropped after the sun went down, but it was still in the low sixties. A trolley car full of tourists rounded the square, and we heard the patter of the tour guide over her microphone, explaining the history of Troup Square.

We stood on the street outside Babalu, gazing at the hundreds of tiny twinkling lights that illuminated their storefront.

"I can't believe anything on Fifth Avenue will be any prettier than this," I said, giving both men a hug. "Thank you so much for agreeing to take care of all the wedding stuff. I can't tell you how much I appreciate all you're doing for us. Just remember—it's only a wedding, right? Not some Broadway extravaganza."

Manny sighed dramatically. "Well, it's your party," he conceded. "But so far your version sounds like a perfectly grim affair."

"Positively Mormon," Cookie agreed.

"Or Mennonite," Manny said.

# Chapter 11

✦

# Weezie

I squeezed my way through the crowds at LaGuardia's baggage claim
and inched toward the carousel, craning my neck to look for my
black suitcase with the jaunty red bow tied to the handle. But two beefy
men with European accents and thick gold chains around their necks
blocked my vision. I tried to sidestep them, but was cut off by a tall
bored-looking blonde in a full-length mink coat and tall, black patent-
leather boots with six-inch spike heels.

It was noisy and stuffy, and people were jostling me around like
I didn't exist. Finally I gave up and started jostling back. Fifteen minutes passed. The crowds gathered their luggage and dispersed, until
there were only three battered black suitcases circling the conveyor
belt—and none of them were mine.

"Excuse me?" The baggage clerk in the Delta office was busily texting on her phone and didn't look up.

I coughed loudly. "Ma'am? Excuse me. I came in on a flight from Savannah, and my bag wasn't on the conveyor belt."

She still didn't look up. "Flight number?"

I had to check my boarding pass. "Twenty-seven-eleven."

She finished sending her text, put the phone down, and checked the computer monitor in front of her. "All bags on that flight have been unloaded."

"Not mine." I handed her my baggage claim check.

She slid a piece of paper in my direction. "Fill that out. Put your cell phone number or the phone number where you'll be staying in the city. Also the address. Your flight was full, so maybe your bag is coming on a later flight. We'll give you a call when it arrives, and have it sent out to you."

"Today?" I asked hopefully. "All my clothes are in that suitcase." I'd dressed hurriedly that morning, blue jeans, a white shirt, red cashmere pullover sweater, and my favorite shoes, a pair of gorgeous black crocodile Stuart Weitzman loafers I'd picked up at the Junior League thrift store in Atlanta for five dollars. I was thankful that I'd kept BeBe's coat with me on the flight.

She shrugged. "Whenever. It's Christmas season, you know." Satisfied that she had exerted the absolute minimum requirement for fulfilling the absolute minimum amount of customer service, she looked over my shoulder at the people lined up behind me. "Next."

* * *

It didn't seem possible, but the terminal was now even more crowded than it had been an hour ago. I moved with the crowd, like a salmon swimming upstream, heading for the exit doors. I felt a hand tugging my sleeve.

"Miss?" A man I could describe only as short, thin, and swarthy gave me an eager smile. "You are needing a car?" He was wearing a faded black suit coat, white dress shirt, and skinny black necktie. He looked semi-official to my untrained eyes.

"Well, a taxi."

"I have car. Much better. You are going where?"

"Um, the East Village, I think, but I was just going to take a cab."

He shook his head vigorously. "Car is nicer. I take you. Very fast. Very safe." He put a hand at the small of my back, and I tried to shrink away, but he kept it firmly in place, steering me out the doors of the terminal.

Where a cold blast of arctic air nearly sent me running back into that hot, noisy terminal. BeBe had been right. The temperatures must have been in the teens, and the air was raw and damp and howling. Something cold and wet touched my cheek. A snowflake.

"Wait," I said, struggling to don my heavy coat. He stood, shifting impatiently from one foot to another. When I'd barely managed to get my arms into the sleeves, he was tugging at my arm again. "This way to car."

He led me past a long line of yellow cabs, across two strips of tarmac, to a parking area. I had to trot to keep up with him. Finally, we came to a row of parked black sedans. Still pulling at the sleeve of my coat, he led me to a black Buick that had seen better days.

He opened the back door with a flourish. "Car."

I gazed out the grime-smeared window, eager for my first glimpse of the big city. It soon struck me that I wasn't actually in New York. Yet. My first impression was of a world etched in charcoal. Gray highway, gray sky, black cars, twisted leafless gray trees, the only real color was from the yellow taxis packed in on the road ahead and beside and behind us. The snow was falling softly, wiped away by the sedan's screeching windshield wipers. A lifelong Southerner and native Savannahian, I'd seen snow, of course, mostly while I was living in Atlanta during my first marriage. But only once or twice. That snow was innocuous, fluffy, and white, a thin covering barely enough to coat streets and yards before it vanished in the next day's sunshine.

Traffic was the thickest I'd ever seen, a solid unmoving mass of cars. The driver muttered to himself, laid on his horn, and swung the car sharply to the right, directly in the path of a long black limousine beside us. I closed my eyes, already feeling the inevitable collision. The limo honked back, but somehow the driver forced his way into the lane.

The sedan's radio was tuned to a sports talk station, and the discussion, mounted at top volume, seemed to be a heated debate about the prospects for the Rangers, which left my driver in a fury. He was screaming obscenities and pounding the steering wheel. "Fuck the Rangers. Nobody care about Rangers." He jabbed at the radio's push-button controls, changing stations, tuning now to an ear-splittingly loud rap music station with a thumping bass that made the whole backseat vibrate. My temples began to throb.

"Could you please turn that down a little?" I asked timidly. No response. Finally, emboldened by the driver's bad manners, I tapped his shoulder.

"Hey! Turn it down, please. Okay?"

He glanced at me in the rearview mirror, and I could see his scowl, but he did finally turn the volume down.

The Buick's thermostat was turned up to the blast-furnace setting, and I could feel perspiration beading up on my face and neck, and sweat trickling down my back. My driver was sweating too, but he seemed oblivious to the thick garlic-scented fumes wafting through the car's interior. I tried rolling my window down for a breath of fresh air, but the crank window handle was broken. Out of desperation, I shed the heavy coat, laying it gingerly across my lap.

We paid some tolls, and eventually we merged onto an elevated highway that seemed to cut directly through a gritty gray morass of industrial buildings and tenement houses shoved right up against the highway's edge. At one point, as we inched along, I looked over to the right and found myself staring directly into an apartment window, eyeball to eyeball with a fat man in a greasy undershirt who appeared to be standing at a stove cooking something. I looked away, embarrassed to intrude on his privacy, but when I looked back, he gave me a jaunty salute with his spatula. So far, it was the friendliest encounter I'd had since landing at LaGuardia two hours earlier. I smiled and waved back.

Suddenly, the driver floored the Buick's accelerator, zipping in and out of lanes, alternately speeding and tailgating. I was desperately searching for my seat belt when the car hit a pothole so deep, it bounced me nearly off my seat.

"Hey!" I said sharply, but the driver didn't even turn around. Anyway, the search for a seat belt was fruitless, so I simply hung on to the cracked plastic seat back and prayed we'd reach our destination before I got jounced out of all my dental work.

After we left the elevated highway we were on an ancient steel truss-work bridge which the signage declared to be the Williamsburg Bridge. This, I concluded, was definitely not the scenic route to Daniel's apartment. Snowflakes swirled around in the air outside, and I longed for just a lungful of what I was sure was cold, clean air.

We drove through dense, urban streets. No signs of Christmas here. Just more stunted trees, soot-blackened buildings crowded up against streets, and sidewalks heaped with bags of trash, which were now receiving a picturesque frosting of snow. I saw street signs, but of course, they meant nothing to me. My driver hunched over the steering wheel, muttering in a low voice and an unfamiliar language.

"Excuse me," I said brightly, thinking he was addressing me. It was then that I noticed he was wearing a headset, and actually talking into his phone.

We'd been driving for at least thirty minutes, and I was becoming more and more uneasy with each block. Shouldn't we be in Manhattan by now?

"Excuse me," I said loudly, but the driver had no reaction. I leaned forward and tapped him on the shoulder. "How much longer?" I said in a loud, distinct voice. Ridiculous! He was foreign, yes, but not deaf.

"Yes," he said, nodding, his eyes meeting mine in the rearview mirror. "Very soon. We arrive."

"How soon?" I asked. "I looked up the address last night. On the Internet it says it's only twenty minutes from LaGuardia."

"Internet not know everything," he said.

Ten minutes later, he pulled the car onto a street lined with what looked to me like rows of abandoned storefronts. The shop windows were covered with steel pull-down grates, and the brick and concrete walls were riddled with spray-painted graffiti. I saw what looked like a large bundle of rags dumped up against a vacant storefront, and was horrified to realize, on closer examination, that the bundle was actually a man, sleeping on a pallet of flattened cardboard beer crates.

The driver rolled slowly down the block, then pulled alongside the grimmest, most decrepit building I'd ever seen.

"Here," he said triumphantly. He turned to me. "We are here."

"Here?" I blinked. This looked nothing like the Greenwich Village I'd always pictured. I craned my neck to read the print on the nearest street sign, which read "Avenue C."

"This isn't Stuyvesant Street," I protested.

"No. Is Avenue C. You say Avenue C. I take you here."

"I never said Avenue C. I don't know where this is. I asked you to take me to the East Village."

"East Village?" He shrugged. "East Village is not here."

"I realize that. You've brought me to the wrong place."

"I take you where you say." He picked up a pencil and a tiny spiral-bound notebook and began jotting figures. He frowned, erased, scribbled some more. Satisfied, he tore off the slip of paper and handed it to me.

In large numbers, he'd written $130.

"What's this?"

"Is fare. You pay."

"A hundred and thirty dollars? This can't be right."

"Is right. I pay tolls, gas. You pay one hundred thirty now."

I was scared. But I was starting to get angry. Obviously this driver had deliberately targeted me. An out-of-town rube, a woman traveling alone, who would be ripe for a rip-off. Or possibly selling into white slavery.

"I am not going to pay you anything," I said, clearly enunciating every word. "Until you take me to the right address on Stuyvesant Street in the East Village."

His eyes narrowed. "You pay!" he screamed. "I call police if you no pay. Police put you in jail."

"Call the police," I said, crossing my arms over my chest. "I'll tell them you took me to the wrong address and deliberately tried to overcharge me." I glanced around at his dashboard, thinking I would write down his unit number, or however private cars were regulated, to report him, but for the first time realized there was nothing resembling a meter or anything like a permit to indicate my driver was actually licensed.

"You'll be the one to go to jail," I said. "You don't even have a license to carry passengers, do you?"

"You pay," he repeated. "You pay and get out my car."

"I am not getting out of this car until you take me to Stuyvesant Street," I repeated.

He gave it some thought. "You pay half now. Seventy bucks. Then I take you." He'd started the car again, and we were slowly rolling forward again, but he was still turned halfway around in the seat, glaring daggers at me.

"Not even one dollar. Not until you take me to the right address." I pulled my cell phone from my purse and held it up for him to see. "Or I'll report you to the authorities."

This, as it turns out, was not the winning strategy I'd hoped for.

He muttered something else under his breath. The car traveled another hundred yards, and suddenly he slammed on the brakes, sending me ricocheting off the back of his seat.

"Out!" he screamed, turning to me again. "Out, out, out! Out right now."

I knew I'd lost, but I was determined to have the last word. "I'll get out," I said finally. "But I'm not paying you."

I swung the door open and put my right foot down, but before I was completely out of the car, the driver sped off, sending me toppling face-down onto the sidewalk.

I managed to scramble to my feet. "Come back here!" I screeched, but the Buick was already halfway down the block. With my borrowed black camel's hair coat stowed safely in its backseat.

"Psst." The hoarse voice startled me so that I jumped. I looked down. A person who'd been sleeping on a nearby grate was now sitting up.

It was a man. "You got any smokes?" he asked, giving me a toothless grin.

"Sorry," I said, taking a step away. "I don't smoke."

"Maybe a sandwich?"

I shook my head no. It was bitterly cold. The nice, warm fleece-lined leather gloves BeBe had loaned me were in the pocket of her now-departed coat. I tucked my hands up beneath the edge of my sweater sleeves.

"Maybe some spare change?"

I reached into my purse and fished out a dollar bill and gave it to him. I looked up and down the street, but there was no other sign of life anywhere. "Look. That cabdriver was supposed to take me to the East Village, but instead he dumped me out here. Can you tell me where we are?"

He looked down at the dollar, and then back at me. "I could. If you had, say, five bucks."

# Chapter 12

✳

Reluctantly I handed my new tour guide a five-dollar bill. He eyed it carefully, turning it over and over with hands encased in greasy yellow wool gloves with the fingers cut out. "You're in Alphabet City. Avenue C. Between Fourth and Fifth," he said finally. "But if I was you, I wouldn't plan on sticking around. This ain't exactly Park Avenue."

"Thank you," I said. I turned and started walking down the block, hoping he wouldn't decide to follow. At the corner, I looked up and down the intersecting streets. Cars zoomed past, but I didn't see many taxis, and anyway, I wasn't really confident I actually knew how to hail a cab. I looked up at the sky, which was lead gray, with low, ominous-looking clouds. The snow was falling faster now, and my sweater was getting damp. My feet squished inside the loafers, and my toes were beginning to feel numb. My nose and cheeks burned from the cold.

If I stayed on this corner any longer, I feared I'd be frozen to the spot. Reluctantly I pulled out my cell phone and called Daniel.

His phone rang three, then four times. I felt my mouth go dry. What if he'd gone out? Or was asleep? He'd sounded so awful the night before, he was hoarse and had a dry, hacking cough. I'd urged him to take some cold medicine and try to get some sleep.

Finally, on the fifth ring, the phone picked up. "Hello?"

I was stunned. It was a woman's voice.

"Hello?" she repeated. "Anybody there?"

"Sorry," I managed, finally. "I must have a wrong number. I was trying to call Daniel Stipanek."

"This is Daniel's number," she said smoothly. "Who's calling, please?"

Again, I was stumped. I looked at my watch. It was 9:30 a.m. Why was a woman answering Daniel's phone at this hour?

"This is his fiancée, Eloise Foley," I said. "And who is this?"

"This is Carlotta," she said. "I just came over to drop off some soup to Daniel. He looks like hell, so I made him go back to bed. Maybe you could call back later? After he's had some rest? Say . . . after lunch?"

"Later?" I felt the blood rushing to my face. Who the hell did this woman think she was?

"I really need to talk to Daniel. Right now," I said, making my voice steely. "It's kind of an emergency."

"Oh. Well, in that case . . ." Her voice trailed off, and I could hear footsteps on what sounded like a wooden floor, and then her voice, somewhat muffled.

"It's your fiancée, Eloise. She says it's an emergency. But I really don't think . . ."

"Weezie?" Daniel's voice was little more than a croak. "What's wrong? Are you all right?"

At the sound of his voice, my steely reserve melted like a Southern snowflake, and I was instantly reduced to a big, blubbering baby.

"I'm lost," I wailed. "I wanted to surprise you, but this driver ambushed me at the airport. He deliberately took me to the wrong address, and when I wouldn't pay him, he kicked me out of the car and took off. I'm freezing and I'm terrified . . ."

"Weezie, slow down, for God's sake." Daniel's next words were lost in a spasm of coughing. "What are you saying? Exactly where are you? Airport? What airport?"

"LaGuardia," I said, wiping at my nose, which was now running nonstop. "But I'm not there anymore. I'm someplace called . . ."

"LaGuardia? Here? You're here in New York? Right now?"

"I took the first flight out of Savannah this morning. I was going to take a cab over to your apartment, but this driver . . . he accosted me. And the next thing I knew, I was in his car, and I know I told him I needed to go to the East Village. He drove off with my coat. BeBe's coat."

"Hold on a minute." He coughed for what seemed like another three minutes. "Did you say you're in Alphabet City?"

I could hear the woman's voice in the background. "She's in Alphabet City? Oh my God. What the hell is she doing in that neighborhood? Tell her to flag down a cab."

Daniel was back. "Carlotta says . . ."

"I can't flag down a cab," I said. "They won't stop. They just go speeding right past me."

"Never mind," Daniel said. "I'm coming to get you. Is there a store or something—like a bodega, where you can wait for me? At least get in out of the cold?"

I walked back to the middle of the block. Metal grates were pulled down over most of the storefronts. But across the street, there was a storefront. I could see a light through the window plastered with ads for cigarettes, lottery tickets, and malt liquor.

"There's a store—but it's pretty seedy-looking . . ."

"Never mind that. Just go over there and wait for me. Buy a newspaper or something. I'm getting dressed right now, and I'll be there as soon as I can. Give me that address again?"

He wasn't dressed? And Carlotta was there?

I was walking toward the store. I repeated the address. "Hurry, please," I said. And then. "I'm sorry. I know you're sick . . ."

"Just get inside and get warm," Daniel said. "It's gonna be all right, baby. I'll be right there."

A middle-aged woman was perched on a backless stool behind the counter, her dark hair pulled back from her face with a faded red scarf. She shot me a uninterested smile, then returned to the stack of papers spread out on the counter before her.

The store was tiny, with narrow aisles stocked with typical convenience store items. Tall coolers stocked with soda and beer ran across the back of the store, and on the counter adjacent to the cash register sat a coffee machine. I closed my eyes and inhaled the scent of the coffee. Near the coffee machine was a glass display case of pastries—muffins, croissants, bagels, and gooey-looking sugar-drizzled danishes.

My stomach growled. I'd had no dinner and no breakfast, only a cup of weak, lukewarm coffee on the early-morning flight.

"Get you something?" the woman asked, her pen poised over an order blank of some kind.

"Could I please have a large coffee—and a muffin?"

She nodded, got to her feet, and poured me a cardboard cup of coffee. While I poured two pods of artificial creamer and two packets of sugar into my cup, she took a waxed paper envelope and wrapped it around a muffin and handed it to me. "Six dollars," she said.

I cradled the steaming cup of coffee between both hands, held it up to my nose and inhaled, letting the rich warmth wash over me. I sipped, and was rewarded with a scalded tongue.

The clerk went back to her order forms, glancing up at me occasionally as I stood and nibbled at my breakfast. The muffin was sawdust dry, with no discernible flavor, and the coffee was strong enough to strip paint, but I didn't care. For the moment, I was warm and semi-dry and safe.

"Anything else?" the woman asked after ten minutes had passed.

"Uh, maybe a newspaper?" I spied a stack of tabloid newspapers on a wire rack near the door and grabbed the top one.

SERIAL SLASHER STALKS CITY, screamed a boldfaced black headline on the front page of the *New York Post*.

I was handing her the money when Daniel rushed in and I threw myself into his arms.

After he'd wrapped me in his old navy pea coat and his own suede gloves and hustled me into the cab he'd left waiting at the curb outside, Daniel hugged me close to his chest.

"You're crazy, you know that?" He stroked my damp hair. "Flying all this way without even telling me?"

I pulled away and looked into his eyes, which were red-rimmed and set with dark circles. "I had to come. You sounded so bad last night, and lonely. And I missed you so much. I couldn't stand the thought of you sick and alone up here. I wanted to surprise you. Are you mad at me?"

He laughed hoarsely, which set off a short fit of coughing. "At you? Never. I just hate what you've been through. When I think what could have happened to you . . ."

I shuddered and tucked myself under his arm. "But nothing did. I'm fine. Just cold and wet."

He looked down at my red sweater and my jeans and frowned. "I know you said the driver took off with your coat, but what about your luggage? Don't tell me he took that too . . ."

"Thank God, no. The airline seems to have misplaced my suitcase. I filled out a form, and they said it was probably on the next flight, and they promised to deliver it to me this afternoon."

"Let's hope they find it," Daniel said. He gestured out the cab window.

"We're supposed to get maybe six inches of snow by tonight. We'll have to get you a coat before you freeze to death."

He gave me a wolfish smile. "Unless you plan to stay holed up in the apartment with me, night and day."

I gave him a chaste kiss on the cheek. "You're sick, remember? I came up here to make sure you're taking good care of yourself."

He kissed me back, not so chastely. "I'm feeling better already, now that you're here. And I've got a great idea of how you can take care of me."

We settled back into our seats, and Daniel pointed out the neighborhoods we were passing through—all of which were a huge improvement over the one he'd rescued me from.

"How far away is Rockefeller Center?" I asked. "The big Christmas tree—that's the first thing I want to see. And ice skating. Can you take me ice skating there? I know it's corny, but I'd love to see the Rockettes. Also, Cookie says we've got to walk down Fifth Avenue so I can see all the Christmas windows. And I've got to see a Broadway show. A musical, I don't care which one. And I want to eat roasted chestnuts . . ."

"Slow down," Daniel said. "That's a lot of stuff. How many days are you going to stay?"

"Just till Friday," I said. "I know I shouldn't have come, not with everything else going on, but this might be the only chance I get to see New York at Christmas."

"I'm glad you came. I just wish I had the whole week to do all that stuff with you."

"Never mind," I said, sighing. "You're sick. I can't drag you around doing all my silly touristy stuff. We're going to go back to your place and put you right to bed."

He raised one eyebrow. "Now you're talking."

# Chapter 13

✦

# BeBe

**M**onday morning, Harry astonished me by emerging from our bedroom in a pair of sharply pressed gray slacks, a pale blue dress shirt, a red-and-blue-striped rep tie—and yes—wait for it—a navy blazer.

My eyes goggled. The piece of buttered toast I'd been about to nibble on fell onto my plate.

"Don't look at me like that," Harry said. He went to the coffeepot and filled his chrome travel mug. "You've seen me in a coat and tie before."

"What are you up to?"

"I told you last night, I'm getting a real job."

"Yes, some time in the future, in an abstract sense," I said. "After the baby comes, you meant."

He shrugged. "I didn't want to say anything before, just in case it didn't work out, but I'm starting today."

I still couldn't wrap my mind around the sight of Harry dressed like a banker, right down to a pair of polished black loafers. "Starting what today?"

"My job. I'm a seafood broker," he said patiently. "For Joey Catalano."

J. Catalano and Sons Seafood is the oldest seafood wholesale market in Savannah. It had been around so long that my great-grandmother had bought seafood from Joe Catalano Senior's grandfather. I could remember accompanying my mother as a little girl to the Catalano Market, downtown on Bull Street, with its huge neon sign of a cat pawing at a fish suspended from a fishing pole. My strongest memory was of a six-year-old me, staring with a mixture of horror and fascination at the displays of whole fish mounded on piles of crushed ice behind the glass display cases.

"I wish you wouldn't do this," I said with a sigh.

He bent down and dropped a kiss on the top of my head, and I could smell an unfamiliar aftershave. "What? Wear a tie? I thought all you Country Day girls liked preppy dudes in coats and ties."

I reached up and grabbed the end of said tie, and tugged until his cheek was right next to mine. "Not this girl," I said sharply. "I've had preppy, remember? I like you just the way I found you—unshaven, grungy, in a ball cap and beat-up jeans and T-shirt."

Harry eased down onto the chair next to mine. "And smelling like a bait bucket—like you said I did last night?"

"Last night I might have been emotionally overwrought," I admitted. "But I never, ever meant that you should give up fishing just because we're having this baby. Fishing isn't just what you do, Harry, it's who you are."

"Was," he said, helping himself to the piece of toast I'd abandoned. He chewed slowly. "Starting today, I'm a seafood broker. Steady paycheck, Monday to Friday, nine to five."

"Next thing I know, you'll be driving a Mercedes and taking up golf," I said glumly. "You'll probably have an affair with your secretary too."

He grinned and headed for the door. "Never happen. And you know why? My truck is paid for, I suck at golf, and you'll be happy to know we don't *have* secretaries at J. Catalano and Sons. What we do have is Joey's mom, Antoinette—who lends new meaning to the term 'fishwife.'"

"And?" I lifted one eyebrow.

"And I'm hopelessly in love with the mother of my child, and just a little bit afraid of what she might do if she ever thought I was messing around on the side, not that I would."

"Good answer," I said. "What would you like for dinner tonight?"

He stuck his head back around the kitchen door. "Anything at all. As long as it's not fish."

As soon as Harry was gone, I headed into town to see Weezie's uncle.

James Foley listened carefully to the tale of my crazy mixed-up marriage mess, his hands folded on his desk, his kind blue eyes twinkling out at me from behind his thick-rimmed glasses, and I knew somehow he would make things right.

James had that effect on people. Maybe it was because he'd been a priest for so many years before resigning from his order and returning home, to Savannah, to practice law. He'd probably heard much worse stories than mine from his side of the confession booth.

He took some notes in that kind of careful handwriting the nuns instilled in parochial school children, then looked up at me.

"The first thing we'll do is check with the clerk's office to see if your divorce decree was ever issued. Maybe you're right, maybe Richard Hodges did hire another lawyer. Or maybe the decree just never got mailed out. Stranger things have happened."

He half stood from his desk. "Janet?"

A moment later, his longtime secretary popped her head in the door.

"Feel like taking a walk?"

She shook her head. "Still haven't finished your Christmas shopping?"

James laughed. "Don't start. No, I haven't finished yet. Could you go over to the courthouse and check in the clerk's office for a divorce decree under these names?"

"Certified copy of the decree if I find it?" she asked.

"Please." He hesitated. "As long as you're out . . ."

"Jonathan has been hinting about wanting the new Nathaniel Philbrick book about Bunker Hill. I'll stop by Shaver's and get them to giftwrap a copy. And I saw some really unusual estate jewelry in the window at Levy's that might be nice for Weezie."

"The courthouse is job one," James said. "Call me and let me know what you find. After that?" He reached in the top drawer of his desk and rifled through some papers.

"I already have your Amex card if that's what you're looking for," Janet told him.

The Chatham County courthouse was only a ten-minute walk from James Foley's office. We sat and chatted for a while, discussing the efforts of his partner, Jonathan, to make him spruce up the house they shared on Washington Avenue.

He was still grousing about having to get rid of thirty-year-old curtains when the phone on his desk rang. He looked at the read-out screen. "That's Janet."

He punched a button to put the phone on speaker. "What's the word?"

"I'm afraid it's not good," Janet said. "There's no divorce decree on file. I did find the initial filing, but since it had gone five years without being processed, the case was dismissed."

James winced. "I was afraid of that. Okay, thanks."

I felt sick. I gripped the arms of the chair I was sitting in and willed myself not to throw up.

James, alarmed, jumped up and went into the other room, rushing back with a bottle of water and a wad of paper towels.

I took a small sip of water and waited.

"I'm all right," I said when I could finally trust myself to speak again. "Now what?"

"We get you a divorce," James said.

"And how do we do that? Like, yesterday?"

"I'm afraid I don't have the power to practice retroactive law, BeBe.

But it shouldn't be too complicated. We file our own divorce decree. Do you have an address for Richard?"

"God, no! The last I heard, he was still locked up in prison."

"You don't happen to know which prison?"

"Not really."

He made another note, then swiveled his chair and started typing on his computer. "I'm checking the Department of Corrections database. If he's still a guest of the state, that'll tell us exactly where he is."

"Behind bars, I hope," I muttered.

"Hmmm." James looked over at me. "Paroled. Twenty-two months ago."

I felt the blood drain from my face. Richard wasn't violent. But the thought of him out of prison, living anywhere within a hundred miles of me, made me feel queasy all over again.

"Don't panic," James said gently. "We'll track him down, and we'll file for divorce ourselves."

"What if we can't find him?" I asked.

"We file an affidavit with the court stating that. We advertise for two consecutive months, and then your divorce is final."

"Advertise?" I cried. "You mean, like, in the newspaper?"

"In the legal ads. In very tiny print. Nobody except lawyers reads that."

"Are you kidding? *Everybody* I know reads the legal ads. Who's getting divorced, who's bankrupt or had their house foreclosed? It's the best-read part of the Savannah paper."

James had gone back to typing.

"We subscribe to a couple of databases. I'll look to see if there's a recent address for Richard Hodges. You don't have his social security number, do you?"

"No," I said dully.

"Date of birth?"

I closed my eyes and managed to conjure up a repressed memory. Richard, reading his horoscope aloud from the morning paper.

"He was a Scorpio," I said, scowling. "His birthday was October 31. We actually met at a Halloween party. So his date of birth is October 31, 1970."

"Makes sense. Scorpios are secret keepers. And there's supposedly something sexual about that scorpion tail," James said.

"You're into astrology?" I asked.

James blushed slightly. "Silly, isn't it?"

He went back to reading his computer screen. "Hodges is a pretty common name," James said. "Does he have any family locally? Maybe they've heard from him."

"His parents are both dead. He has a sister, but they weren't very close."

He looked over the top of the computer at me. "Her name?"

"Cindy. Cynthia. Patterson was her married name, but I heard she got divorced, so maybe she went back to calling herself Hodges."

"This is all helpful," James said. "Janet is a whiz with the computer. I'll put her onto tracking Richard Hodges down when she gets back to the office."

"Thank you," I said. "I know I've already said it, but we have just got to get this settled. I can't stand the idea that I'm still married to that vermin. It makes me physically ill."

James nodded solemnly. He started to say something, then pressed his lips together.

"What?" I asked, leaning forward. "What were you going to say?"

"I was just wondering when the baby is due."

"Not for another four weeks. Why do you ask?"

"It's just a technicality," he said.

"About the baby?" I heard my own voice, shrill and pinched.

He nodded, looking truly miserable.

"Tell me," I whispered.

"It's just that . . . well, there's a statute in Georgia that states that any child conceived or born during marriage is presumed by law to be child of the husband and wife."

"But that's crazy," I protested. "I haven't seen Richard in years and years. He's been in prison! I thought we were divorced. This baby is ours. Mine and Harry's."

"I'm sorry," James said, reaching across the desk to take my hand. "I'll start the paperwork today. We'll track your ex down, serve him notice, and in sixty days, you'll be divorced."

"But in the meantime . . ." I had to swallow to choke back the wave of nausea threatening to engulf me. "If something were to happen to me . . . that's what you're saying, isn't it? If something were to happen to me, before the divorce . . . Richard could claim to be the legal father of my baby?"

"But he wouldn't, would he?" James said soothingly. "He's had no communication with you, and clearly, the last thing he'd want is a new-born baby. And anyway, nothing is going to happen to you."

"No," I said, gritting my teeth. "Nothing is going to happen to me. I promise you that."

"Good," James said.

I released his hand and stood, somewhat unsteadily.

"I've got to go. But you'll call me, right? When you have any news at all?"

"I will," James said. "I definitely will."

# Chapter 14

✦

# Weezie

I sat on the edge of the severely modern (and severely uncomfortable) sofa bed in Daniel's speck-sized apartment on my first full day in New York and watched as he hurriedly pulled on his black-and-white-checked pants and white chef's jacket.

"But I thought you didn't have to go in this early," I protested.

"I don't, normally. But that text was from Carlotta. The sous-chef has the flu, and our fish order didn't come in, so now I need to go to the Fulton Fish Market and the green market to pick out the stuff for tomorrow and get everything prepped. But don't worry, it's not for the whole day. I should be back midafternoon."

He sat down beside me on the edge of the bed and kissed me gently. "I know it's not how you planned it, but when I get back, we'll go out and have some fun. Get a late lunch, some shopping. Didn't you say you want to see all the Christmas windows?"

He was right about one thing. Nothing about this last-minute trip had gone exactly as I'd planned, starting with our reunion.

"It's just like the movies," I exclaimed as we got out of the cab on Monday. "Like Meg Ryan's place in *You've Got Mail.*"

Daniel's apartment was in a picturesque ivy-covered nineteenth-century brick building, with a high marble stoop and charming window boxes planted with dwarf evergreens. A huge boxwood wreath with a discreet bow of olive-colored satin hung on each side of the dark-green-painted double doors.

"It's okay, I guess," Daniel said. I followed him up the steps as he fumbled in his pocket for the keys. He opened the door and I followed him inside to a high-ceilinged vestibule with checkerboard marble floors and flocked damask wallpaper. We faced two grandly carved doors, with brass nameplates and knockers, but he opened neither one of them.

Instead, he unlocked a not-so-grand door, and I found myself standing in a dimly lit stair hall.

He gestured toward the stairs. "Sorry. It's on the top floor."

"How many floors?"

He winced. "Four."

When we reached the top floor, he was pale and wheezing, and I was just plain exhausted. He pulled out his key ring again, then touched my cheek lightly.

"Look," he said, "I don't know what Meg Ryan's place looked like in that movie, but I'm pretty sure it doesn't look like this one. This is what they call a junior studio in New York. Carlotta just keeps it for when she has out-of-town company. It's nothing fancy. I think it was probably actually the servant's quarters for one of the bigger apartments, back in the day."

"I don't care," I assured him. "As long as we can be together."

He gave me a glum look. "We'll be together, all right."

Nothing could have prepared me for what I found on the other side of that door.

We were standing in a single narrow windowless room. The walls were painted a pale gray. There was a gray carpet on the floor, and a charcoal-gray sofa with an unmade pulled-out bed. There were some framed photos of the New York skyline on the walls and a small, wall-mounted flat screen television.

"Home sweet home," Daniel said, throwing his arm across my shoulder.

"You're kidding," I said finally. "Where's the rest of it?"

He opened a door that was painted the same gray as the walls. "Bathroom." I poked my head inside. There was a dinky little sink, a wall-mounted commode, and a shower approximately the size of a phone booth.

"Cozy," I managed. "Kitchen?"

He took five steps in the other direction and pulled aside a curtain I hadn't noticed earlier. Mounted in an alcove that had once been a closet was a shallow Formica countertop. A two-burner hot plate stood on one end of the counter, and the world's smallest kitchen sink was at the other end. Beneath the countertop was a dorm fridge.

"Le Cordon Bleu it's not." Daniel laughed. "But I don't need much, because I'm not here much."

"Where do you keep your stuff?" I asked. "Is there a closet?"

"You mean my dressing room?" He pulled the curtain a little wider to reveal a clothes pole just wide enough to hold Daniel's three sweaters, two shirts, two pairs of pants . . . and, oh yes, that dinner jacket. Beneath the closet rod was a three-drawer dresser.

"Good thing I don't have any luggage or clothes to store," I said, trying to sound cheerful. But Daniel wasn't listening. He was tugging me by the hand, toward the bed.

"I thought you were sick," I said as he slid the coat off my shoulders and pulled my sweater over my head.

"I'm better already," he said.

I touched the back of my hand to his forehead, which was still warm to the touch, but he caught my hand in his and gently pushed me backward onto the bed.

Later we slept. And Daniel decided he should prove to me how very much better he was feeling.

"You're my penicillin," he said, kissing my bare shoulder. "I'm getting hungry. And you must be starved. Where shall we go for dinner?"

I glanced over at the rumpled pile of my clothing on the floor. "I don't exactly have the wardrobe to be out on the town," I reminded him. "And what if the airline delivers my suitcase while we're gone?"

"We'll order in," he declared. He climbed out of bed and walked over to the makeshift kitchen, and I sat up with the sheet gathered beneath my arms, grateful for the opportunity to appreciate his well-muscled back and buns. He turned and caught me looking, and I blushed, as I always did at such moments.

He dumped a stack of take-out menus on the covers. "Were you leering at me just now?"

"No," I lied.

"I think you were. But it's okay. I like that you like what you see."

"I do," I said. "I always have."

He fanned out the menus. "Chinese. Thai. Pizza. Ethiopian. Sushi. Burgers. Vegan. Soup. Soul food. Gyros. What do you feel like?"

"There's a whole restaurant that serves nothing but soup?"

He laughed. "This is New York, Weezie. Whatever you want, you can get. For a price."

"Soup. After hanging around on that street corner, I feel like I might never get warm again."

Daniel had chili and surprisingly decent corn muffins and I had an amazing potato-leek soup. And we ate it sitting up in bed, with me dressed only in Daniel's one good white dress shirt, and I didn't dare tell him how happy it made me—feeling like I was living out an old Doris Day movie, but maybe costarring Colin Firth instead of Rock Hudson.

But the best part of all came when we turned on the television. He was flipping the channels when I caught just a glimpse of a black-and-white Barbara Stanwyck.

"Ooh, stop. Back up. It's *Christmas in Connecticut.*"

He rolled his eyes, but he flipped back in time to catch Barbara and Dennis Morgan, who were getting all cozy in a horse-drawn carriage in the midst of an obviously ersatz snowstorm that even to my untrained Southern eyes had to have been made from soap flakes.

"This is my favorite Christmas movie," I said.

"I thought you said *Miracle on 34th Street* was your favorite."

"I can have more than one favorite."

"But I also seem to remember you claiming *White Christmas* was your favorite."

"Favorite Christmas musical," I corrected, looking up at him. "You're such a Grinch, I bet you don't even have a favorite Christmas movie of your own."

"Sure I do."

"What is it?"

He considered. "*The Ref.*"

"*The Ref*? That hideously depressing movie with Denis Leary and the nasty bickering married couple and the whole dysfunctional family thing? I know you're not big on the holidays, but that can't be your favorite. Come on. Pick something else. Something nice. Something cheerful."

"I like *The Ref.*"

"No, really. You have to have a favorite movie that can be part of our annual Christmas tradition. Like, every year, when it comes on, we'll put on our pjs and have hot chocolate and popcorn and decorate the tree."

"You can watch your movie, and I can watch mine."

"That's not a movie we can watch with our children," I said primly.

He looked so shocked I had to laugh. "No, silly. I'm not pregnant. Not yet, anyway. I'm just thinking about the future. When we watch happy, cheerful holiday movies with our pink-cheeked cherubs."

"As they knock over the tree and spill hot chocolate on the sofa and whine about having to watch your sappy black-and-white stuff."

"Probably," I said, unfazed by his cynicism. "So what's it gonna be?"

He gave a huge, martyred sigh. "How 'bout *Home Alone?*"

"Perfect."

After Daniel left for work, I got dressed and walked downstairs and peered out the front window of the town house. The sky was the color of the carpet in our junior studio—dull gray. Melting snow was piled along the curb outside, and I watched as a stylishly dressed woman walked past in fur-lined boots, pushing a bundled-up toddler in a baby carriage. Why couldn't I be the one out walking, seeing the sights of the big city at Christmas?

My suitcase still hadn't arrived, but I wasn't about to hang around waiting on them all day. I dug through Daniel's meager wardrobe and outfitted myself for the weather. I pulled on his ancient black leather bomber jacket, rolling up the cuffs three times, and knotted a red wool scarf around my neck. I took the key he'd given me that morning, slipped an extra ten-dollar bill in my bra—just in case of an emergency—and went out to experience the city all on my own.

\* \* \*

The subway entrance was at 8th and Broadway. I'd studied the New York City Transit Authority's maps before leaving the apartment, and memorized my route, so I knew that if I took the R line and got off at Fifth Avenue, I would arrive at my destination.

I had the correct fare in the pocket of Daniel's jacket, but I stood there, in a fear-induced trance, for at least fifteen minutes, trying to get up the courage to descend the stairs to the subway. People rushed by me, some of them deliberately bumping me or brushing me aside in annoyance. It was as though my feet were frozen in place. Finally, I turned to leave, my cheeks flushed with shame over being such a chicken-shit.

And then I saw them—a pair of girls no older than ten or twelve, in their parochial school plaid skirts and sweaters, swiping their Metro-Cards into the readers. "If they can do it, so can I," I thought.

I followed the girls through the turnstile and we swam upstream through a stream of urban fishes until I reached the train platform. I took another deep breath and climbed aboard my train.

# Chapter 15

✦

# Weezie

When I emerged from the dim recess of the subway station I found myself squinting in the sunlight and under a now crystal clear blue sky. The sidewalk was jammed with people, and it was all I could do to merge myself into the throng and hope that I was moving in the right direction.

But when I saw the tree line of Central Park and the granite walls looming ahead, I knew, without looking at the signs, that I'd arrived.

Everything about the scene there delighted me. I strolled the lineup of horse-drawn carriages, snapping photos of the drivers in top hats and mufflers and the horses, their coats gleaming in the sunlight, their harnesses and the carriages themselves arrayed with red ribbons, tinsel, and holiday wreaths. I shopped the street vendors, picking out an inexpensive pencil sketch of St. Patrick's Cathedral for Uncle James, a sparkly holiday brooch for Mama, and a silly "I ♥ New York" onesie for BeBe's baby.

For myself I picked up a pair of stretchy one-size-fits-all synthetic red gloves and a pair of obviously bootleg Chanel sunglasses with the interlocking C logo on the side picked out in large tacky rhinestones.

Suddenly ravenous, I bought a hot dog dripping with all the trimmings and a cup of hot chocolate from a cart, and headed into the park. Passing runners, Rollerbladers, and brigades of nannies and young mothers pushing strollers, I made my way to the Wollman Rink, found a seat on a bench, and sat down to enjoy my alfresco lunch and the ice show.

I stayed for what seemed like hours, watching the skaters twirling and circling, racing and swooping across the ice. The cold air left my nose red and runny and my toes, in their inadequate fake wool socks, numb. But I didn't care. The prerecorded music floated out over the treetops and people drifted on and off the ice. Teenagers did crazy loops and improvised break dances to "Rocking Around the Christmas Tree," and then the music and tempo changed.

I recognized the melancholy strains of "Have Yourself a Merry Little Christmas" just as an elderly couple made their way onto the ice rink.

He was tall and thin, even in a thick quilted black jacket, and quite bald, with a beaklike nose and an erect bearing. His partner was short and round, with a lime green beret parked at a jaunty angle on her silver curls. Her fancy white figure skates had red-and-green pom-poms and she was dressed in a red sweater, red tights, and an old-fashioned-looking calf-length green skirt that flared in the breeze. They twined their arms around each other's waists and began a slow but purposeful dance around the rink, seemingly oblivious to the hundreds of other skaters who shared the ice.

As they built up speed, he gave her a gentle push-off, and she spun away, executing a creaky arabesque, and now the other skaters slowed or stopped to watch the show.

When they were together again, they were in waltz position, and I marveled as she glided backward around and around the rink, her eyes never leaving his face as they slid easily into a choreography they obviously knew by heart.

As the song drew to a close, he gave her another push-off, and now she did an abbreviated slow-motion spin, with him doing the same, twirling in the opposite direction. Finally their spins wound down, and at the exact last note of the song, she dug the toe of her skate into the ice, and still panting from the exertion, she slid into a low curtsy while he bowed and grinned and doffed an imaginary hat in tribute.

The other skaters clapped and whistled and cheered. Without thinking, I stood up, pounding my gloved hands together in noiseless applause. I found myself blinking back silly sentimental tears, picturing Daniel and me as that couple, our own arms intertwined, years and years from now, in this same magical scene.

The music segued into "I Saw Mommy Kissing Santa Claus," and the spell was broken. Reluctantly I moved on.

I found the Plaza Hotel with no trouble, but as I approached the entrance, I noticed cabs and limos drawn up on the street outside, spilling out elegantly dressed women in full-length furs, clutching the hands of equally dressed-up little girls.

Obviously, I thought, they were going to some kind of special holiday tea party at The Plaza. Just as obviously, dressed as I was, I would have been glaringly out of place.

I was paused at the corner of Fifty-seventh and Fifth when Daniel texted me.

*Stuck @ work. So sorry. What r u doing?*

It was nearly three, but I found myself not minding nearly as much as I expected. I'd successfully navigated the subway, ticked off two items on my New York City bucket list, and I still had lots of Manhattan to explore.

I had to remove my gloves to tap out a reply.

*Out on the town. See u 2nite.*

# Chapter 16

✦

## BeBe

BeBe? James Foley here. I hope it's not too early to be calling you?"
I yawned and glanced over at the clock radio on Harry's empty side of the bed. It was nearly eight o'clock on Tuesday morning.

"Not too early," I said, struggling to sit up. "Especially if you have good news for me. Did you find out anything about Richard?"

"No news about him," James said. "But I think Janet might have tracked down that sister of his."

"Cindy? Have you talked to her?"

"Not exactly. We can't find a phone number for her, but with cell phones these days, that's not unusual. We did track down an address for a Cindy Patterson who could be your ex's sister, though."

"That's great. Is she local? Can you go talk to her and ask her about Richard?"

There was a long pause from the other end of the phone, which I didn't quite know how to interpret.

"The Cindy Patterson we found has an address way out in the county, on the Little Ogeechee River."

"Great," I said, yawning. "Practically in my own backyard."

"The thing is, neither Janet nor I can possibly get away to go speak to this woman, not this week, anyway. I've got all these court documents to file before the Christmas break."

"No apologies necessary," I said. "I'll go see her myself. Cindy and I were never what you could call friends, but it's probably best if I show up at her door, instead of a lawyer."

"I'll text the address as soon as we hang up," James said. "But I hate to think about you doing this by yourself. Are you sure you don't want to take Harry into your confidence about this?"

I put the palms of my hands across my stomach and breathed in and out, and as I looked down, I could see the distinct rise and fall of my belly, beneath which a tiny foot was rhythmically kicking away. The prospect of visiting my hostile sister-in-law wasn't a pleasant one. But I had no choice. I had to get myself disentangled from Richard Hodges, once and for all.

"I know you don't approve, James. But no, I just can't tell Harry about any of this right now. I can't let him know his baby might not legally be his. You understand, don't you?"

James let out a long sigh. "I guess I do," he said. "Call me if you need anything."

* * *

The address James texted meant nothing to me. But after I plugged it into the GPS in my car and found myself on Ogeechee Highway, it struck me that I actually did know where I was going.

By the time I met Richard, his grandparents were long dead. But I knew he'd spent his childhood summers at Oak Point, their farm on the Little Ogeechee River.

I'd actually been to Oak Point a couple of times for family picnics, but when I pulled up to the weather-beaten structure at the end of the long oak-lined driveway that led off Ogeechee Road, the house I found there bore only a faint resemblance to the neat white-painted frame farmhouse I remembered.

Just the faintest remnants of white paint still clung to the farmhouse's now-gray clapboard siding, and the sagging porch roof appeared to be held up by a pair of unpainted two-by-fours. A white van was parked in the shade of a denuded dogwood tree. Three mismatched wooden rocking chairs lined the porch, and as I got out of the car and approached the house, I saw that a huge calico cat was slumbering quietly in the chair nearest the door.

The previous day's sunny weather was gone, and now it really felt like December, with low clouds gathered in the gray winter sky, and a cold wind whipping through the pine saplings and scattered weeds that marked what had once been Richard's grandmother's old-fashioned flower beds.

I tugged at my sweater to try to ward off the chill, and as I stepped onto the porch, the cat rose and stretched, and I could see by her distended belly that she was probably expecting, with a due date not far from mine.

Bright blue paint blistered on the wooden front door, and as I was about to knock, the door was jerked open, leaving my hand fluttering ridiculously in midair.

A woman with pale blond hair scraped back from her high forehead by a plastic headband stood in the doorway scowling at me. She was dressed in faded blue jeans and a new-looking Atlanta Falcons red sweatshirt, white socks, but no shoes.

"What?"

Apparently, my absence had not made my former sister-in-law any fonder of me.

"Hi, Cindy," I said. "It's me, BeBe."

"I saw you pull up. I know who you are, but what I don't know is what the hell you're doing here."

"I'm trying to track down Richard."

Her laugh was short and nasty and ended in a racking cough. Her eyes watered and her face was pink when the coughing fit ended.

I glanced around the porch. "Do you happen to know where he's living these days?"

"What do you care where he's staying? You walked out on him, didn't you?"

"That's between Richard and me," I said, trying to keep my voice pleasant. "I've got a legal matter I need to discuss with him. So, Cindy?

I'm asking nicely. Do you happen to have an address, or maybe a phone number for your brother?"

She leaned forward and grinned, exposing a pair of freakishly short incisors, so small they were like baby teeth. Her eyes were a pale brown, with light green rings around the irises, the exact same shade as Richard's eyes. I felt a chill run down my spine at the sudden family resemblance. I took a half step backwards.

Her breath on my face was hot and smelled like burned coffee. "Listen, BeBe Loudermilk. I don't like you. I never liked you, and I never knew what my little brother saw in you. Richard, he got in some trouble, and you walked out on him, the minute things got a little dicey. Right? All that stuff about 'in sickness and in health'—you forgot about all that, didn't you? Just left him flat."

Before I could try to answer her rant, a quavery voice called from inside the house.

"Cindy? Who are you talkin' to? Who's that at the door?"

Cindy rolled her eyes and turned sideways. "It's nobody, Opal. Just somebody sellin' crap we don't want."

"How do you know what I do or don't want?" I heard a muffled clumping sound, and it was coming toward us now.

"She was just leaving, Opal," Cindy said, and she moved to close the door, but a pale gnarled hand jerked the door inward.

The old lady wore a stiffly starched housedress with a pattern of bright red poinsettias. Her frizzy silver hair hung down to her shoulders in a pair of plaits. She had a green handkerchief pinned to the bosom of the dress, and her spaghetti-thin legs were encased in white anklets and scuffed brown leather loafers. She was pushing an aluminum walker.

Bright blue eyes peered out at me through thick-lensed glasses. "I know you," she said, pointing a finger at me. "You're that Loudermilk girl that married our Richie."

"Hello, Aunt Opal," I said, smiling widely. "Yes, it's me. BeBe. How've you been?"

Richard's father had died when he was only twelve. Was that when he'd gone bad? His mother, along with her two maiden aunts and Richard's two older sisters, had coddled and spoiled him and spared him the trouble of ever having any real-life responsibilities—or suffering the consequences of any of his actions. Wasn't that how it worked? When a son turned out badly, wasn't it always the mother's fault?

Richard had been the apple of his great-aunt Opal's eye, and when he'd brought me home to introduce me to the rest of the family, she'd instantly welcomed me into the family. She'd be in her late eighties now, and I'd just assumed she was deceased.

"Bet you thought I was dead, didn't you?" she said now, with a cackle.

I laughed. "Obviously, I underestimated you."

She looked me up and down, and I already knew what she was going to say.

"About nine months gone, aren't you?"

"A little less than that," I said, feeling myself blush.

"Ain't that something," Aunt Opal said. "I always wished Richie'd had children. He was the sweetest baby in the world. Wadn't he, Cindy? Wadn't Richie a sweet baby?"

Cindy's face hardened. "He was a handful. That's what I remember. BeBe was just leaving, Opal." She gently pushed the older woman's walker out of the doorway.

"Aunt Opal? I'm looking for Richard. I need to see him about something important." I blurted the words out. "Can you tell me where to find him? Or let him know I'm looking for him?"

"Richie?" Momentarily confused, she glanced at Cindy for direction.

Her niece's reaction was swift and cold. "I already told her, we don't know where Richard is. And if we did know, we sure as hell wouldn't tell that bitch."

"Cindy Lynn Hodges!" Opal looked shocked.

Cindy maneuvered her aunt sideways a few more inches. "I was just talking to BeBe, Cindy," Opal protested. "We were going to have a nice visit."

"Not with her we're not," Cindy snapped. She caught the old lady under the arm. "You're getting yourself all worked up over nothing, Opal. Go on back in your room now. If you keep getting yourself all wound up like this, you'll be too tired for church tomorrow night."

Opal looked stricken. "I can't miss service tomorrow night. It's my turn to read scripture."

Before she could say anything more, Cindy managed to move her aunt clear of the doorway. The next moment she slammed the door in my face.

So much for happy reunions.

# Chapter 17

✦

## BeBe

Driving back to Tybee, I had just enough time to puzzle over my encounter with Richard's sister Cindy. I hadn't seen her in close to six years, and she clearly hadn't gotten any fonder of me. But her behavior this time around was different.

In the past she'd chosen to ignore me, which is how well-bred Southern ladies deal with life's little unpleasantries. But this time around, she'd been hostile, even rude. And I wasn't convinced it was just because I'd walked out on her slime-ball brother. There was something else at work here. I was certain she was operating out of fear as well as good old-fashioned loathing. But fear of what? Me?

There was definitely something afoot at Oak Point. Something that would bear closer examination, and soon. I was determined to get some answers out of Cindy—or maybe dear old Aunt Opal.

* * *

The roofers were just clambering down off their ladders and the floor guys were loading equipment in their vans when I pulled up outside the Breeze Inn.

So the day hadn't been a total loss—even without me there to supervise and issue dire threats.

Miles, the flooring contractor, walked over to meet me at the foot of the deck stairs at the new house. "We got all the floors stained and a first coat of poly down today," he said. "We've got fans running in all the rooms, and if it sets up like it should, we can sand and do another coat tomorrow."

"That's wonderful," I said. "Did the kitchen sink get installed before you got started on the floors?"

"Yes, ma'am, the sink is in, and your plumber got the water lines run to your laundry room too."

"Finally," I said.

He finished putting his equipment in the truck and climbed into the driver's seat. "Uh, ma'am?"

"Yes?" I tried not to fidget, but it had been a long drive back from Oak Point, and I really, really needed to get to the bathroom.

"There was a black-and-white-spotted dog over there at the Breeze Inn when we got here this morning."

"Yes, it's my friend's dog. Jethro."

"And you know that little white dog of yours?"

"Jeeves?"

"I didn't catch the little guy's name," he said apologetically. "The thing is, I heard a commotion coming from over there, and when I went to check, it looked like the little dog was kinda nipping and yapping at the big dog. I opened the door, you know, to try to settle them down a little, and when I did, that big dog took off running down the street." He pointed north, down Butler Avenue, the island's main drag.

"Did you go after him?"

He shrugged. "Well, by the time I got to my truck to go looking, he was long gone. And I'm already one man short on my crew, so I couldn't really spare the time. Sorry."

I really, really needed to pee. "Jethro's gone? He never came back? And nobody thought to try to call me to let me know?"

"Guess not." I glared at him.

"Thanks. Guess it's up to me now, huh?"

He was too embarrassed to say anything else, so he started the truck and drove away. As for me, I sped into the house for a quick potty stop—and an even quicker dirty look at Jeeves, who didn't seem at all bothered by it, and then got in my car to go hunt down Weezie's dog.

I don't know why I was surprised that Jethro had taken a powder. He's sweet but a notorious escape artist, who'd run away from Weezie's town house on more than one occasion—once even managing to knock up her neighbor's purebred pooch, Ruthie, while on the lam.

The bad news was that Jethro had been gone at least three hours by the time I went looking for him. The good news was that Tybee is only about three and a half miles long, and I still had a couple hours of daylight left in which to track down his shaggy butt.

Before I set out, I made a quick call to the Tybee Police. I recognized the day shift dispatcher's syrupy drawl as soon as she answered. Angela Anderson had worked as a housekeeper at the Breeze Inn for a year after splitting up from an abusive boyfriend and moving to the island. I'd hated to lose her, but since she was a single mom with two school-age daughters, I totally understood her need to have full-time work and city benefits.

"Tybee Island Po-leece."

"Angela? It's BeBe Loudermilk."

"Oh my Lord, BeBe. Is it the baby? I've got a car just down the block from you. I'll get Leo there right now. Did your water break? Can you tell if you're dilated?"

"Calm down, Angie! I'm not dilated and I'm not in labor. I've got a runaway dog, is all."

"Jeeves ran away?"

"Not Jeeves, Jethro. He's my friend's dog and I'm watching him while she's out of town, but Jeeves picked a fight with him, so Jethro took off a couple hours ago. I was calling to see if anybody around the island spotted him. He's just a mutt, medium-sized, black with white spots and kinda goofy. He's wearing a tag with Weezie's name and phone number, and he's microchipped too, but I'm hoping to round him up before my friend finds out he's missing."

"Black and white and goofy. Answers to Jethro," she said. "I'll get on the horn to the Animal Control guys and tell them if they pick up the dog not to take him to the county pound."

"Thanks, Angela," I said. "How are the girls?"

"Tara made honor roll, and Scarlett won the school spelling bee," she said proudly. "They don't have a lick of their sorry daddy's DNA."

"Good for them," I said. "You'll let me know if anybody spots him?"

"Sure thing."

I cruised up and down the streets around the Breeze Inn with my windows down, hollering Jethro's name. I drove down Tybrisa and The Strand, which accounts for the island's abbreviated business district, and I drove behind every restaurant and even our grocery store, the Tybee Market, thinking maybe a chowhound like Jethro might be hanging around the Dumpster or back door, hoping for a handout. I saw approximately thirty feral cats and stopped half a dozen neighbors out walking their own dogs, to ask if they'd seen Jethro, but I came up with absolutely nothing.

With a heavy heart (and a full bladder) I drove back to the Breeze, hoping maybe Jethro had changed his mind and come back.

Lillian, our part-time desk clerk, was packing up to leave when I walked into the office. She shook her head no before I could ask.

"Not here," she said. "I think that one," she said, tossing her head in the direction of Jeeves, who was sitting in a chair pulled up to the window, with his nose pressed up against the glass, "is suffering from a guilty conscience. He hasn't moved from that spot since you left."

I scooped Jeeves up and scratched his ears. "You can't be picking on the big dogs," I told him. "They get their feelings hurt and run away. He's only here till the end of the week. So once he comes back, play nice. Okay?"

Jeeves licked my hand and wagged his tail, and I truly believed he was repenting his sins.

"We've got a full house," Lillian said. "The Dowlings are in from Indiana, and I put them in unit two. They're going to Hilton Head for dinner, and that nice older couple from Boston checked into unit six. They're headed into Savannah to visit with their cousins, and said they wouldn't be back until late."

"Good," I said, relieved. We usually have a happy hour get-together in the office-lounge weekdays from five to seven. I set out wine and a fruit and cheese platter and let the guests help themselves, but tonight I was happy that our regulars wouldn't be in residence and therefore wouldn't expect me to join them.

Because, frankly, I was exhausted. At five, Harry texted me that he'd be home late. Only his second day at the new job, and already he was all in, but that was Harry. I was tempted to take a nap, but instead I caught up on the inn's bookkeeping, paid some bills, and then began rooting around in the fridge for something to cook for dinner.

Mindful of Harry's no-fish request, I found a package of boneless, skinless chicken thighs, which I chopped up and sautéed in a Dutch oven, along with diced onion and red bell pepper. I drained the meat and veggies, then dumped them back in the pot, along with a big container of chicken broth, a can of drained and rinsed cannellini beans, a can of Ro-Tel tomatoes, and a packet of white chili seasoning mix. I put the pot on simmer, threw together a quick green salad, and went back outside to look around for any sign of Jethro.

Jeeves trotted at my heels as I circled the block, whistling and softly calling Jethro's name. After twenty minutes, it was getting cold and my lower back was starting to throb. Reluctantly, I walked back home.

Harry was just pulling into the parking lot when Jeeves and I walked up. He kissed me hello and grabbed up Jeeves for a head scratch.

"Long day?" I asked as we walked into the office and through to our living quarters.

He shrugged. "It was all right. I'm still learning the ropes, and there's a pretty steep learning curve. What about you? How are things going over at the house?"

"Better." I filled him in on the day's progress.

"You look a little tired yourself," he observed after we'd finished dinner. "Are you feeling okay?"

"I'm fine," I insisted. "Just a few spasms in my lower back."

"Should you be out walking if your back hurts?" he asked.

I hesitated, then told him about Jethro's disappearing act.

"How did he get out?" Harry asked.

I paused. I didn't want to lie to Harry about where I'd been earlier in the day, but there was no way I was going to tell him about my mission at Oak Point.

"I'd run into town to do some errands, and the floor guy heard Jeeves over here yipping and snapping at Jethro. He opened the door to break it up, and Jethro took off running."

Harry frowned. "And there's no still no sign of him?"

I sighed. "Not yet. I don't know what I'm going to tell Weezie if he doesn't turn up. She adores that dog. She'll never forgive me if he's truly lost."

Harry got up from the table and started loading the dishes into the sink. "Look, why don't you go run a hot bath and climb into bed? I'll take another stab at finding him."

"No!" I protested, trying but failing to suppress a yawn. "You've just worked a twelve-hour day. This is my problem. Jethro is my responsibility."

"Your problems are my problems," Harry said. He came around to my chair and helped pull me to my feet. "Now go on. I'll call you when I find him. And when I get back, you'd better be tucked in bed, young lady. I'll bring you up your supper."

Harry was right about one thing, I was absolutely exhausted. As pregnant as I was, it was nearly impossible to find a comfortable position to sleep in, and when I did finally manage to doze off, it seemed like I had to get up to go to the bathroom every hour.

So I did as I was ordered. I took a warm shower and climbed into bed. Jeeves hopped up on the bed and settled himself at my feet. Harry had been gone nearly an hour, and there was still no word. Jethro, it seemed, might be gone for good.

With dread in my heart, I reached for my phone on the nightstand. But Weezie beat me to the punch.

"Hey!" I said. "How's the Big Apple?"

"It's great," she said. "And how's my little mama?"

"Big as a house and growing," I replied.

"And how's Jethro? I hope he's not being too much of a bother. Sometimes when I'm gone, he'll hardly eat. Is he eating okay for you?"

"He eats everything in sight. Listen, Weezie..."

"Please tell me he hasn't tinkled in the house. You know, he gets overexcited and sometimes he forgets..."

"No accidents in the house," I assured her. "But speaking of Jethro..."

"And he's getting along with Jeeves? I swear, Jethro is such an only child—he just doesn't like to share his toys."

"Jethro's been a model citizen. I wish I could say the same for Jeeves," I said. Jeeves, hearing his name, stood up on the end of the bed, wagging his tail, but I gave him the stink-eye and he dropped down and buried his head in his paws.

"That's a relief," Weezie said. "But really, I was calling to check in on the whole d-i-v-o-r-c-e situation. Any news?"

"Not any good news, I'm afraid. James checked at the courthouse, and it seems like Inez Roebottom was correct. So Richard is still, literally, my old ball and chain."

"Oh no. I was afraid of that."

"It gets worse," I said, leaning to look out the window to make sure Harry hadn't gotten back yet. "If I don't get this divorce finalized before the baby comes, in the eyes of the law, Richard would be assumed to be the baby's legal father."

"Whaaaat? You haven't seen him in years. How can that be?"

"It just is," I said glumly. "The only way out of this mess is to file for divorce all over again. But first I've got to track Richard down. The only thing I know for sure is that he was released from prison two years ago."

"Well, how do we go about finding him?" she demanded.

"I tracked down Richard's sister. She's living with his great-aunt at Oak Point, an old family farm out on the Little Ogeechee River."

"Cindy? That's the oldest of the sisters? She didn't like you much, did she? Refused to be a bridesmaid in your wedding?"

I had to laugh. "She refused to *attend* our wedding, that's how much she loathed me."

"Did she tell you anything?"

"She basically told me to scram," I said. "But Richard's aunt Opal is living with her now, and she always liked me. She got all misty-eyed when she saw I was pregnant, talked about what a precious baby her Richie was. I think she would have talked to me if Cindy hadn't literally shoved her out of the way and slammed the door in my face."

"That's kind of extreme," Weezie said.

"That's what I was thinking," I said. "It's almost like she was hiding something. Aunt Opal wanted me to come in and visit, but that's when Cindy really got agitated."

"What could they be hiding in the house?" Weezie asked. "You think they've got Richard locked up in a closet? Oooh. Or maybe the old lady was actually Richard—dressed up as Aunt Opal. You know, like Anthony Hopkins at the Bates Motel in *Psycho.* "

"This isn't a Hitchcock movie, Weezie. But I do think there's something fishy going on there."

"What's your next step?"

"I'm not sure," I admitted. "I think if I could just get Aunt Opal away from Cindy for a few minutes, she'd spill her guts about her little Richie. Or if I could just get a look inside that house . . . maybe I'd find *something* that would lead me to Richard . . ."

"If only I were there," Weezie said. "We could break out our black catsuits again. Remember when we went sneaking around that warehouse back in the day . . ."

"Even if I could find my catsuit, I doubt it would fit my big toe," I said. "Anyway, you're up there and I'm down here. How's it going up there, by the way? Was Daniel glad to see you?"

"He was surprised," Weezie said. "Things got off to kind of a rocky start. The airline lost my luggage. A gypsy cabdriver dumped me off in a bad part of town, and Daniel had to come rescue me. And the apartment he's staying in is the size of a broom closet—seriously. But yesterday I figured out how to take the subway, and I walked all over Central Park, and I watched the skaters at the Wollman Rink. And then I went over to the zoo. They have the most adorable polar bears. And I saw the seals and the penguin house. And then I walked over to the Plaza Hotel, which is right there near the park . . ."

"I've stayed at the Plaza," I reminded her. "Did you go inside and have tea in the Palm Court? And get your picture taken in front of the portrait of Eloise?"

"No," Weezie said, sounding a little sad. "They were having some kind of fancy society soiree, and there were hundreds of lady lunch types all dressed to the nines in designer duds and jewels and furs—

and there I was in my ratty jeans and Daniel's bomber jacket. I just peeked in the door long enough to see the lobby. Which was gorgeous."

"You mean the airline still hasn't delivered your suitcase?"

"It came late last night," Weezie said. "Thank God. Daniel's working tonight, of course, but we've got tickets to a Wednesday matinee, and I can't wait."

"What are you going to see?" I asked. "Don't tell me Daniel is actually going to sit through a musical with you . . ."

"I didn't even ask," Weezie said. "And I don't care. I just want to see a Broadway show."

She was rattling off a list of potential shows, but I'd been looking out the window while we chatted, on the lookout for Harry's truck. Now a car with blue flashing lights was pulling into the Breeze parking lot.

I got out of bed and stared out the window. Our visitor was a Tybee police car. And there, silhouetted in the front seat, was a familiar-looking wayward black-and-white dog.

"Jethro!" The words were out of my mouth before I realized what I was saying.

"What? What's he done now?" Weezie asked.

"Not a thing," I said with a grateful sigh. "He's just a very good dog, that's all."

# Chapter 18

✦

## BeBe

James Foley was not a happy camper. We were in his car, in a convenience store parking lot opposite the long unpaved drive that led to Oak Point. I was wearing a big floppy hat and using Harry's binoculars to watch for Cindy Hodges's van; he was fidgeting and using his smart phone to look up sentencing guidelines for breaking and entering.

"Do you see this?" he demanded, brandishing his phone. "We could get eighteen months to five years! And that's assuming we get a friendly judge."

"Relax. We're not really going to break in. I was just here yesterday. That house is so old and rickety, we can probably just pull back a board and crawl inside."

"I should never have let you and Weezie talk me into this. I'm an officer of the court! I could get disbarred as well as imprisoned."

"You didn't have to come," I pointed out.

"Weezie would never let me hear the end of it if I'd let you do this alone. What if something happened? What if somebody caught you breaking in, or God forbid, you went into labor?"

"For Pete's sake! Why does everybody keep expecting me to go into labor? The baby is weeks away. And nobody is going to catch us."

"John will never speak to me again if we get caught. What if somebody in the DA's office finds out you roped me into this caper of yours? It could ruin his career. And I hate lying to him. He thinks I'm playing bridge tonight. What about you? Where did you tell Harry you were going?"

I sighed. I'd hated lying to my partner as much as James hated lying to his. "Harry thinks I went to do some last-minute Christmas shopping."

James shook his head and tsk-tsked some more. Just then, the minivan pulled onto the road opposite us. I raised the binoculars and liked what I saw.

"See there? That's Cindy driving, and that's Richard's aunt Opal sitting in the front seat right beside her. Aunt Opal is hard-shell Baptist, and they're going to Wednesday-night prayer service. They won't be back for at least an hour or more."

James started the car but he didn't stop fussing. "What if they're skipping church? What if they're just running out to get a carton of milk?"

"Cindy wouldn't go to the trouble of loading Opal and her walker into that van just for a trip to the store. They're going to church. Now, can we pleeeease get moving? I hate to mention it, but I need to use the bathroom again."

I glanced over and saw his ears had turned crimson.


"Kill the headlights," I said as we rolled up to the house.

"I thought you said the coast was clear," James said.

"It is. But there's no reason to take chances."

He switched off the headlights.

"Park with the car facing out toward the road. Just in case we have to make a fast getaway," I said.

"Dear Lord!"

I traded the floppy hat for a black knit ski cap and handed him a matching model.

We got out of the car, and it struck me what a very odd-looking couple we made. James Foley was dressed in baggy black faded slacks and a long-sleeved black shirt that looked like relics from his priest days. His thinning silver hair glowed in the moonlight. I'd tucked my hair up under the cap, but there was no way I could tuck away the baby. I wore black maternity leggings, one of Harry's oversized navy blue sweatshirts, and a pair of black flats. I carried a flashlight. James carried a lifetime of Catholic guilt.

"Look," he whispered, pointing to a dilapidated shed on the east side of the house. "There's a car under there! Somebody's home. Let's get out of here."

"Shh." I walked as quickly as I could toward the shed, with James a couple of steps behind. The car was an old beat-up blue Honda Accord. I played my flashlight over it. The hood and trunk were covered with dust, spiderwebs, and pine needles.

"It's a junker," I said. "Probably been here for years and years. Come on, let's go take a look at the house." I had a dim memory of a wide back porch that ran the width of the old farmhouse, with a glass-paneled door leading into the kitchen.

"This way," I said. We made a wide berth around the front porch and picked our way through overgrown shrubs and foot-high weeds. Each time a twig snapped underfoot, James froze.

"Relax," I muttered.

The undergrowth was so dense here, I felt sure nobody could spot us even if they'd been looking. I switched on my flashlight and we followed a faint footpath that had been beaten through the brush.

In a few minutes, the back of the farmhouse loomed before us. If the front of the house looked bedraggled, the back looked worse—forlorn, even abandoned. As I played the light over it, it appeared that the roof had caved in on an ell that curved out from the porch—a room I remembered had once been Richard's grandmother's laundry room. Most of the paint on the house was long gone, and the brick steps leading up to the porch were broken and crumbling. But the kitchen door was right where it should have been.

"Come on." I gestured toward the porch. As we got closer, I could see that it was in bad shape too. The floorboards were warped and rotten—a large sheet of plywood had been clumsily placed atop what must have been a particularly questionable spot on the floor.

I started toward the steps, but James grabbed my arm. "Let me go first. If one of those boards gives way beneath you ..."

Was he making a crack about my weight? I didn't care. It was a sweet gesture, and I wasn't exactly eager to test just how sturdy the floor-boards were.

I handed him the light, and he climbed the steps slowly. He put one foot on the first board and tested it, then another, then another. I followed close behind, until we were now standing in front of the kitchen door.

He played the light over the door, which had pale blue blistered paint. "Just so you know, I'm not picking any locks. I draw the line at that."

I reached around him and turned the knob. Rusty hinges rasped, but the door swung slowly open by a few inches and then stopped. I stepped around James and gave the weather-warped door a shove with my hip and almost fell into the kitchen.


Not much had changed on the inside of the house. The olive green lino-leum floor was faded and worn—but clean, as was the rest of the kitchen. The dark pine cabinets and red Formica countertops were as I remembered them. There was a wire dish drainer in the sink, with a dish towel placed neatly atop the still damp dinner dishes.

"Be back in a minute," I told James. I found the downstairs bath-room with no trouble, and afterward, dried my hands on a prim mono-grammed linen hand towel that screamed faded fortune.

James was standing in the living room. A lamp on an end table gave off a weak light, but it was enough to see what we needed to see. An old-fashioned lumpy brown sofa stood on a threadbare Oriental rug. A leather recliner faced the television, with duct-tape repairs on the arm and a crocheted afghan neatly folded on the chair back.

I leafed through a stack of magazines on the coffee table, unsure of what I was looking for—some sign, I guess, that Richard was in residence. But there were no back issues of *Hustler,* just some well-thumbed *Reader's Digest*s, a five-year-old copy of *Guideposts*, and the December issue of *Southern Living*.

"What now?"

I pointed toward the dining room. A massive antique banquet-sized mahogany table was too large for the room, and the ornately carved Chippendale chairs looked out of place in such a simple farmhouse. The furniture had probably come from Richard's parents' home—a beautiful circa 1910 house on the bluff at Isle of Hope where our engagement party had been held—and which had been sold shortly after the end of our ill-fated marriage.

There were three place mats at one end of the table, and the other end held neat stacks of papers and file folders—as though it were being used as a makeshift office.

"I'll go through the papers to see if there's any mail for Richard, or any other signs he's been here," I said. "Why don't you go check in the bathroom and bedrooms?"

"Check for what?" James glanced uneasily around the dining room and checked his watch for the tenth time since we'd entered the house. *Note to self—never invite a priest, even a former priest, along for any extra-legal outings.* James made the world's worst accomplice.

"Signs that a man is living here," I said. "You know, like men's clothes or a shaving kit or pornography—if you find any smut, give a holler. That means Richard is either living here or hanging out here."

Rifling through the mail was a depressing project. Lots of bills, most of them marked past due, final notice, etc. If the sad condition of the house hadn't been enough to convince me that Cindy and Aunt Opal had fallen on hard times, reading their mail did the job.

At the bottom of a thick stack of catalogs and junk mail I found a tidy package of mail bound tightly together with rubber bands—all of it to Richard Hodges and sent to this address.

I held my breath as I unsnapped the band and looked through the envelopes. None of it was particularly interesting. There were bank statements, credit card offers, even, ironically, half a dozen unopened solicitation pleas from various nonprofits, including the American Heart Association, the World Wildlife Fund, and Richard's alma mater, William & Mary.

Naturally, I checked the bank statements. Richard had a checking account with a local bank, and the October statement showed a balance of less than $200. Not surprising, but it did make me wonder if he'd been able to find a job after his release from prison.

I thumbed through the mail a second and third time, hoping to find something like a pay stub or any indication of employment, but I found nothing.

"BeBe?" I turned to see James standing in the doorway from the hall. "Something down here you might want to see."

I followed him down the hall, past two small but tidy bedrooms, to the last door at the end of the hall. The door was ajar, so I peeked in.

The room was starkly furnished. There was a single narrow four-poster bed, with a heavy woolen blanket stretched taut over a sagging mattress, and two wafer-thin pillows in white cotton cases. On the wall opposite the bed was a chest of drawers with a mirror. A wooden kitchen chair had a neatly folded stack of white bath towels. The closet door was open. Wordlessly, I walked in and thumbed through the garments hanging on wire hangers.

I pulled out a heavily starched white cotton dress shirt. The label was from John B. Rourke's men's shop. It was a long-sleeved white oxford cloth button-down, size 14½/36. Richard had shopped at Rourke's since his freshman year at Savannah Country Day. He never wore anything but white oxford cloth button-downs, and he had an unusually thin neck and long arms.

I held the shirt up to my nose and sniffed, then dropped the shirt as though I'd been burned. My hands were shaking and my heart was beating a mile a minute. I sank down onto the bed.

James sprung into action. "BeBe? Are you all right? Talk to me. What's going on? You're not going to faint, are you?" He was patting my hand and fanning my face at the same time.

"He's here," I said finally, nodding toward the closet. "Those are his clothes. His shirts. His aftershave. Richard's, I mean."

I had a fresh crop of goose bumps on my arms.

James sat down on the bed beside me. "You're sure?"

For a moment, I couldn't speak. Somehow I felt Richard's presence pressing in on me, sucking the breath out of my chest. And then I was right back in that dark place again, in a marriage to a man who'd managed to hide his true self from me for months and months, until I was forced to face the awful truth of who he truly was.

And then I felt a tiny little butterfly kick to my rib cage. And I remembered, somehow I'd managed to survive that time. Richard was the past. I'd rebuilt my life from the ground up, in a new place with a new man, and there was a new life force just waiting to make an entrance into this world.

I took a deep breath and the darkness receded.

"I'm fine," I said, squeezing James's hands. I looked around the room one last time. "Really. Now I know he's living here, I'll come back. I'll make him sign the divorce papers. Then I never have to see Richard Hodges or deal with him. Ever again."

"Do you want to wait around for a while? See if he shows up?"

"Better not." I stood up and took one more look around the room. "It's nearly nine now, and Harry worries about me. If we hurry, we can stop at Target and do a little Christmas shopping."

"Sounds good," James said. "You don't happen to play bridge, do you?"

# Chapter 19

✴

# Weezie

By my third day in the city, I was starting to feel like an old pro. I'd successfully managed to ride the subway to and from Central Park without getting lost or mugged; I'd window-shopped down Fifth Avenue and eventually found my way to Rockefeller Center to admire the Christmas tree.

I'd even slipped inside St. Patrick's Cathedral and sat for a few minutes in a pew, admiring the magnificent vaulted ceiling and stained-glass windows. Uncle James, I thought, would love this place. Not long after moving home, James met Jonathan McDowell, a dashing, ten years younger assistant district attorney. To my parent's astonishment and my own delight, he and John had become a couple only weeks after meeting.

James had given up his collar, and although his church would never recognize or approve his relationship with Jonathan, he still attended mass every Sunday, often picking my parents up at home and ferrying them to Blessed Sacrament Church and then out to lunch afterward at their favorite all-you-can-eat buffet. It was the high point of their week—especially Daddy's, since I knew it was likely to be the most edible meal of the week.

Sitting in that pew, watching tourists file through, stopping to genuflect before the altar or drop some coins in the poor box, I thought about Daddy now. I hadn't heard anything from Mama all week. She was probably mad at me for leaving this close to Christmas and the wedding. It didn't take much to get her mad at me, but I decided I wouldn't dwell on that now.

That morning I pawed through my long-lost suitcase, trying to decide what to wear for my Broadway debut. I knew it was only a matinee, but I wanted to look nice, especially since it would be the first time this week that Daniel had seen me dressed up.

Despite his best intentions, we hadn't seen much of each other at all. He'd had to work most of Tuesday and by the time he got home at two in the morning, I was fast asleep. Today would be different, though, he promised. Carlotta had given her word that she'd make sure he could sneak away from the restaurant by no later than one, sharp. The plan was for me to meet Daniel at the restaurant, where we'd have a special lunch, and leave in plenty of time to make the two o'clock curtain. Two o'clock curtain!

I finally decided to wear the only dress I'd packed for the trip. It was a vintage 1960s long-sleeved peacock blue tissue-weight wool dress with a close-fitted bodice, a wide black patent belt at the waist, and a narrow skirt. It no longer had a label, but from the quality of the fit, workmanship, and fabric, I felt sure it had to have been the work of a major designer. As soon as I zipped it up and stepped into my black suede pumps with the gold buckles on the toes I felt glamorous and, yes, positively soignée. Like something out of a *Mad Men* episode. I added a pair of vintage gold Chanel button earrings, and finished off the outfit by fastening the rhinestone Christmas tree brooch I'd bought the Christmas Daniel and I got engaged.

The day before, on my walk around the Village, I'd found a tiny vintage clothing boutique on Sixth Street, but when I stepped inside the shop, I realized the merchandise wasn't really my kind of thing.

The shop was so narrow that you could stand in the middle aisle and touch the racks lining both walls. And those racks? Stocked with dozens and dozens of pairs of gnarly blue jeans, seventies rock concert T-shirts, leather garb, and vintage eighties fashions. Waaay too hipster for me.

I was about to turn around and walk out when I spotted a lone garment hanging on a hook near a curtained-off dressing area; it looked nothing like the other clothes in the shop.

It was a circa 1950s black lamb shearling car coat, with dolman sleeves and a high funnel neck. I tried it on. It fit like it was made for me. And then I checked the price tag and almost choked. Only $30. Could that be right?

I found the shop's proprietor sitting on a high stool behind the cash register. I handed her the coat and dug my billfold from my pocketbook.

"Is that the correct price?" I asked timidly, afraid that maybe I'd overlooked a missing zero.

"I could do twenty bucks if you've got cash," she said. I handed her a twenty-dollar bill and donned the coat as I was walking out the door. It had a red satin lining, and for the first time in three days I finally felt warm.

And by Wednesday, I was ready for a day on the town with Daniel.

He'd written the restaurant's address on a slip of paper before leaving for work that morning. "Take a cab," he'd advised.

But I hated to waste money on a taxi. As soon as I stepped outside the town house, I was thankful for my new coat. It had snowed again overnight, and although the temperature had risen enough to start melting the snow, the wind was still cold and raw. I picked my way carefully down the sidewalk to the subway entrance, but after only a block or so, my beautiful black suede pumps were soaked from the accumulated slush.

Still, I couldn't help feeling smug as I went through the turnstile and stood on the subway platform, telling myself I looked just like any other seasoned commuter. When my train pulled up, I stepped inside and found the last available seat in the car. The doors slid shut, and we were all jammed inside, shoulder to shoulder, hip to hip. Music wafted back from an unseen source at the front of the car, a horn solo of "Silent Night." I found myself humming along under my breath, checking the faces of nearby passengers to see if they were doing the same, but everybody else seemed preoccupied, texting on phones, checking e-mails, or reading books or newspapers.

Me? I clutched my purse tightly on my lap and watched the scenery. Ten minutes later, I had to forcibly shoulder my way through the throngs to exit at my stop.

Emerging from the subway station into daylight, I stepped under a nearby overhang to try to get my bearings. The earlier sunlight had faded and it had started to sleet. Did I turn right or left? I wasn't certain, so I turned left, but after a block realized I'd done the exact wrong thing. I did an about-face and headed right, the sleet coming down so hard it felt like needles piercing my bare head and face.

The sidewalks were as jammed as the subway car, and I felt myself being carried along with the tide of humanity. We came to an intersection. The light turned and I stepped down from the high curb and into the street. And into a six-inch puddle of melted black slush.

The shock of cold startled me so that I gave a quick, sharp shriek at the same time I hopped out of the puddle. I looked down just in time to see my right shoe go floating off down the street in a river of slush. It bobbed along for a few feet, with me in hot pursuit, but as I watched, it flowed right into a large metal storm drain and disappeared.

I stood and stared at the drain for a moment in disbelief. But only a moment, because my shoeless right foot was freezing. I hop-walked for the next block until finally I spotted a cheery red-and-green-striped awning with the Cucina Carlotta logo.

Never had I been so happy to see a restaurant. I pulled the heavy plate-glass door open and stepped inside. It was barely noon, but the foyer was already crammed. I tucked my one remaining shoe in my pocketbook and in my wet stocking feet edged my way over to the maître d's stand.

The hostess was tall and willowy, with a cascade of long auburn hair and huge eyes fringed with extravagant black lashes. She wore a short, tight black dress with a plunging neckline and thigh-high black patent leather boots right out of a dominatrix catalog. She held a phone to one ear and was staring down at the open reservation book on the stand. I waited patiently for her to finish listening, conscious that my wet hair was plastered to my face, and what little makeup I'd applied that morning had probably washed away, like my shoe. I looked like a drowned rat, I was sure.

I edged closer so she could hear me in the din of the room.

"Um, hi," I said, glancing around the room. "I'm looking for Daniel Stipanek."

She continued writing something in the book. "Danny? You mean our chef?"

"Yes, that's right. Daniel. I'm meeting him for lunch." Danny? The only people who called him Danny were his brothers—and his mother.

Now she glanced up, and I realized I was talking to the restaurant owner and namesake, Carlotta Donatello.

The tabloid picture hadn't done her justice. She was even more stunning in person. Her eyes were a deep cobalt blue, and she had a small mole just at the right corner of her full lips.

"Ohhh. Oh yes! You must be the fiancée. He told us you were coming in for lunch today."

"That's right. I'm Weezie."

She looked me up and down, and I began instantly regretting every single wardrobe choice I'd made that day. The blue dress was dowdy, the fabric too clingy, the color too bright. My big gold earrings looked tacky compared to the tasteful square-cut diamond posts with large silver hoops that glittered from her own earlobes.

I felt like what my meemaw used to call "country come to town."

Carlotta's glittering eyes lingered on my feet. "What happened to your shoes?"

I felt my cheeks burn with embarrassment. "Storm drain."

She burst out laughing, a big, braying belly laugh. People around us stared and then looked away, to be polite.

She grasped my forearm. "Sorry! I'm not laughing at you. Oh my God. That same exact thing happened to me last summer. I was wearing these insanely expensive sandals, and it was raining like crazy, and one minute I was walking down the street and the next, one of my shoes went floating down the street. It was August, and here I am, wearing only one shoe on Central Park South."

"What did you do?" I whispered.

She shrugged. "I chucked the surviving shoe in the trash and hobbled over to the nearest Duane Reade and bought a pair of two-dollar flip-flops."

I looked down at my bare feet. "I don't think I'm going to find any flip-flops this time of year."

"What size shoe are you?"

"I'm a seven."

She laughed that belly laugh again, and improbably, I began to like her for it. "I was going to offer to loan you a pair of the flats I keep in my office, but I'm a nine and a half. So that won't work."

"Probably not. I'd just lose them again."

She clutched my arm again. "Look, as you can see, we're having sort of a crush of lunch business today, and Danny's in the weeds back in the kitchen. Tell you what. I'm going to seat you at my table in the front dining room and let him know you're here. And I'll send my assistant out for another pair of shoes for you."

"Oh no, I couldn't," I protested. "If he's busy, I'll just go find a shoe store myself..."

"Barefoot?" She shook her head. "No way. Claire can just run out and buy a pair. It won't take but a few minutes. Some nice stylish flats, black, right?"

Before I could manage an answer, she was towing me through the dining room, toward a prime seat in front of a broad picture window.

She grabbed a passing waiter by the arm. "Arnie, this is Danny's fiancée, Ms. Foley. Would you please get her drink order right away? She's having a rough morning."

"Sit!" she said, pointing to a chair. "I'll just let Daniel know you're here."

I shot her a look of gratitude and took the chair she'd indicated, finally taking a moment to soak in the atmosphere in the dining room. The décor was what I'd describe as early Tuscan ruins, rough-textured stucco walls painted in a warm yellow-pumpkin shade, dark wood floors, and simple but heavy olive-green-and-russet-striped drapes. The room was buzzing with conversation. I asked for a glass of white wine, and Arnie disappeared.

Five minutes later, he was back with a carafe of wine, a basket of bread, and a cruet of olive oil, but no menus. He fussed with the table setting for a moment and poured my wine. "Daniel said to tell you he's fixing something special for your lunch," Arnie confided. "We've got kind of a backup in the kitchen, but he promises he'll be out by the time you finish your salad."

The salad he brought me was one Daniel had tinkered with for weeks back home in Savannah. Two fat slices of cornmeal-crusted fried green tomatoes sat atop a bed of baby greens. The dressing was a sort of remoulade, and there were polka dots of creamy goat cheese and shards of crisp lean applewood-smoked bacon scattered across the whole affair.

Glancing around the room I could see diners at adjacent tables diving into the same salad with what can only be described as reverence.

I took a bite and chewed slowly. I took a sip of wine and another tiny bite of salad. It was that good. I could have taken a bath in the dressing.

The room grew more crowded. I finished the salad and glanced down at my watch. It was 12:30. The room was at full capacity and the noise level matched it. I looked around for Arnie, but he was busily taking orders at a nearby table of six chicly dressed women.

Finally, at quarter to one, Daniel came rushing up to the table, a plate of food in hand.

I stood and he set the plate on the table and kissed me, nuzzling my neck for a moment and whispering in my ear. "Sorry, sorry, sorry."

I sat back down and he took the chair opposite mine. I gestured at his empty place setting. "You're not going to eat?"

"Can't." He pointed at the plate he'd brought me. "Dig in."

"What is it?"

He helped himself to a gulp of my wine. "Braised quail breast with a portobello-prune stuffing and a reduction of bourbon and figs, over a grits cake, with bacon-braised bitter greens."

I speared a bite of the quail, closed my eyes, and chewed.

"Divine," I pronounced.

"Glad you like it," he said. "It was the special and we sold out within thirty minutes of opening. I had to fight the waiters to save you this last plate."

"It's great that it's such a success," I said, between bites.

"Almost everything on the special today is from Georgia," he said proudly. "We sourced the quails from a farm down near Thomasville, the grits are from North Georgia, and the greens and dried figs are from a family-owned farm in Ellabell. I'm doing a chocolate pecan tart for dessert, and the pecans are from Baxley."

I smiled and waited for what I'd already guessed was coming.

He got that serious look on his face. "Look, honey, I feel terrible about this . . ."

I held up my hand to cut him off at the pass.

"I know. You're too busy to go to the theater with me."

"There's just no way. We're totally slammed out in the kitchen, and if I don't get back out there in like five minutes, we'll never catch up."

I sighed. "Doesn't matter. I can't go either. I don't even have any shoes."

"What?" He peeked under the table and came up looking puzzled.

"I lost my right shoe just as I was crossing the street to get here.

And it was my favorite pair of heels too. I guess it wasn't meant to be. This whole week was probably just a really, really dumb idea."

Daniel looked stricken. "Don't say that. Please! It's great that you came up. I love having you here. Honestly. And I was looking forward to going to the show with you today. I've never been to a Broadway show either, you know."

He reached into the pocket of his white coat and brought out a pair of tickets. "Orchestra level, third row, on the aisle. It's a revival of *South Pacific*. Carlotta's idea. She said everybody ought to see a Rodgers and Hammerstein show on Broadway, at least once in their lives."

"You don't even want to know what I had to do to get those tickets either." We both looked up, and Carlotta was standing behind my chair, holding out a shoe box.

"Here," she said, thrusting the box toward me. "Put those on, finish your lunch, and then you two need to get out of here. There's a cab waiting for you out front."

I opened the shoe box, and nestled in a fold of pink tissue were a pair of black flats with a distinctive round gold logo buckle that I recognized instantly.

"No," Daniel said. "I can't leave. We've got three big parties coming in the door right now . . ."

"I've got it covered," she said, yanking him up by the collar of his coat. "Lend me that, will you? I'm the messiest cook on the planet, and I hate to ruin a six-hundred-dollar dress with bacon grease."

Daniel was protesting at the same time as he was unbuttoning his jacket. "This won't work, Carlotta. We appreciate it, but really, I don't feel right about leaving."

"These are Tory Burch flats," I said, holding one up. The price sticker was on the sole of the shoe: $350.

"They were on sale," Carlotta said. "Put them on. A gift from me to you. Go. Hurry."

"I can't accept these," I started, but she cut me off again.

"Just go," she said, shooing us toward the door. "Have a good time, and then I don't want to see either of you back here tonight. Understand? You're taking the night off, Danny."

# Chapter 20

✴

# Weezie

Dusk had fallen on Broadway by the time we emerged from the theater. People around us were smiling and laughing and chatting about the play—even Daniel, I realized, was humming "There Is Nothing Like a Dame."

I squeezed his arm and laughed. "That was your favorite song? In the whole show?"

"What's not to love about a song that features bearded sailors dressed up in coconut shell bras and grass skirts?" he asked. "Let me guess, you liked 'Some Enchanted Evening.'"

"Hard to decide. There were so many sweet songs, but yeah, I loved that and 'Younger Than Springtime.' I swear, I could turn right around and go see it a second time, it was that good. Come on, admit it, you loved it too."

"It didn't suck too bad. For a musical. So, was it everything you expected?"

"And more," I assured him. "After this, you don't even have to bother with a Christmas gift for me. Because nothing you could do could top taking me to see *South Pacific*. On Broadway. At Christmas." I wrapped my arms around his neck and gave him an enthusiastic kiss to emphasize just how happy he'd made me.

He returned the favor, and as we stood there, kissing right there in the middle of Broadway and 42nd Street, people just kept walking right around us, as if we didn't exist.

Finally I peeled myself off Daniel's chest, and we drifted down the sidewalk, traveling through Times Square.

"Where to now?" he asked. "It's kind of early for dinner."

I hesitated.

"Come on, I know you still have at least a dozen things you want to do, and I've been such a jerk, too busy working to spend time with you. What do you really, really want to do?"

"Well . . . I've always wanted to go to the Metropolitan Museum . . ."

"Oh man . . ."

"I promise I won't drag you through the whole museum. I just want to see the big tree with all the hand-carved angels and cherubs and the fancy eighteenth-century Neapolitan crèches."

He heaved a huge, martyred sigh. "Theater and a museum, all in the same day? That's asking a lot of a good ol' boy from Savannah, Georgia."

"You are so *not* a good ol' boy," I said. "But if you really don't want to go..."

"Who said I don't want to go? I just have to give you grief, because otherwise you'd start taking me for granted. Is it too cold for you? Should we grab a cab?"

"Not too cold at all. We've been sitting in that theater for three hours. It'll feel good to stretch my legs."

"It'll probably be mobbed with people," Daniel commented, but he kept walking.

"I know."

"We probably won't even get close enough to see anything."

"I bet we will. Anyway, it won't hurt to try."

We started walking, looking for a cab.

We passed a place called Joe Allen's. Daniel pointed at the sign. "That's a famous restaurant, you know. According to Carlotta, lots of actors show up there after shows. We could stop in, warm up, get a drink..."

"Maybe after? You know how I get if I have a drink in the daytime. I'll need a nap..."

"A nap? We could go back to the apartment and I'll tuck you in..."

I punched his arm. "And neither of us will get any sleep. I know you, Daniel Stipanek."

"Later?"

"Much later," I promised.

\* \* \*

As he had predicted, the great hall where the Christmas tree was set up was mobbed—and even as we paid our admission, we were told the museum would close in fifteen minutes.

"Fifteen minutes? That's all we get?" I tried not to look as disappointed as I felt.

"Fifteen minutes of Christmas is about all I can take. Come on," Daniel urged, tugging me gently into the swirl of people, all apparently headed in the same direction as us—the Medieval Hall.

The sounds of hushed voices and the scuffling of feet on the marble floor echoed in the high-ceilinged hall, and from somewhere you could hear piped-in music from some kind of stringed instrument. Lutes maybe? After all, this was the medieval room.

We were packed in shoulder to shoulder, with what seemed like thousands of people, and slowly we managed to edge our way closer and closer to the tree, which we could see, towering in the middle of the room, propped in front of a baroque altarpiece. It was crowded, yes, but people were in a holiday mood, polite and reverent.

Finally we managed to inch our way within sight of the display. The tree, a twenty-foot blue spruce, was magnificent, hung with dozens and dozens of carved and jeweled angels and cherubs out of some Pre-Raphaelite fantasy. Just the angels and the tree itself were so gorgeous, so baroque and gilded and golden, it was difficult to take it all in. At some point, I realized my jaw was hanging open.

Set up at the base of the tree, the crèche figures were arranged in a kind of grotto scene, with the manger and the Holy Family at the center, and then ringed around them was a whole village of characters straight out of the story of Luke. The angels and archangels were there, and the three Magi, and barnyard animals and the shepherd and their flock, and villagers... all of it hand-carved and gilded in the most exquisite detail.

Daniel was being patient, but at some point, I realized he'd been shifting from one foot to the other. Luckily for both of us, we heard the closing gong sounding, and security guards appeared to help empty out the hall.

The first snowflakes of the day were falling as we came out of the museum. "Come on." Daniel pulled me in the direction of a street cart, where the smell of something being grilled over charcoal wafted into the cold air.

"Roasted chestnuts!" I cried when he handed me a waxed paper packet, inhaling the scent. He showed me how to eat them, and we walked arm in arm down the street.

"Now where?" I asked.

"You'll see."

Snow was falling harder now, and I was glad of my coat, warm gloves, and Daniel's scarf, which he wrapped securely around my neck.

He stepped out into the street, raised his arm, and whistled—but nothing happened. Buses, cars, and taxis inched past us in the traffic, but no cab pulled over. We walked on two more blocks, finally stepping under the parapet of a hotel, where Daniel discreetly handed the door-man a five-dollar bill. The doorman stepped into the street, blasted a shrill tweet on a silver whistle, and a moment later, we were being handed into a cab—with a fully functioning heater. Heaven.

Ten minutes later we pulled alongside a park bristling with tents outlined with Christmas lights.

"Where are we?" I asked as we got out of the cab.

"Bryant Park. It's a Christmas market," Daniel explained. "I know you wanted to go to a real New York flea market, but they're only on weekends, so this is the best I could do. Carlotta said sometimes vintage dealers set up here."

"That's so sweet. But I know you hate to shop. We can skip it if you want."

"No way," he said gamely.

We strolled around the park, stopping in the tents, which all had zipped-down sides—and space heaters. We found a church-sponsored booth with crafts made by senior citizens, and I bought the tiniest hand-knitted sweater, cap, and booties for BeBe's baby. Daniel bought New York Yankees baseball jerseys for his brothers, and when Daniel wasn't looking, I bought him a Yankees cap—and a beautifully illustrated coffee table cookbook.

After we'd wandered and shopped for an hour my feet were cold and wet, and for the first time in my life, I realized I was all shopped out.

"You hungry?" Daniel asked.

I nodded gratefully.

"Carlotta told me about a great little restaurant just around the corner. She even offered to call and make us reservations."

A black-and-white awning marked the entrance to the restaurant, whose name, Daniel assured me, roughly translated to "beautiful garden" in Italian.

The single dining room was tiny, with a low ceiling, whitewashed brick walls dotted with vintage Italian travel posters, and less than a dozen tables, all covered with red-checked tablecloths. Candles glowed from raffia-covered Chianti bottles on each table.

"This is so romantic," I said, after the waiter seated us and brought us individual carafes of prosecco. "It reminds me of *Lady and the Tramp.*"

He tried to look offended. "A Disney dog cartoon? Weezie, this is a four-star restaurant."

The waiter came back with a basket of bread and a beaker of olive oil, and I let Daniel order our dinner while I sat back in my chair and soaked up the atmosphere.

"*Lady and the Tramp* isn't just a dog cartoon," I said after the waiter left. "It's about acceptance, and opposites finding their true love. It could be about us. My favorite scene is where they're sharing a bowl of spaghetti in this little Italian bistro, and a strolling accordionist comes over, and they gaze into each other's eyes . . ."

Daniel grabbed my hand. "I'll do anything for you, Weezie Foley. I'll

sit through a three-hour musical, get stomped to death in a museum so crowded you can barely breathe, let alone see anything. I'll even Christmas-shop with you. And you know how I feel about Christmas. But I draw the line at ordering spaghetti with red sauce in a four-star Manhattan restaurant."

He hadn't even noticed the waiter hovering over his shoulder. "Sir? The lady would like to change her order?"

I turned around and beamed up at him. He was stocky with an elegant black handlebar mustache and a spotless white apron that barely stretched across his generous belly. In short, he looked exactly like my memory of the waiter in *Lady and the Tramp*.

Daniel sighed. "Cancel her capesante. Spaghetti it is."


The waiter brought thimble-sized glasses of grappa and biscotti. I tasted both and nearly swooned. "This," I pronounced, "was the most perfect, most bestest New York day ever."

"I'm glad," Daniel said. "Look. Since we're on the subject of New York, there's something we need to talk about." His face was solemn.

"What is it?"

"Don't get that panicked look," he said. "It's nothing bad. It's actually pretty cool. Carlotta offered me a job, Weezie. She wants me to stay on and be the chef at Cucina."

"Stay on? Like, past Christmas?"

"Stay on, like, forever. Like live in New York and everything. What do you think?"

What did I think? Live in New York? No effing way! I wanted to lean across the table and grab my fiancé by the neck. New York was everything I'd wanted to see and more. Too much more, really. I hated clichés, but this one was true. The city was a nice place to visit, but I definitely didn't want to live here. Now I just wanted to drag Daniel back home to Savannah. To our home. Where my dog was waiting to lick my face, and I could climb in my beat-up truck and go wherever I wanted to go and not have to bribe a guy five bucks to get me a cab. Snow was fine, but I'd seen, and walked through, enough already. I didn't want to trade in my flip-flops for galoshes.

But how could I tell Daniel any of that? I felt a stabbing sensation in my gut, but I managed to form a frozen smile. "What do you think?"

# Chapter 21

✦

## BeBe

By Thursday morning, Jethro and Jeeves had made an uneasy peace with each other. Jethro had taken up residence under our dining table, while Jeeves commanded Harry's leather armchair in front of the shell-encrusted fireplace.

Jethro snoozed on, snoring softly, oblivious to my existence. But Jeeves raised his muzzle and gave me a quizzical look as I tiptoed out of the bedroom. "Shh!" I cautioned. It was only six o'clock. I wanted to get out to Oak Point as early as possible, in hopes I might catch Richard by surprise. And I didn't want to have to explain to Harry where I was going or what I was doing.

Too late. The bedroom door opened and Harry stepped out, dressed in boxers and a white T-shirt. His hair was mussed, and he yawned widely. "What's up?" he asked, looking as surprised as Jeeves was about my unusual early-morning appearance. I was dressed in my warmest maternity leggings, one of Harry's old oversized flannel shirts, work boots, and a down-filled parka, which wouldn't quite zip.

I had hoped not to have to use it, but I had a pretext planned and ready.

"Weezie called yesterday. There's an estate sale at one of those old plantation houses down near Richmond Hill. She got the sale flyer, and she's all hot and bothered about some old crap they're selling. Since she won't be back until Saturday, I promised her I'd go take a look."

"At six in the morning?"

I poured a mug of coffee and handed it to him. "It's one of those once-in-a-lifetime sales. Like the one out at Beaulieu—where she sweet-talked me into camping out with her. The doors won't open till ten, but Weezie says all the dealers start lining up way before then."

Harry sipped his coffee and stared at me over the rim of the mug. I tried to look innocent.

"Okay, well, I better go," I said, picking up a big tote bag I'd set out as part of my charade. I patted Jeeves on the head and kissed the end of Harry's nose. "See you later, Dad."

He shook his head. "I still can't believe you got up at six in the morning to go stand in line at some estate sale. Weezie's going to owe you big-time."

The sun was just coming up as my car bounced down the bumpy drive leading toward Oak Point. The track ran through an abandoned field surrounded by rotting fence posts and rusted barbed wire, and as I rounded a bend in the road, I spotted a group of deer standing at the edge of the field, in the shadow of a cluster of pine trees. I rolled to a stop to watch them. Harry says deer are so prolific in the countryside around Georgia they've become a nuisance, but I never get tired of seeing them.

This group looked to be a doe and two fawns. They were nibbling on some kind of greenery, and at one point, the doe raised her head, pricked up her ears, and gazed in my direction.

"Hi, Mama," I murmured. "I'm not gonna hurt you or your babies. Just passin' through."

I parked the car a few yards away from the farmhouse. Cindy's van was gone, but a thin plume of smoke rose from the crooked brick chimney, so somebody, I hoped, was home. Did I hope to see Richard? I honestly couldn't have said.

My hands were clammy as I knocked on the door. I waited a moment, then knocked again. And again.

"Aunt Opal?" I called loudly. "It's BeBe. Are you there?"

My hand rested lightly on the doorknob. Should I try and go inside? "Aunt Opal?"

I heard a sliding noise, and then a thump, followed by another slide.

"Hold your horses," came the old woman's voice. "I'm a-coming."

The door opened a few inches, but she had the chain lock fastened. Opal was dressed in a pink flowered housecoat that hung down past her knees, with a moth-eaten man's cardigan buttoned all the way to the neck. Her white hair was unbraided, and there were toast crumbs on her chin.

"I'm not supposed to let you in," she announced, narrowing her eyes suspiciously.

"Is Cindy home?" I asked.

"I'm not supposed to say."

I held out the package I'd tucked in the pocket of my jacket. It was a small, unwrapped box of chocolates, a Whitman's Sampler, which I remembered she loved.

"That's all right," I said. "I just wanted to bring you a little Christmas gift. You can have sweets, can't you? I mean, you're not diabetic, right?"

"Doctor says my blood sugar is perfect," Opal said. Her hand snaked out and snatched the candy back inside like a flash.

She balanced the box on a little makeshift shelf on her walker and lifted the lid, surveying the contents. She plucked one of the candies and held it up for inspection.

"I don't get much chocolate these days. Cindy says it makes my bowels lock. The square ones—they're the caramel, idn't that right?"

"I think so."

She popped the candy in her mouth, closed her eyes, and chewed slowly. I waited.

"Aunt Opal, I really need to find Richard. It's very important. He's here, isn't he?"

She kept chewing, but opened her eyes. "That one was a cherry cream. I had a beau once, a long time ago, he'd bring me a whole box of chocolate-covered cherry creams. He got kilt in a car wreck out on U.S. 17. I don't never eat a chocolate-covered cherry that I don't think about that boy."

"I'm sorry," I said, not knowing what else to say. "About Richard. He's been staying here, hasn't he?"

She was staring down at the candy, her gnarled finger poised over this one, then that one.

"Aunt Opal? Please?"

"Cindy told me not to say nothing."

"She's not home right now, is she?"

"Gone to work. At the Waffle House. I can't let nobody in this house. No matter what."

"Not even me? Just to see Richard?"

Her pale eyes met mine. "Just how far gone are you?"

"Eight months. And that's why I need to see Richard. Because of the baby. Do you understand?"

"He ain't here," Opal said.

"Then . . . where?"

She closed her eyes, and for a moment or two, I thought maybe she'd fallen asleep, standing up.

Opal unchained the lock and opened the door all the way. She pushed the walker onto the porch, shivering in the early-morning chill.

She raised her right arm and pointed off to the left. "He's out there, in the garden, back near the river. But don't you go telling Cindy I told you."

I looked in the direction she'd pointed. "I won't," I promised.

There was frost on the ground, and drifts of dried fallen leaves crunched loudly underfoot. The wind shifted, and I could smell the tang of salt water and mud and marsh. Birds flitted about in the tops of trees. This had all been a grassy lawn at one time, but time and neglect had changed that. Sapling pine trees had sprung up in the place of Richard's grandmother's flower beds, their roots upending her carefully placed borders of sun-bleached seashells and rocks. I pushed aside branches and dead vines and kept walking.

The underbrush grew thicker, a nearly impenetrable thicket of privet, pines, palmettos, and other bushes whose names I didn't know.

At one point, from somewhere up ahead, I heard what sounded like a footfall.

"Richard?" I called. "Is that you?"

No answer came. I walked on, and briers tore at my clothes and scratched my face and I heard the snap of a dead branch. "Richard?"

Finally I pushed through the underbrush and found myself standing on a sandy knoll. Directly ahead of me I could see an expanse of golden-green marsh grass, and past that, the brackish waters of the Little Ogeechee River. A dock stretched out over the grass, its silvery gray boards collapsed and rotted in places, and on the muddy bank nearby I spotted the bleached remains of an old john-boat.

Just in front of the bank was a small roped-off rectangle. Unlike the rest of Oak Point, this little patch had been lovingly maintained. A rough, whitewashed fence surrounded it, and waist-high evergreen shrubs marked each corner. A gate stood ajar, and I looked around for any signs of movement or life.

I pushed through the gate and into the garden. Waist-high dried corn- and okra stalks stood in straight rows, and rusted tomato cages held the remains of the summer's crop. My boot struck something solid underfoot, but it was obscured by fallen leaves.

I bent over to see what I'd stepped on and saw a glint of pale stone. With the toe of my boot, I kicked away the foliage. A silvery-gray rectangle of chipped granite sparkled in the early-morning sun. There was writing—not carved, but handwritten in block letters with what looked like some kind of black marking pen. A thick covering of dirt obscured the words.

I dropped to my hands and knees and with both hands brushed away the rest of the dirt and leaves.

The writing had faded, but the letters were large enough to make out now.

**_Richard Hodges—February 17, 1966–April 22, 2011._**
**_Loving son and brother._**

A twig snapped and I looked up sharply, expecting to find Cindy Hodges glaring back at me.

Instead, Harry stood by the garden gate, his hands shading his eyes from the direct glare of the sunlight.

# Chapter 22

Harry knelt down in the dead leaves and lightly touched the make-shift grave marker. His eyes met mine, and his brow was furrowed.

"Is that . . ."

"Richard. Yes, my ex."

He nodded slowly. "So . . . there was no estate sale?"

"No. I lied to you."

"This morning. And last night too."

"You knew?"

"Lamest story ever, Babe. Since when do you go Christmas shopping at night? And come home with a single bag from Target?"

"I know. Dumb, dumb, dumb. I'm sorry. I hated lying to you."

"Then why did you? Why not just tell me what was going on?"

I bit my lips and looked down at the scrap of granite that marked Richard's last resting place.

"I was ashamed. Ashamed and embarrassed. And oh, dear God, I was desperate."

"Over this guy? He's dead."

"But I didn't know that. Not until just now. I thought..." I pressed my lips together and closed my eyes for a moment.

When I opened my eyes, he was standing up, holding out his hand to me. I took it, and he hauled me to a standing position, then folded me gently into his arms. He held me for a long time. I felt the wind whipping off the river and heard the rasp of dried cornstalks rustling together. And my own sobs, muted against his chest.

We found a moss-covered concrete bench in a corner of the garden that faced out toward the river, so we sat, and that's where I told him the whole sad, stupid story.

Harry listened and nodded. He was almost as good a listener as James Foley.

"You could have told me," he said when it was all over. "It wouldn't have made any difference to me."

"I know. But it seemed like a huge deal to me. Insurmountable. All I could think about was finding Richard and getting that stupid divorce over and done with. And then there was the baby to think about. Our child! If Richard were still alive—legally, he would have been considered the father. And if anything had happened to me..."

I shuddered.

"Nothing's going to happen to you. I won't let it," Harry said. And I knew he believed he could absolutely prevent anything from happening to me. "Anyway, it's done now. Right?"

We heard a rustling behind us, and I halfway expected to see another deer when I turned around.

Cindy Hodges, grim-faced, stood at the garden gate.


"I guess y'all are gonna call the cops on me now, aren't you?" She stood in front of us, arms crossed defiantly over her chest.

Harry raised one eyebrow. "Why would we do that?" He pointed toward the grave marker. "Did you kill him?"

"No! He just . . . up and died. He hadn't been out of prison three months. Richard didn't have anyplace else to go when he got out, so he moved in here with us. He was in bad shape when he got out. Congenital heart failure, the prison doctors told him. Our daddy had the same thing. I guess it runs on his side of the family. We finally got Richard on disability, and he was getting social security checks. Which helped a lot. As you can tell, things have gone downhill pretty bad around here."

"Your husband?" I asked.

"Gone." She shrugged. "Not that he was much use when he was around. So good riddance. Daddy left us pretty well fixed when he died, but Mama, well, she thought the Hodges were still what we used to be. She just had to keep up appearances. The big house in Ardsley Park, the country club memberships, it all cost a lot of money. And when she got sick, I'd promised her she'd never go into a nursing home, so between staying home and taking care of her, and the doctor bills, that ate up all the rest of the so-called Hodges family fortune. By the time Richard got out, it was all gone."

"Except Oak Point," I said.

"Which Daddy left to Richard," Cindy said, her voice bitter. "I moved out here with Aunt Opal right after Mama passed. You can see how run-down it's gotten. Richard, he had all kinds of grand schemes about fixing it up, selling off the land and building a subdivision with fancy million-dollar houses. But with the economy the way it was, and then, he really didn't have any energy, as sick as he was."

"When I came looking for him this week, why didn't you just tell me he was dead? Why pretend he was still alive?"

Her face colored. "I was afraid, if you found out, you'd make trouble."

"Trouble over what?" Harry asked.

But I already knew the answer to that one.

"You couldn't tell anybody Richard was dead. Because then the disability checks would stop. So you buried him yourself and left his room just as it was, in case anybody like me came snooping around."

"Which you did," Cindy said. "I was pretty sure when we got home from church last night, somebody had been in the house. I found one of Richard's shirts on the floor of the closet. You came back out here last night, didn't you?"

"You actually broke into this house?" Harry asked, looking alarmed.

"The back door was unlocked," I said, giving Cindy an apologetic look. "I didn't take anything. I just wanted to find Richard. I knew you were lying when you said you hadn't seen him."

"That part wasn't a lie," Cindy said. "He's been gone a long time."

"What happens now?" Harry asked, looking from me to Cindy.

"I guess I start looking for a new place to live," Cindy said.

"Why would you do that?" I asked.

"Because Opal and I have been living here on borrowed time," Cindy said. "I'm tired of hiding out, worrying about the day you'd show up and kick us out."

"I still don't understand what's going on here," Harry complained. "How could BeBe kick you off your own family farm? Richard didn't leave it to her, did he?"

"Richard? He never had a will. He was lousy at any kind of paperwork. Which was part of why he went to prison. Anyway, my little brother never really believed he'd die," Cindy said. "Even as sick as he was, he was hatching schemes right up till the end."

"You knew he'd never followed through on our divorce, didn't you?" I asked.

"I buried him, and then I went looking through his papers, to see if he had a will or maybe a bank account we didn't know about. I found the divorce papers in a file folder, along with the letter from that lawyer telling him he'd stopped doing the work because Richard's check bounced," Cindy said. "So as far as I knew, you two were still married. No will—that meant anything Richard had, including this farm, belonged to you."

She looked around at the overgrown garden, the collapsing dock, and then back at the farmhouse. The rooftop was just barely visible above the tree line. "It's not much, not to you. But it's all Opal and I have."

"I don't want it," I said hastily. "The only thing I ever wanted from Richard was a divorce. The farm, anything else, it's yours. I'll get James Foley, he's my lawyer, to draw up the papers right away. In the meantime, I don't see why anything has to change."

"What about him?" Cindy asked, giving Harry a hard look. "How's he feel about you signing away a farm like this? Twelve acres, right on the river? The economy's better now. People are building houses again. You could sell off the rest of the land around us, if you wanted to."

Harry put his arm around my shoulder. "BeBe makes her own decisions. I know she'll do the right thing." He stood up then. "I'll leave the two of you to hash this out."

I flashed him a grateful smile.

Cindy watched him go. "He seems like a decent guy. He's the baby's father, right? So now nothing stopping you two from getting married."

"He's the best thing that's ever happened to me," I agreed. "But marriage? That's not what any of this is about."

"No? What is it about, then?" she asked.

That stopped me cold. I'd been so frantic to make sure I had no legal ties to Richard Hodges, I hadn't had a lot of time to really question my own motives.

"I'm sorry about Richard," I said, pointing toward his grave. "Despite your opinion of me, I know what it's like to lose family. My parents are both gone, you know. It must have been hard, losing your only brother like that."

She was tough, that Cindy. With a brother like Richard, she'd had to be. She brushed off my sympathy the way she'd brushed me off the first time we'd met.

"Opal misses him. He was always her pet," Cindy said. "Me? I'm gonna miss that disability check of his. Unless . . ."

And here I'd thought Richard was an anomaly, the only Hodges to ever go bad. But it turned out big sister Cindy had more than a little larceny in her soul too.

"I'm not turning you in, if that's what you're worried about," I said. "But I am going to need some proof that Richard is deceased—if only to deed the farm over to you. And that'll probably mean an end to the government checks."

She frowned and I could already see the wheels turning. But it was time for me to leave Oak Point, and the Hodge family farm. Past time, really.

# Chapter 23

✦

# Weezie

Daniel brought a cup of hot tea and sat it down on the floor beside the wretched sleeper sofa.

He brushed a kiss on my forehead. "Gotta get to work. You'll be okay by yourself, right?"

"Mmm," I said sleepily. "I'm still exhausted from yesterday. I might just stay in bed all day to rest up." I tried to pull him down beside me, but he just laughed and stood up.

"Wish I could," he said. "But there's no telling what the kitchen will be like today, after Carlotta ran things last night. She likes to think of herself as a chef, but she's really strictly a front-of-the-house type."

"I guess that's why she needs somebody like you."

"Probably."

"When do you have to give her an answer about the job?"

"She'd like an answer yesterday. You know these New Yorker. Everything is hurry up, right now! Get it done!"

"Right." I tried to gauge what he was thinking, but Daniel was wearing his poker face.

"I'll call you later," he said, as he headed out. "Lock the door after me. And the dead bolts."

"And the dead bolts," I repeated.

Somehow the streets of New York did not beckon me that day. I did go back to sleep. At lunchtime, I ordered Chinese and felt positively decadent eating in bed, still in my pajamas, at one in the afternoon. I watched *The Muppet Christmas Carol* on television and was starting to think about yet another nap when my cell phone rang.

I winced when I saw the call was from my mother. Mama calls me every day at home, sometimes two or three times a day, but I couldn't convince her that long-distance calls on her cell phone were free. So she never called when I was out of town. Except now. I knew it had to be bad news.

"Hi, Mama. What's wrong?"

"It's your daddy," she said, her voice shrill with barely contained panic. "Something's happened to him. I just know it."

"Did you call an ambulance? Is he breathing?"

"How should I know? He's been gone since ten thirty this morning. It's two now, and there's no sign of him!"

"Gone, where? Calm down, Mama, and just tell me what's going on."

"How can I be calm? This is all my fault. He hardly goes out at all these days. But today was the Christmas lunch with his post office buddies, at Johnny Harris. He wasn't going to go, but I convinced him it would be good to see the guys. Weezie, he left here at ten thirty. Said he wanted to get the car washed and waxed before lunch, which was at eleven thirty. You know old men, they have to eat early. Anyway, I waited and waited for him, but he's still not home."

"Maybe they all got to talking and having a good time," I suggested.

"No. I called Harold Andrews, his old supervisor, and Harold said the party broke up right at twelve thirty. He said everybody was real glad to see your daddy, but that Joe was acting kind of funny. Distracted, he said."

I stood up and paced around the tiny apartment, trying to think where Daddy might have gone.

"Maybe he stopped by to see one of your neighbors," I offered.

"He didn't. I've called everybody, and I've been driving around for the past thirty minutes, but nobody has seen him. As soon as I hang up from you, I'm going to start calling emergency rooms to see if he's been in some kind of accident."

"That's a good idea. Tell you what, you call St. Joseph's/Candler and I'll call Memorial, all right?"

"Thank you. Call me right back, you hear?"

\* \* \*

Mama called back five minutes later. "He's not at St. Joe's," she said breathlessly. "What did you hear?"

"Not at Memorial either," I said.

"I just know he's dead in a ditch somewhere," Mama said. "I never should have let him drive by himself. I didn't want to tell you, but he hasn't been himself this week. Sometimes I find him just standing out in the yard, looking around like he doesn't know where he is. I should have driven him to the party myself. But I wanted to finish working on your wedding dress..."

"Oh, Mama. It's not your fault. Daddy has a mind of his own. He wouldn't have liked you dropping him off like that. It would have embarrassed him in front of the guys."

"Well, I'm going to call the police. Maybe they can put out a lookout for him."

"Are you sure? Won't he be awful upset if it turns out he just stopped off somewhere?"

"Better upset than dead," Mama retorted.

"How about this? Why don't you get in your car and drive over to Johnny Harris right now. Drive the exact route Daddy would have taken to the restaurant from your house. And just look, all along the way. Maybe he pulled over at a store or something. Okay? Will you do that? Call me back."

It was a very long twenty minutes before she called back. I hadn't wanted to upset Mama, but my mind was reeling with all kinds of awful possibilities. Maybe Daddy had suffered a stroke or heart attack while driving...

Mama was in tears. "I've looked and looked, Weezie. And his car just isn't anywhere. I am at the end of my rope. I think I'm just going to go home and call the police and light a candle and pray."

"Let's think about this a minute. Maybe Daddy got confused and took a wrong turn somewhere. Are you still in the car?"

She sniffed. "Yes."

"Where are you right now?"

"I'm on Victory Drive, headed east. But I already checked the Target store. He loves Target. I swear, before he started getting all fuzzy-headed lately, he'd go there two or three times a week, just pushing that red plastic buggy around and looking at all the stuff."

"So, you're almost to the Thunderbolt bridge?" I asked.

"That's right."

I mentally retraced the route Daddy would have taken to go home from Johnny Harris's, the barbecue restaurant where he'd met his friends for lunch.

"I bet he did take a wrong turn," I said suddenly. "Mama, take a left, instead of the right he should have taken."

"Joe knows the way home, Weezie."

"He used to. But you said he's gotten forgetful. If you take a left, where does that put you?"

"On Bonaventure Road. This is ridiculous. You know that just goes to the cemetery. Why would he go there?"

"Isn't that where Grandmamma and Granddaddy are buried?"

"But Joe hasn't been out there in years. Your uncle James sees to their burial plot."

"It won't hurt to look, will it?"

Mama sighed. "I guess not. I don't remember where the Foley family plot is, it's been so long."

"I remember it's in the Catholic section, with all those other Irish families," I said. "Stop in the sextant's office. They've got a map. And call me back."

While I was waiting to hear back from Mama, I called the airlines. It wasn't fair for my mother to have to deal with my wedding, plus Daddy's increasing "fuzziness" alone. I got put on hold, of course, so I put the phone on speaker and started packing my suitcase—which I'd gotten only two days ago. After forty minutes on hold with Delta, I hung up in disgust.

And as soon as I disconnected, Mama called back.

"I found him! You were right. He was at Bonaventure. He wasn't at the Foley plot, though. I found his car parked there, but there was no sign of him, so I started walking. He was just sitting on one of those benches they have on the bluff there, looking out over the river. He'd fallen asleep. When I woke him up, he was mad as blazes. Said I'd made him miss the end of the ball game."

"Dear God," I murmured.

"Weezie, he didn't have any idea where he was. I think he thought he was at home sleeping on our sofa in front of the television, like he does all the time."

"What did you do?"

She was weeping softly. "I sat there with him for a while, and we looked out at the river. After a while, he was his old self again. He said he'd been thinking about his mama and daddy and feeling bad that he hadn't visited their graves in such a long time. And he did go to Target, I was right about that part. He went in and bought a pot of plastic poinsettias to put on their headstones. He visited with them, and then he went for a walk, and then he said he got tired and just sat down on that bench where I found him. It was such a pretty day, he sat and watched sailboats out on the water."

"It's been snowing here in New York," I offered. "Off and on all day."

"Sixty-five and sunny here in Savannah," Mama said. "There were even jonquils popping up on some of the headstones."

"Twenty-six in New York. You've never seen so many people in your whole life. I went to St. Patrick's Cathedral the other day. It was so beautiful. I wish you could see it, Mama. I lit a candle for everybody in the family."

"I bet it wasn't any prettier than St. John the Baptist right here in Savannah," Mama said. "And I hear they have muggings in churches up there. I don't know how folks live up north in weather like that. I've been worried about you all week. Are you locking the door on that apartment? You're not carrying any money around, are you?"

"I'm fine," I assured her. "We're having the best time. Daniel took me to see a Broadway show, and we went to see the most magnificent manger scene at the museum . . ."

"Well, I'm glad you're having a nice time. I don't know how this dress is going to look on you, though, since you never would stay home long enough for a final fitting . . ."

Time to change the subject, I thought.

"What are you going to do about Daddy?" I asked.

"Do? I'm not going to do anything. He'll be fine. He just gets over-tired some days. I guess maybe I won't send him to the store by himself anymore, though."

"You don't think you should get him to see a doctor?"

"What would a doctor tell me?" Marian said, her voice sharp. "That I should put him in a home? Take away his car keys? Is that what you'll do to me the first chance you get?"

"No! I just want you to figure out what's going on with Daddy. Maybe there's some drug they can give him or something the doctors can sug-gest. There's a lot of new research on dementia these days. I was read-ing a story about it in the *New York Times* . . ."

"You just worry about you, and I'll worry about your daddy and me," Mama said. "When are you thinking about coming home? There's still a lot to do about this wedding, and I can't be worrying about your daddy and Christmas and all this wedding stuff."

"I'm flying home on Saturday." I did not dare tell her that Daniel was considering a job offer that might make my trip home to Savannah a temporary one.

"Saturday! That doesn't give me any time at all to hem your dress. And I've got so much else to do. I'm baking Daniel's groom's cake, and I need you to figure out what kind of cake plate you want to serve it on . . ."

"Excuse me just a minute, Mama."

I put the phone down, went into the tiny bathroom, climbed into the phone-booth-sized shower, and screamed my head off for fifteen seconds. Then I went to the sink and splashed cold water on my face and examined my hair to see if any of it had turned white during my conversation with my mother.

"Okay, I'm back. What were you saying?"

"About the groom's cake. I pinned a recipe out of Pinterest for a chocolate fruitcake . . ."

*Sweet baby Jesus! Mama's regular fruitcake was bad enough, but add chocolate to it and you would have a full-blown disaster on your hands.*

"Now, Mama, I don't want you worrying about a cake. We don't even need a groom's cake. I've already baked the wedding cake. It's in the freezer and I'll frost it Sunday morning. Most of the food is coming from Guale. Remember, we're just doing heavy appetizers."

"I have no intention of letting you get married without a groom's cake. It's bad enough that you're not getting married in a church in front of a priest. And on a Sunday! What will people think if I let somebody else do all the food for my only daughter's wedding?"

*They'll be incredibly relieved, I thought. Especially anybody who'd ever had a taste of Marian's unfortunate home cooking.*

"We've been over this already," I said, trying to be patient. "This is not my first rodeo, remember? I want to get married in my house, and I want Uncle James to marry us this time. He wants it too. He even went and got himself named a justice of the peace to make it all legal."

"James is a *former* priest. And I just don't think it's right."

"I think it's right," I said gently. "And Daniel does too. We're adults, Mama. I respect your ideas and beliefs, so I hope you'll respect mine."

"Doesn't mean I have to like them. Anyway, back to the cake. I've already bought all the ingredients. I'm making it, and that's final. So what cake plate?"

"Just a sec, Mama."

I put the phone down, threw myself on the bed, covered my face with a pillow, and practiced my primal screaming for maybe ten seconds.

"I'm back now."

"Good heavens, Weezie. Is something wrong with your phone?"

"I might need to charge it. If you insist on doing the cake, just use a nice cut-glass cake stand. But it doesn't need to be very big. We're only having forty people, remember?"

"How could I forget? Your cousins in Pooler and over there in Swains-boro are absolutely crushed that they didn't get invited. And I can't even look at the women in my rosary guild, since you snubbed all of them."

"I haven't seen any of those cousins since my first communion. And as for the rosary guild, you'll just have to tell the old biddies that you have a rude and thoughtless daughter."

"What makes you think I haven't already told them that?"

"Good-bye, Mama. See you Saturday."

# Chapter 24

✦

## BeBe

"M iz Loudermilk? You want to take a look at this kitchen back-splash and tell me if it looks all right?"

Benny, the tile contractor, was standing on the porch of the new house, hollering down at me. I was standing at the foot of the staircase, rubbing my aching lower back and wondering if I had the energy to climb those steps one more time.

It was Friday morning, ten o'clock, and I'd been awakened at seven with the cheerful whine of a table saw coming from our construction site. Not that I'd gotten much sleep. No position was comfortable for me these days, and when I did doze off, the baby managed to kick me awake soon after.

Harry had headed off to work in the predawn hours. I was starting to wonder when the nine-to-five part of his new office job was going to kick in. So in addition to running the inn I'd also become construction manager.

I hauled myself up the stairs and picked my way carefully through the construction debris in the living room.

Benny stood proudly by the kitchen counter, pointing at his handiwork, neatly laid and grouted gray and white penny tiles on the backsplash.

"Oh no." I felt a stabbing pain in my lower back.

His face fell. "You don't like it?"

"I liked it fine for the guest bathroom floor. This is the wrong tile, Benny."

"Huh?"

I picked up one of the cardboard cartons he'd discarded on the floor and pointed to the label I'd written in one-inch-high letters: GUEST BATH FLOOR. Then I walked over to the stack of tile boxes that had been delivered earlier in the week.

KITCHEN BACKSPLASH was labeled on the side of the box. I took out one of the tiles and showed it to him.

"Two-by-four white subway tile. *This* is what's supposed to be on the backsplash."

He took the tile and turned it over and over, like it was the first time he'd ever seen one.

"The penny tile looks right nice, though, don't it?"

"Subway tile for the backsplash, please, Benny. I'm sorry, but you'll have to take the penny tile down, and you'd better do it fast before that grout sets up. In the meantime, I'll call the tile place and reorder more tile for the guest bathroom floor. Do we have enough thin-set?"

"I reckon so." He turned abruptly and began mounting an attack on the backsplash with a crowbar, his feelings obviously hurt.

I walked away, shaking my head, to check on progress in the nursery. Finally I had reason to smile. The walls had been painted the soft seafoam green Weezie and I had picked out. The hardwood floors had been stained and given a soft matte finish. Morning sunlight splashed on the floors, and I could feel the tension knot in my stomach begin to relax.

Tomorrow morning I'd get Harry to start moving in the furniture. I was itching to put the crib in place and dress it in all the bedding Marian had sewn for it. I wanted to put the rag rug with its pastel stripes of butter yellow, green, and coral on the floor, and I wanted to fill the wooden bookcase with all the picture books I'd been collecting for our little sprout.

In short, I was ready to nest. The painters had left a ladder in the corner. I had the curtain rods in a box out in the hall. I even had my own cordless drill. It wouldn't take me more than half an hour to hang those rods. I eyed the ladder and pictured myself teetering on the top rung. Maybe I'd just wait for Harry to get home. If he ever came home.

As if he knew I'd been thinking about him, the cell phone in my pocket buzzed. Speak of the devil.

"How's it going?" Harry asked.

"About the way it usually goes," I said. "The tile guy installed the kitchen backsplash—using the tile that's supposed to go on the floor of the guest bath."

"Damn."

"But on the other hand, the baby's room is ready for furniture and drapes. I hope you don't have any plans for tomorrow morning."

"I'm all yours," Harry said. "But I do have a little bad news. I can't meet you for your doctor's appointment this morning after all. Remember Wayne Templeton? The thoracic surgeon from Syracuse? He's in town and he's insisting I take him fishing. I'd really rather not, with everything else going on, but I just can't see turning down the kind of money he's offering to pay for one fishing trip. If I go, I'll cut out of work around lunchtime."

"Go catch your fish," I said. "I'm a big girl. I can go to the doctor all by myself."

"I like going with you."

"It's strictly routine. All they're going to do is take my blood pressure and weigh me. And that's not a number I want to share with anybody. Especially you."

"If you're sure you don't mind. This is absolutely my last charter. I'm not crazy about going with Weezie still out of town . . ."

"I'll call you after I leave the doctor's office," I said, cutting him off. "All I ask is that you make sure your phone is charged."


Michael Garbutt wheeled himself away from the exam table, washed his hands, and made a note on the laptop computer open on the desk.

I clutched at the cotton sheet draped over my mostly naked torso and struggled to sit up again.

"Your blood pressure is up," he said, running down the notes on my chart.

"No wonder, after I had issues with my contractor this morning. It'll probably come back down after I make sure he gets the right tile for my bathroom floor," I said.

"Harry's not your contractor, I hope," Michael said. He and Harry had been long-ago high school classmates at Benedictine Military School in Savannah, and had somehow survived their wild teen years. Michael had surprised everybody in town when he came home from his freshman year of college and announced his intention of becoming a doctor.

"I wish Harry was my contractor. But no, he's too busy with the new job. I'm kind of overseeing things on the new house, and it's not going very smoothly."

Michael brushed a lock of graying blond hair off his forehead, looked over the top of his horn-rimmed glasses at me, and frowned. "Tell Harry I said he needs to fire you from being a supervisor. Your blood pressure is up, and that's not good. Bebe, I'd really like you off your feet, if possible."

"Not possible," I said, cutting him short. "I've got the inn to run, plus the new house to finish. And my best friend is getting married Sunday. Honestly, Michael, the blood pressure is just temporary. It'll probably go right back down after I leave here."

He made some more notes on the laptop and turned back to me. "Also? The baby's started to drop a little."

"Already? But I'm not supposed to be due till next month."

"First babies come when they want to come," Michael said. He pointed his pen at me. "I want to see you back here Monday morning. If your blood pressure's still elevated, I'm putting you to bed."

"Fine." I stuck my tongue out at him and began to gather my clothing.

"Harry's not doing any fishing since he took the new job, is he?" Michael asked.

"He was taking a charter client out today, but he claims it's his last run," I said.

Michael made some more notes on my chart. "It better be. He's gonna be a daddy again pretty soon here." He laughed at the very idea. "You know, some of the guys in our BC class are having grandbabies right about now."

"And some of the guys in your class are also totally bald with hip replacements and bad hearts," I reminded him. "Harry's young at heart."

He patted my shoulder. "More importantly, he's got a good heart. You guys will be great parents. Just remember—take it easy for the next couple weeks."

# Chapter 25

✦

# Weezie

I stood on the top step of the town house and looked out at the street. The previous day's snow had turned to slush and the sky was the color of a dirty dishrag. But I buttoned my coat, slung a huge plastic tote bag over my shoulder, and donned my gloves, scarf, and hat. Today was my last day in the city and I was determined to do some New York–style junking, weather be damned.

I'd done an Internet search for nearby vintage and antique shops, and I had a list of likely addresses, along with directions to get where I was going. More important, I'd finally broken down and bought a pair of inexpensive boots—and heavy woolen socks.

Eight blocks away from the town house, I found what should have been my street of dreams. Both sides of the street were lined with antique shops. My pulse raced at the concentration of vintage goodness.

The first storefront I stopped at had a window filled with artistically stacked old wooden packing crates. Spilling out of the crates, amid shreds of brown paper excelsior, were more pieces of old Jadeite than I'd ever seen in one place.

There were green Jadeite divided dinner plates, chop platters, coffee mugs, and soup bowls. There were nesting sets of mixing bowls, cups and saucers, cream pitchers, and sugar bowls. Hundreds and hundreds of pieces. There were rare Jadeite pieces I'd only ever seen on eBay listings or in Martha Stewart's magazine, pieces like canister sets and spice jars. The shop was called Miscellanea.

I pushed through the heavy plate-glass door and was hit with a telltale odor. Not the scent of mildew or mothballs I always hope for in a junk shop. No, this was an expensive-smelling lavender-scented aromatherapy candle. I turned toward the window display, snaked my hand behind the burlap coffee sack backdrop, and brought out a sugar bowl. One glance at the laser-printed price tag told me I was in the wrong place. The price for the sugar bowl? A hundred and fifteen dollars. I quickly tucked the bowl back in the window and turned to go.

And bumped into the salesclerk. She had on a white lab coat like the clerks at the Clinique counter at Macy's, and a name tag identifying her as Esme. "Do you do Jadeite?" she asked.

"Um, I sometimes *buy* Jadeite when it's affordable. I'm a dealer," I added apologetically.

"Then you know how *amazing* these pieces are," she said, gesturing toward the window. "It's dead stock, from an old warehouse in Indiana. Those are even the original packing crates. I can sell you one of those for three hundred fifty dollars—but I'm warning you, they won't last at that price."

"Well, I'd love one, but I'm flying home tomorrow, and that's not exactly a carry-on piece."

"We ship all over the world," she offered.

"Thanks, it's all lovely, but I don't usually *do* crates." Then I fled the premises.

I window-shopped the rest of the block and quickly discovered that New York junk was priced from five to ten times higher than what I could sell things for at Maisy's Daisy.

It was fun to look, and I got great ideas from the artistic displays in all these high-end shops, but after a couple hours of the look-but-don't-buy routine, I was getting nostalgic for good old rusty, crusty Southern junk prices. Wasn't there *anything* here that I could afford?

I wandered for what seemed like miles. The cheap boots were rubbing blisters on my heels, and the sky was looking threatening. I was about to wave the white flag and splurge on a cab ride back to the apartment when I spotted a cobblestoned lane so narrow I wondered if it was an alley rather than a street. I stood in the entrance to the lane and peeked down it. There were storefronts, but most of them were darkened.

In the middle of the block, though, I saw a large old neon sign in the shape of a lady's high-button boot. The name LaFarge & Sons blinked on and off, beckoning me to investigate.

The shop window was caked with what looked like Reagan-era dust. The display was a haphazard jumble of stuff from a cavalcade of decades—1980s-era mannequins dressed in polyester disco stacked on top of shiny 1930s-era mahogany sideboards, shoved up against 1950s metal high school chemistry lab tables on top of which were stacked 1920s oak pressed back kitchen chairs.

A set of tarnished brass sleigh bells attached to the door jingled merrily as I stepped inside and into another era—and zip code.

The interior was dim, lit only by a scattering of vintage chandeliers hanging from the high pressed tin tile ceiling. Furniture had been shoved into random corners, and everything was stacked four and five items high. Dust filmed every surface, cobwebs festooned every corner.

I smiled. No pomegranate-scented candles flickered, no chic sales-clerks hovered. I flipped over an ugly 1960s florist vase and saw a yellowing masking-tape price tag. Fifty cents!

The echo of my footsteps was the only sound in the high-ceilinged room. I wandered around, touching battered dressers and rickety chairs. My general impression was that the phantom shopkeeper had been pillaging garage sales for the past fifty years and then dumping his finds into this space.

Wandering in circles, I came to a turquoise Formica-topped dinette table in a 1950s-era boomerang shape. The price? Ten bucks. I could have wept. Back in Savannah, I could easily sell a table like this for $250. But there was no way to get it home.

An old army-green footlocker sat atop the table. Idly, I opened the lid and began to paw through the contents. I'd half expected to find some old soldier's war memorabilia—maybe an army blanket or canteen, or some yellowing newspapers announcing VICTORY IN JAPAN.

But these looked like the peacetime souvenirs of a well-traveled civilian. I opened a dusty cardboard shirt box and found dozens of sheets of unused vintage hotel stationery. The kitschy logos and letter-heads looked to be from the forties and fifties, gathered from hotels and motor courts ranging from Cheyenne to Omaha to Poughkeepsie to Montpelier to Clearwater. The box would fit easily into my suitcase. I set it aside and kept digging. Another shirt box held hotel "Do Not Dis-turb" door hangers from eight different hotels, all with fabulous old graphics. I added the box to my pile.

Peeling back the layers of the box I found half a hatbox. Careful not to tear the brittle old floral-printed cardboard, I heard a clink of glass as I removed the box from the trunk.

Lifting the lid, I saw folds of the palest pink tissue, which revealed a cluster of old mercury-glass Christmas ornaments. I exhaled slowly as I set each one on the tabletop. There were four little Christmas cottages, each in a different tarnished pastel color—pink, blue, green, and a dusty rose. Four more ornaments turned out to be mercury glass churches, complete with tiny steeples. Beneath the next layer of tissue were a baker's dozen of mercury glass clip-on bird ornaments with hand-painted detailing and real feathers applied as wings and tails. Tiny bits of the feathers floated into the air, even as I added them to the pile of other ornaments.

More tissue layers revealed a whole forest of vintage bottle-brush

Christmas trees. Each had a wire base screwed into a tiny red wooden pot. On the underside of one was the original McCrory's price tag. Nineteen cents. Some of the trees were green, but others were tinted in pastel colors, with globs of snow dusted all over them. Others had the teeniest glass ornaments glued on, or fine coatings of silver, gold, or green glass glitter. There were fourteen trees, the largest ten inches tall, the smallest less than an inch.

Jackpot.

I examined the footlocker lid for a price, finally spying $5 scrawled in black grease pencil on the underside of the lid. But there were no prices on any of the contents, and I guessed that the trunk had probably never been opened since it had been purchased.

"Hello?" I walked toward the back of the shop, hoping to find a salescounter.

A set of old wooden shutters cordoned off the rear of the shop from what looked like a back office. A grungy glass display case sat in front of the shutters, and behind that was an old black vinyl sofa. Stretched out on the sofa, softly snoring, was a very tall, very slender old gentleman with a scruffy white beard.

"Hello?" I called softly again. And then louder, "Sir?"

He sat bolt upright and stared right at me.

"What's that?" His voice was hoarse, phlegmy. He rubbed his eyes. "Who are you?"

"Uh, I'm a customer. The door was unlocked, so I've been doing a little shopping. You are open for business, aren't you?"

"Of course." He walked around the counter and shook my hand. I saw that he was wearing a tattered red sweatshirt, red corduroy pants, and black boots.

"Frances LaFarge. What can I do you for?"

"I found some things in an old footlocker and was wondering about prices."

He followed me through the maze of furniture until we'd reached the boomerang table.

He pointed at the footlocker. "You're not talking about that, right? Because that's not for sale. Definitely not."

"Well, I don't want the trunk." I pointed out the hatbox and the cardboard boxes beside it. "I really just want these things."

I'd hoped he'd glance at the pile and make me one price. In my dreams!

Instead he opened each box, rifling the contents. He pulled on his beard, coughed five or six times. Rifled through the boxes again and sighed.

"This trunk came from a very dear lady I met out in Connecticut," he said. "She'd been an actress in her youth, with a traveling theatrical troupe. I cleaned out her house shortly before she died. These were her special treasures, you know."

I nodded gravely. "I love old things like this. These sweet vintage ornaments and the old hotel stationery—they just speak to me."

"And what do they say?" he asked.

"Buy me!" I answered, with what I hoped was a winning smile.

"For how much?" he countered.

I did some quick math in my head. If I offered too much I'd never get my investment back, too little and I risked insulting him.

"How much were you thinking?" I asked.

"Hmm." He ran his hands over the hatbox. "How's $12.38? Cash."

It was an odd number and a crazy cheap price. I reached for my billfold. "That sounds like a very fair price." I handed him a ten and a five. "Please keep the change."

"Merry Christmas," he said, giving me a wink. I winked right back.

With my plastic tote bag bulging with my newfound bargains, I stepped out of the shop, directly back into reality.

Snow was falling. Not just falling, sheeting down. The sidewalk was already coated, and the cobblestones in the lane were blanketed.

I heard a ding coming from my phone, dug it out of my purse, and read the text message. It was from Daniel.

*"U busy?"*

I had to remove my gloves to tap out a reply.

*"What's up?"*

He texted back. *"Meet @768 Fifth Ave. Take cab."*

# Chapter 26

✳

I had to walk several blocks through near white-out snow before I could finally get a cab. The city seemed eerily quiet, with snow muffling the usual Manhattan street racket.

The taxi's heater was blasting and the noisy wipers were mostly ineffective at keeping the windshield clear. The cab crept along the streets with the driver hunched forward, trying to see through the curtain of snow.

It wasn't until we'd pulled over at the curb and I stepped out of the cab that I realized where I'd arrived. It was the Plaza Hotel.

Daniel stood in the lobby, leaning against one of the marble columns, trying to look nonchalant.

I rushed over and threw my arms around his neck. "You remembered!"

We worked our way through the throng of fur-coated women and little girls dressed in their Christmas best red velvet frocks and patent leather Mary Janes, all of them waiting to enter the fairyland-looking Palm Court.

As befitting the holiday crush, service was agonizingly slow. But eventually the waiter brought us glasses of champagne and a three-tiered stand of dainty finger sandwiches, miniature elaborate frosted cakes and sweets, and jewel-colored fruits. As scenic as the food was, I was more impressed with the room itself. Enormous glittering crystal chandeliers lit the room, and overhead, the domed ceiling was made entirely of stained glass.

"How on earth did you manage to get us in here?" I asked after I'd polished off two glasses of champagne and about a million calories worth of tea cakes.

"Dumb luck," Daniel said. "And BeBe. She texted me yesterday, asking if I'd taken you here yet. Everybody warned me that I'd never get a reservation—not this time of year. But I just kept calling, and right before I texted you, I managed to get through—and they'd had some cancellations for this afternoon. Probably because of the weather."

"This place is divine," I said, trying to appear nonchalant while I leaned over and unzipped a boot, easing my blistered right foot out of the faux-leather casing.

Daniel pointed at my tote bag. "What's all that?"

I told him about my junk jaunt and showed him one of the bottle-brush Christmas trees.

"Are those to sell or to keep?"

"I'm keeping all of them! They'll be my souvenir of my first trip to New York, Christmas, everything."

"I'm glad the trip wasn't a total bust," he said, glancing down at his watch. It was past five.

"You need to get back to the restaurant, right?" I tried not to let my disappointment show.

"I'm worried about getting a cab in all this snow," he admitted. "Traffic's gonna be a bear."

He paid up and we made our way toward the lobby exit, where a huge throng of people were standing around, staring out the window—at a sea of white.

"Damn," Daniel said. "I can't believe it's snowing even harder than when I got here."

I clung to his hand as we made our way through the crowd. Stepping out of the overheated hotel lobby felt like stepping into a deep freezer. The temperature had continued dropping, and a bitter cold wind sent gusts of snow whirling through the darkened night, even under the covered hotel parapet.

A quartet of scarlet-coated doormen stood out on the street, whistling ineffectively at the occasional cab that happened by on the oddly quiet street. But none stopped, and after ten minutes, we went back inside to get warm and regroup.

Daniel pulled out his cell phone. "I'll call the car service Carlotta uses. I'll get a Town Car to drop me at the restaurant and then take you back to the apartment."

He listened without speaking, then hung up, his expression glum.

"Nobody answering the phone," he reported. "I got a recording saying they weren't dispatching cars due to inclement weather."

"What do we do now?" I was starting to feel uneasy about all that snow. It had been a beautiful novelty earlier in the week, but now it seemed somehow ominous.

He was already working the phone again. "Carlotta has a four-wheel-drive. Maybe she can come get us."

"Hi," he said suddenly. "Look, we're stuck at the Plaza. Cabs are non-existent and the car service has shut down. Any chance?" He listened intently, shaking his head.

"You're kidding?

"For real?

"What about all the dinner bookings?"

He nodded again.

"Okay. Talk tomorrow. Good luck getting home."

"What?" I asked. "Bad news?"

"The snow's worse than we knew. The weather service is calling it a full-blown blizzard. None of the rest of the staff can get into work, so Carlotta closed down the restaurant an hour ago. She was trying to drive back to her place on the Upper East Side, but there were so many abandoned cars she just pulled over to the side of the street to walk the rest of the way home."

"Oh wow," I said weakly. "A blizzard? What are we gonna do?"

He looked around the lobby and spotted a small brocade-covered settee on the opposite side of the room. "Go stake us out a place on that couch. I'm gonna see about getting us a room here."

"For the night? At the Plaza? Can we afford that?"

"I don't think we have a whole lot of other choices," Daniel said. "We're snowed in."

Snowed in! How romantic. How terrifying. I was getting married in forty-eight hours. And I was scheduled to fly home in less than twenty-four. How would a blizzard affect the airlines?

I stayed on hold with the airline for forty-five minutes, listening to a recorded voice tell me how very important my call was to them. Every once in a while I looked up, to see Daniel, working his way through the line of people standing in front of the hotel desk.

Neither of us seemed to be making much progress.

I was still on hold when he drifted back across the lobby, his dejected posture telling me the situation without words.

"No luck?" I asked as he slumped down onto the settee beside me.

He shook his head. "The hotel's completely sold out. I tried to get on a waiting list, but the desk clerk just laughed and called it a 'quaint notion.' I called some other hotels nearby while I waited. No go. Everything in Manhattan is booked solid. Who are you on hold for?"

"Delta. What if they start canceling flights?"

"They already have," he replied. "I thought about the same thing.

There's a notice on the website saying all flights out of LaGuardia are canceled."

"What about the other airports?" I asked. "JFK? And how far away is Newark?"

"Everything in the tristate area is shut down," Daniel said. He leaned his head against the back of the settee and tucked his arm around my shoulders. "Better get comfortable. I think we're in for a long night."

I must have dozed off. When I awoke some time later, Daniel was standing over me, calling my name softly. He held out his hand to me.

Groggily, I took it. "What's happening? Where are we going?"

He held out a large bronze key. "To our room. C'mon."

People were camped out in various stages of sleep all over the lobby. Elegant sofas meant to seat three or four held five and six people, with blankets spread across their laps. Those fur-coat-clad women we'd seen earlier in the Plaza Court were sleeping sitting up in wing chairs, their daughters resting on their laps, the coats serving as makeshift comforters.

"How did you manage to get a room?" I asked, as Daniel led me toward the elevator.

"Dumb luck once again," he said wearily. "I went up to the concierge desk to ask if they had an extra charger for my phone, and I even offered my credit card to pay for the thing. The guy looked at my card and remembered me."

"You know the concierge here?" I was duly impressed.

"Not really. But he knows the chefs at all the important restaurants in town. It's his job. He sent one of their guests over the other night, without a reservation, and Carlotta gave the guy a good table. So he's giving us a room."

"But they told you they were sold out."

"They always hold a few rooms back for emergencies. He swears this is the last one left in the joint."

The elevator doors slid open, and we were on the hotel's top floor.

"The penthouse? We're staying in the penthouse at the Plaza?"

"Don't get yourself too worked up," Daniel warned. "The concierge said it's actually a maid's room."

I trailed behind him down the long carpeted hallway. He stopped before a narrow door marked "Hotel Staff."

"Wow. The maids in this hotel must all have been Munchkins," I said, edging into the room behind Daniel. "Not that I'm complaining," I added hastily. "I'm just grateful to have a room and a bed."

The bed, a double, was tucked under the sharply sloped ceiling and took up most of the windowless room. There was a nightstand on one side of the bed, and a battered painted dresser that held a seventies-era television. Daniel opened a narrow door. "There's a bathroom," he reported. "Kinda."

I looked over his shoulder and saw an old-fashioned cast-iron claw-foot tub, a high-backed commode, and a sink smaller than the one in Daniel's apartment.

"A tub," I said wearily. "An honest-to-God tub."

He reached into the jacket of his pocket and handed me a small zippered bag. "The desk clerk gave me this when he saw that we were stranded. Toothbrushes, toothpaste, soap, shampoo. A razor for me."

"Excuse me," I said, inching the door shut. "I think I have an appointment with this tub."


The water was hot and the soap was some lovely scented stuff, and I laid back in the tub and soaked and felt the day's tensions ebbing from my bones.

The bathroom door opened. Daniel stood there, wearing nothing but a smile.

"Got room for me?"

# Chapter 27

✴

At some point I became aware of a persistent ringing from somewhere close by. I sat up in bed, totally disoriented. The room was pitch black. The ringing seemed to be coming from the other side of the bed.

I lunged across my sleeping fiancée and scrabbled around in the dark for the phone. It kept ringing, but I couldn't find it. I finally climbed over Daniel, turned on the lamp, and saw that my cell phone had fallen on the floor.

"Hello?" I was out of breath.

"Weezie!"

Crap. It was Mama.

"Where are you?" she demanded. "I have been frantic with worry. They're saying it's the biggest blizzard of the decade up there in New York, and that the airports are all snowed in. That can't be right, can it?"

I climbed back off Daniel's back. He was motionless in the bed. I looked around the room, but there was no clock, and with no window, I had no idea whether it was day or night. "What time is it?" I asked.

"It's seven o'clock in the morning. I would have called earlier, but your daddy said you'd be fine and to stop worrying."

"I am fine. Daddy's right. Stop worrying."

"So you're at the airport right now?"

"Not exactly," I admitted. "To tell you the truth, I was asleep."

"How can you sleep at a time like this?" Mama wailed.

"I was tired." There was no way I was going to share with her that Daniel and I were stranded at the Plaza with no luggage—and no way to leave.

"Well, what time are you heading to the airport?" she asked. "I thought you were supposed to be home by noon today. There's still so much to do for the wedding, I'm just frantic with worry."

I yawned widely. "Last night they were saying all of today's flights would probably be delayed. I was sound asleep when you called. I'll call the airline and then I'll call you back."

After I'd disconnected the phone, Daniel rolled onto his side and kissed my nose.

"That was nice last night," he said softly.

"Very nice. We should get stranded in a blizzard more often."

"Just as long as it's at the Plaza, with room service," he agreed.

"I've gotta call the airline and see about getting home," I said regretfully. "Otherwise, Mama is totally going to fall to pieces. You won't really have to work today, right? You can try to come home on the same flight as me?"

"If there are any flights leaving LaGuardia, yes, I'll try to fly home with you," he agreed. "Can't have Marian falling all to pieces this close to Christmas."

He sat up in bed, grabbed the remote, and switched on the television, flipping channels until we found the *Today* show, with Al Roker standing in front of an enormous snowdrift and dressed in a fur-lined parka that made him look like Nanook of the North.

Al was holding a yardstick stuck in the drift, and only a couple inches of the stick protruded. "Record snows for New York City and surrounding areas," he said, sounding absolutely delighted at the news. "Although the snow ceased around one this morning, officials at LaGuardia, JFK, and Newark airports have said flights can't resume until plows get all the runways cleared."

Daniel went downstairs to check on traffic conditions while I got dressed. He came back to the room with two cups of coffee, two toasted whole wheat bagels, and some moderately good news.

"The doorman says most of the streets have been cleared and we should be able to get a cab. I called Carlotta and told her I was going to try and fly home with you this morning, and she agreed that makes sense."

He paused and then sat down on the bed beside me. "I also told her I won't be coming back."

My eyes widened and I put my coffee down on the nightstand. "You did?"

"Yeah. It's a great opportunity, I know, and maybe I'm crazy to turn it down, but this week made me realize I'll never really be happy working for somebody else again. I miss Guale. I miss driving my own damn truck and going where I want, when I want. New York's fun. It's exciting and I learned a hell of a lot working for Carlotta, but this isn't the life I want for us."

"It's not?"

"Not unless you do," he said. "Do you?"

"No." I took a sip of the coffee. They had great coffee at the Plaza.

"Savannah's home. I guess it always will be. I'm like you. I'll never be happy working for somebody else after running my own shop. My family's there. Your family's there. BeBe and Harry are there, and I can't wait for their baby to get born. And Mama? She's a major pain in my butt, but she needs me, Daniel. She's not gonna be able to deal with Daddy and his . . . issues by herself."

"I get that," he said. He pulled me to my feet.

"C'mon, Weezie Foley, let's get on home and get ourselves hitched."

# Chapter 28

## BeBe

Saturday morning, I unlocked the door of the Breeze Inn unit we'd been using as storage for all the furniture destined for the new house. I'd spent the previous night alone, secretly glad when Harry called to ask how I felt about him staying out overnight with his charter client. I still wasn't getting a lot of rest, and there was no sense in both of us having a sleepless night. Besides, I had plans for today, plans he probably wouldn't endorse.

"If the fish are biting, you should stay out there fishing," I'd assured him. "I'm fine. The checkup with Michael was good, nothing exciting to report, except he was bitching at me to take it easy. Which I did. The boys and I had pizza for dinner, then sat by the fireplace and totally vegged out last night."

It wasn't really a lie, not telling him about my elevated blood pressure—more like a tiny little sin of omission. No need for him to worry.

"The boys?" Harry sounded confused.

"Jeeves and Jethro. They're best friends now. Jeeves stays on what's left of my lap; Jethro has commandeered the spot under the coffee table. All I ask is that you call me when you're on the way home tomorrow. Don't forget, we've got Weezie's wedding tomorrow, and I'm sure she'll have a bunch of errands she needs me to run."

"I'll be home before dark," Harry promised. "Take care of yourself—and do what Michael says. Just take it easy, BeBe. I know you're antsy to get the nursery set up, but I can start moving furniture over to the house tomorrow morning, no problem."

I really did mean to take it easy and follow the doctor's orders. But I'd been obsessing about the nursery for days now. Every time the baby kicked, it was a reminder that time was running out. Hadn't Michael warned me first babies come when they want?

What was the harm in moving a few light items over to the nursery? I could hang some pictures, put down the rug, no heavy lifting neces- sary. Now I eyed the white Jenny Lind crib longingly, running my fin- gers over the satin finish on the headboard, but I knew that even if I managed to get it out of the room, there was no way I could lug it up the stairs by myself.

Just then I heard a loud banging and chugging noise coming from the construction site. I knew that racket. It was Benny the tile guy, driv- ing up in his rattletrap 1970s Vista Cruiser station wagon. Benny was scrawny-looking, but looks could be deceiving. All week I'd watched him effortlessly toting fifty-pound sacks of mortar mix and heavy boxes of tile up and down the stairs of the new house.

I met him out in the parking lot. "Good morning, Benny," I said, treating him to my most Madonna-and-child smile. "Is that the replacement penny tile for the guest bath?"

"Yes ma'am." He blushed and looked away. "I feel pretty bad about that mistake."

"No need for more apologies. But if you wanted to make it up to me, I could use one little favor before you get started with the tiling . . ."

By lunchtime, we'd gotten all the furniture in place in the nursery. And when I say we, I mean, he. As in Benny. The crib was set up, the dresser and bookshelf were in place, the antique toy box Weezie had found at an estate sale was in a corner, and the wicker rocking chair and hassock that had been another gift from her was placed near the window.

I'd even managed to sweet-talk Benny into hanging my curtain rods and toting over all the cartons of children's books and toys I'd been hoarding.

"Is that all?" Benny whined. "I really need to get to my tiling. I promised my old lady, I mean, my wife, I'd be back this afternoon to put up our Christmas tree."

"That is absolutely all. For now." I thanked him and shooed him back to his tile chores. I sat in the rocker and admired our handiwork. It would all be perfect—if I just had those drapes hung. And the bedding for the crib. I knew Marian Foley had finished sewing weeks ago and handed everything off to Weezie.

My cell phone rang. Providence was with me again. It was Weezie.

"Hey. How's the snow?" I asked. "I saw about the storm on the news last night. Are you guys going to make it home in time?"

"The snow was . . . epic, to say the least. Everything was delayed, but my flight should leave in a couple hours or so," Weezie reported. "And hopefully, the Atlanta layover won't take too long. Not sure about Daniel's. You know he wasn't supposed to fly home until late tonight, but he's on standby for an earlier flight. It's pretty crazy up here. How are things down there?"

"Weather-wise, we're good. I can't believe it's nearly Christmas. Harry stayed out fishing with a charter client last night, the weather is so calm."

Weezie lowered her voice. "Any news about Richard? Did you manage to track him down?"

"Actually, yes. He's dead, Weezie. He died not long after he got out of prison."

"So . . . that makes you a widow, right? Not a bigamist?"

"Exactly."

She giggled a little, and then stopped herself. "I'm sorry. I know he was your husband. I guess I should have a little more respect for the dead."

"Not on my account," I assured her.

"How exactly did you figure this out?"

"Long story. I'll fill you in when you get home. Your uncle James was a big help. By the way, Harry knows about everything. And he doesn't care. About any of it. Huge relief."

"So glad," Weezie said. "What about little Squirt? Any news on that front?"

"Squirt's good, although Michael Garbutt says the li'l bugger might be here earlier than anticipated. Which is fine by me. I am fed up with being pregnant."

"Early?" She yelped. "How early? Not, like, tomorrow early, right?"

"Relax. Maybe in a couple of weeks, he said. Or not even."

"Thank God for that. Listen, BeBe. Can you do me a huge favor?"

"Anything."

"Can you run into town and check on the wedding preparations? Maybe drop by the house and see if Cookie and Manny have everything under control, then see what Mama needs help with? She's got herself worked into a state about all this wedding stuff. She's been calling me every hour on the hour. I swear, her nervous breakdown is giving me a nervous breakdown."

"I was going to call you anyway. I ambushed the tile guy and made him move all the furniture into the nursery, and I'm about to bust a gut to get the curtains hung and the crib made up with all the bedding your mama made. It's all at your house, right?"

"You can't be hanging curtains in your condition," Weezie said. "Just wait till I get home, and we'll get it all put together."

"You're getting married tomorrow, remember? Anyway, I'm not gonna hang the curtains. Benny is. He just doesn't know it yet."

* * *

"Uh-oh." I glanced over at Jethro, who was sitting in the front seat of my car. I wasn't taking any more chances leaving him home alone with Jeeves. The street in front of Weezie's row house was lined with delivery trucks, caterer's trucks, even—yes, I had to blink to be sure, a landscaper's truck with a pair of ten-foot blooming dogwood trees lashed in the truck bed.

I backed up and drove down the lane, double-parking in back of the sedate silver Buick I recognized as Marian Foley's.

Using my key, I let myself in Weezie's kitchen door. Where I found Marian Foley perched on top of a kitchen chair, ransacking the upper kitchen cabinets. Lined up against the wall were cases and cases of wine, champagne, and liquor. Every countertop held wooden crates of rental glassware and gold-rimmed dishes. The counters were lined with gleaming pieces of newly polished silver serving pieces.

"BeBe! Thank goodness. Do you know where Weezie keeps her cake plates? I know she has her meemaw's plate, which I gave her, but I can't find anything in this kitchen of hers."

Hearing Marian's voice, Jethro slunk quietly under the kitchen table.

"Hi, Marian. I think she keeps cake plates in the Welsh cupboard in the dining room. I'll get it for you, if you like."

By the time she clambered down from the ladder, Marian's face was pink with aggravation, excitement, or stress—or maybe a combination of all three. The shade of her complexion matched the tidy rows of hot pink rollers in her hair, which clashed somewhat with her blue-and-white Frosty the Snowman Christmas cardigan.

She sized me up and down. "Dear, should you be driving around in your condition?"

"I'm fine," I said, making an effort not to grit my teeth. Marian Foley had that effect on me. "I thought I'd just drop by to see how things are coming along with the wedding plans. Weezie said she'll be home in a few hours. Is there anything I can do to help in the meantime?"

"I doubt it," Marian said with a sigh. "I've finished altering her wedding dress, except for the hem, but Lord knows whether or not it will fit."

"I'm about Weezie's size. We could see how it looks on me," I offered.

"I don't think so. Big as you are, you couldn't get that dress on over your ankles, let alone the rest of you."

"I meant we could hold it up to me to check for the hem-length," I said, clenching and unclenching my fists.

"Well, I suppose that could work," she said, clearly unconvinced.

The dress, a froth of ivory lace with a flared tulle skirt, was hanging on the pantry door. Marian had me stand on an old wooden Coke crate, with the dress held up against my front, doing a slow turn, while she checked the length.

"Say, Marian. I saw all those trucks out front of the house when I drove up. What's going on with all that?" I asked.

"It's those Babalu boys," she said, clucking her disapproval. "I knew Weezie shouldn't have put them in charge." She lowered her voice. "You have never seen anything like it."

* * *

For once, I found myself in total agreement with Marian Foley.

When I pushed through the kitchen door into the dining room, I nearly collided with Cookie Parker, who was bent over a makeshift worktable, cutting what looked like lengths of pale gray silk fabric.

I looked around the room. Weezie's expensive vintage wallpaper was now covered with the silver fabric. The ceiling was also tented in the fabric. There were other changes too. Tall plaster columns stood in each corner of the room, topped with gigantic urns filled with cloudbursts of white hydrangeas, orchids, ferns, and lilies. Ropes of ivy dotted with more white and pink flowers swagged out from the urns to the center of the ceiling. The dining room table had been shoved aside, and a workman in a white jumpsuit was hanging the biggest, gaudiest chandelier I had ever seen, in place of Weezie's perfectly respectable 1920s-era rock crystal chandelier.

"Oh my."

Cookie turned and beamed at me. "I know. Isn't it spectacular? Won't she be surprised?"

"Shocked," I said, walking through to the parlor. The front door was open, and Manny Alvarez, dressed in another white jumpsuit, was directing two burly men, who were trying to wedge a heavily lacquered white baby grand piano through the entry. I watched as he coached and bullied the men into placing it at a precise angle between the front windows. Which were now draped with more of the silver silk from the dining room.

Manny stood with his hands on his hips, surveying his handiwork. "What do you think?" he asked, turning to me.

"I'm speechless," I finally said. "Really. I have no words."

"Magical," he said with a happy sigh. "Just magical."

Most of the furniture in the parlor was gone. In the corner opposite the piano, a ceiling-height white-flocked Christmas tree held pride of place. It was draped in ropes of pearls and white lights, and the only ornaments were gigantic live white orchids. The floor had been stripped of its oriental rug. More plaster columns had been placed in front of the fireplace. These were wound with flower-twined ropes of ivy, smilax, and white roses. A white silk tent-looking affair stretched between the columns, and a miniature version of the dining room chandelier hung from the center of it.

"Is that a chuppah?" I asked, pointing to the tent thingy.

"It's a canopy," he said.

"That's good," I said. "Because neither Weezie nor Daniel are Jewish."

"We *know* that," Manny said.

I glanced out the open front door. "Are those giant dogwood trees in the truck out front for the wedding?"

"Yes," he said, his tone getting a little tense. "But they're not *Jewish dogwoods*. Just ordinary secular pink dogwoods. We're going to wind tiny white fairy lights around the trunks, and they're going on either side of the front door."

"Sounds magical," I said, beating a retreat back to the dining room. I managed to dodge Cookie and the electrician, and I fetched the cake plate from the bottom shelf of the Welsh cupboard.

\* \* \*

Marian had set up a sewing machine on Weezie's country pine kitchen table. She was running the dress through it now, straight pins clenched between her teeth. Weezie's daddy sat on the chair opposite her mama, his head tilted back, his mouth slightly ajar, softly snoring.

"I see you've got the dress almost finished," I said. "Is there anything else I can do?"

"As a matter of fact, you could carry in my groom's cake. It's in a big white box in the backseat of my car. But be careful and don't tilt it, or the top layer might come off."

I couldn't resist the temptation. I tipped back the lid of the box. The cake looked perfectly innocuous to me. Three layers high, baked in squares and covered in glossy chocolate icing.

"Here you go," I said, setting the box on the kitchen counter. "I took a peek. It looks gorgeous."

"I had to do something special. Because of Daniel being a chef and all. This is a new recipe I found on Pinterest."

"Really?"

"Oh yes. They have wonderful recipes on Pinterest. You should try it some time. This cake has had over a hundred pins."

"It must be good then."

"It's supposed to be very moist. It's made with six eggs, cocoa powder, all different kinds of dried fruits, and then, of course, the secret ingredient."

"Which is?"

"Baby food!" Marian whispered in a conspiratorial tone. "Two big jars of Gerber's pureed beets."

"Divine," I said, forcing a weak smile.

Later, after I'd retrieved the window treatments and crib bedding, and started the drive back to Tybee, I had to pull off the side of the road. The vision of a chocolate cake with pureed beets and dried fruits would probably haunt me forever.

# Chapter 29

✳

I placed the last of the picture books on the nursery's painted wooden shelf. The Dr. Seuss books I'd loved as a child had pride of place: *The Cat in the Hat, Horton Hears a Who, One Fish Two Fish*. Harry had contributed his own favorite books, most of which featured dogs or horses. And I'd bought a few new books too. My favorites were Mo Willem's *Don't Let the Pigeon Drive the Bus* and Anna Dewdney's *Llama Llama Red Pajama*.

When I was done with the bookshelves, I hung the matted and framed 1930s-era nursery rhyme prints Weezie'd given me, and fluffed and refluffed the crib bedding. By then, my lower back was starting to throb again. I sank down into the wicker rocker and draped Grandmama's baby quilt over my lap. Just a quick catnap, I promised myself. After all, it was four in the afternoon, and I'd been working hard all day.

Two hours later, I awoke to a perfectly still house. Benny the tile man and the electrician had packed up their tools and departed. It was dark outside, and from the window, I could see the flashing "No Vacancy" sign in front of the Breeze Inn. While I was sleeping, a hard rain had blown up out of nowhere, and the palm trees in the parking lot were thrashing back and forth in the stiff wind. By the time I made it over to the Breeze, I was soaked.

I changed into dry clothes and went to the kitchen to fix myself a cup of tea. My cell phone was right where I'd left it, on the kitchen counter. I'd missed a call from Harry at 4:30. But he'd left a voice mail.

"Hi, Babe. We're headed in from the snapper banks. Fishing was so good, we got a little later start than we'd expected. So don't wait supper for me. Go to bed, and I'll see you around eight."

Supper? I was still feeling a little queasy, but I forced myself to nibble on some saltines and eat a banana; then I settled myself on the sofa to wait for Harry's return. It was getting late and I was tired, but I couldn't wait to show him all I'd accomplished over at the house.

I clicked on the television, but nothing kept my interest. With the remote, I flipped idly through the channels. The wind had picked up more, and it whistled and moaned through the trees outside, making both the dogs uneasy. Jeeves planted himself on my feet and wouldn't budge, while Jethro did just the opposite, walking back and forth across the living room, to the kitchen, then back to the front door of the apartment. His ears pricked up every time a car parked.

When my phone rang at 7:30, I grabbed for it, dislodging Jeeves who yelped in protest.

"Hey," Weezie said. "Just wanted to let you know I just landed in Savannah."

"Great," I said, staring out the window at the parking lot, hoping to see Harry pull in. I saw headlights, but then saw a car back out and continue down the road.

"You okay?" Weezie asked.

"Fine. A little tired. I might have overdone it with the nursery today. I'm waiting on Harry to get home so I can show him everything before I collapse in bed."

"He's still at work? On a Saturday?"

"No, he's still out fishing. Remember, it's his last charter on the *Jitterbug.*"

"Right. But isn't it late to be out fishing?"

"He left me a message saying he'd be home around eight," I said, trying not to sound concerned.

"Okay. So—was everything all right at my house?"

"Hmm. Well, your mother finished altering your dress."

"Good."

"And she shared the secret ingredient for her groom's cake."

"Oh Lord. It can't be as bad as the maple syrup in the fruitcake."

"It's certainly healthier. Two jars of Gerber's pureed beets, to be exact."

Weezie made a rude gagging noise.

"I know."

"Did you check on Manny and Cookie? Had they started decorating the house?"

"Ohhh yes," I said. "It's quite a vision."

"Good vision or bad vision?" Weezie asked. "Gimme a hint."

"Manny thinks it's divine; Cookie said it was magical."

"And what did you think? Come on, be honest. I'll be home in twenty minutes. I need to know what to expect."

"Hmm. It's sort of hard to describe. I guess I'd say it was sorta . . . Auntie Mame on acid."

By nine o'clock, there was still no word from Harry. I tried calling his phone, but got no answer. The wind howled, and as I stood at the window, I could see flashes of lightning from off in the distance.

Stay calm, I told myself. No reason to panic. But I didn't feel calm. The dogs sensed my tension. Jethro stood at the door whining to go out, and Jeeves cowered under the coffee table.

By midnight I was flat-out terrified. I'd been watching the weather channel, which reported the same intense weather front that had dumped snow on New York was now wreaking havoc farther south. Seas of three to five feet, gale-force winds out of the northwest. Small-craft warnings.

I tried calling the marina to see if anybody had seen or heard from Harry. Half a dozen other charter boats ran out of Lazaretto Creek Marina, and all the captains knew each other and frequently communicated via their marine band radios. But the phone rang and rang, finally picking up and delivering a recorded message saying that the marina would be closed over the Christmas holidays.

My hands were shaking uncontrollably as I looked up the number for the Savannah Coast Guard.

The dispatcher's voice was crisp and efficient. "Coast Guard Station, Savannah. Is this an emergency?"

"I'm not sure," I said, trying to hold back my panic. "My partner, Harry Sorrentino, captain of the *Jitterbug*, was due back from a fishing trip hours ago. He's not answering his phone, and with this weather, I'm afraid something might have happened."

"Okay, ma'am. Tell me the specifics. What time did Captain Sorrentino leave, and where did he leave out of? Do you happen to know his exact destination? Were there other parties onboard?"

I told her what I knew, gave her the *Jitterbug*'s description and serial number and every other pertinent piece of information I could think of.

"We haven't had any distress calls from that area this evening," she said. "I'll speak to my commander and call you right back."

"Will you send somebody to look?" I asked, fighting back tears. "He's an experienced captain. He wouldn't stay out in this weather unless something was wrong. Please hurry."

After the longest forty-five minutes I'd ever experienced, the dispatcher called back.

"Okay, ma'am. We're dispatching a helicopter to fly over that area, and we'll send out a boat crew also. Do you happen to know if Captain Sorrentino has flares or a GPS onboard that he might activate?"

"Flares—yes! I know he always keeps up with all his safety equipment. He has a radio, of course, but wouldn't he have tried to reach me with that?"

"I can't say, ma'am," she replied. "Just stand by, and we'll let you know something as soon as we can."

# Chapter 30

✦

# Weezie

The Beverly Hills–style lit-up trees outside my Charlton Street front door were visible from two blocks away. If this was their idea of elegant and understated, I could only imagine what awaited inside.

I unlocked the front door and dropped my bags on the marble entry hall floor. The house was darkened, except for the twinkling lights of a Christmas tree in the parlor. I heaved a sigh of relief. Just some nice, simple white lights. Maybe BeBe had been exaggerating when she described the décor earlier.

I flipped the light switch in the parlor and felt my jaw drop.

Holy disco ball! My house looked like the inside of a drag queen's closet. Shiny silver drapes hung at all the windows. The parlor looked like an explosion of white and pink flowers, candles, orchids, pearls, and marabou feathers. Four dozen Louis XIV gilt ballroom chairs were lined up in rows in front of the fireplace, which was now flanked with flower-bedecked plaster columns. And was that a chuppah?

The dining room was just as bad. A chandelier I'd never seen before hung over my dining room table, which was covered with what looked like an acre of living green sod. Flowers spurted out from urns atop plaster columns.

I was almost afraid to see the kitchen. But here, at least, the boys hadn't decorated. They'd merely filled every horizontal surface with silver serving dishes, crates of wine and liquor, and more flowers. On the center of the kitchen island my cut-glass cake plate held Mama's three-layer chocolate cake. It looked pretty enough to taste. And I was starved. But then I remembered the "secret ingredient." Parked right next to the cake was a bottle of chilled Dom Pérignon in a silver champagne bucket. A note in Cookie's flowery handwriting was propped in front of it.

*Welcome home to our favorite bride!*

How could I stay mad at those two? Or at Mama?

I dragged my suitcase upstairs and collapsed into my own bed. Just before I drifted off to sleep it occurred to me that it was my last night as a single girl. And I was good with that.

# Chapter 31

✦

## BeBe

Jethro must have sensed my agitation. He shadowed my footsteps as I restlessly paced the small apartment, then, tiring of that, went to the front door and whined to go out.

I pulled on one of Harry's oversized rain slickers, slipped my cell phone into the pocket, and clipped a leash to Jethro's collar.

The rain had subsided, but the wind pushed at our backs as we worked our way down Butler Avenue. The neon signs of the Shell station and the liquor store were mirrored in the dark, wet street pavement.

Jethro tugged impatiently at the leash and I let him lead me across Butler, which was largely deserted. Winter at the beach is always a quiet time, but the beach, a couple of nights before Christmas, was especially solitary.

We turned down Tybrisa, and at a glance I saw that most of the souvenir shops and bars were closed. Except Doc's Bar, where the red "Open" sign blinked on and off.

Standing beneath the red and white awning I could hear laughter and voices from inside, and the strains of music drifted out on the cool night breeze. I peeked in the window and saw that the bar was decorated for Christmas, with gaudy red and gold strands of tinsel fluttering from the smoke-darkened rafters. The barmaid, a woman I didn't recognize, wore a jaunty fur Santa hat and leaned over the bar, deep in conversation with two grizzled regulars. Half a dozen other customers sat at tables and booths, and a lone couple, oblivious to everybody else in the room, necked at a table near the window.

Doc's was where I'd first met Harry. He was working as a bartender, his boat had been repossessed by his ex-wife, and he was living in the manager's unit at the Breeze, in exchange for acting as general manager and handyman.

Jethro stood and sniffed the nearby fire hydrant. We walked down to the end of the sidewalk and crossed over to the concrete municipal pier. At the end of the pier I stopped and stared out at the ocean. Off in the distance, I could see the lights of a huge oceangoing freighter as it glided toward the port. Waves crashed against the beach and the wind whipped my hair into my eyes.

Harry was out there somewhere, I knew. My fingers curled around the phone in my pocket, willing it to ring and bring me the news that he was safe.

At least it had stopped raining. And was I imagining things or had the wind died down—just a little?

I'd crossed Butler and was on my way back to the Breeze when I felt my phone vibrating in my pocket.

The caller ID screen read USCG.

"Hello?" I said hurriedly.

"This is Petty Officer Brawley," a male voice said. "Is this Ms. Loudermilk?"

"This is she. Do you have news for me? About Harry Sorrentino?"

"Ma'am, our helicopter spotted a vessel in some kind of distress in the approximate location you described, about eight miles out from the sea buoy. We don't know if it's the *Jitterbug* or who is on board, but the boat fits the description you gave us. I was asked to let you know that the passengers on that vessel have been transferred to the Coast Guard Cutter and the cutter is currently towing the disabled vessel back to the Coast Guard station."

"Are they all right? Were there two men on the boat? Can't you tell me any more than that?"

"Afraid not, ma'am," Brawley said. "We've had two more distress calls related to the storm tonight, and we're shorthanded. That's all the information I can give you."

"When can you tell me something?" I cried. "If they're on the cutter, can't you get somebody to ask their names? Please?"

There was a pause. "Ma'am? Stand by. When we have more facts, we will call you. Will you be at this number?"

"Yes. I'll be right here."

\* \* \*

I walked slowly down Butler Avenue, checking my phone every few steps to see if it was ringing. We were walking past St. Michael's Catholic Church when Jethro abruptly sat down on his haunches and refused to move. I jerked impatiently at the leash, but at that point he spread himself flat out on the wet sidewalk.

"Come on, Jethro," I coaxed. "We've stretched our legs. Let's go home where it's warm and dry and wait for some good news."

He sat up reluctantly, but when he started walking, it was toward the church entry instead of home.

"Wrong way," I muttered, but he pulled me along after him until we were standing in front of the church's big carved oak doors. A hanging lamp above the door was lit.

He pawed at the door.

"Oh, for Pete's sake," I muttered. "What is it? Do you smell a cat or something inside there?"

Just to humor him, I yanked at the door handle. I'd expected it to be locked. It was nearly two o'clock in the morning. It didn't occur to me that Doc's Bar and St. Michael's Church would be the only two Tybee establishments open at that hour.

But the door swung open, and the next thing I knew, Jethro was trotting down the main aisle of the church. I tried to pull him back, but being Weezie's dog, he had a mind of his own.

He didn't stop until we were directly in front of the altar, at which point, he plopped himself down onto the floor. I glanced around to see if we were alone. Did churches allow dogs? Especially Catholic churches?

I'd been raised Episcopalian, but hadn't been a regular churchgoer in many years.

Jethro seemed to feel right at home. He rested his brown muzzle on his front paws, and his tail swished contentedly.

"Okay," I relented. "We'll sit. For a little while. Until somebody shows up to chase us out."

I sat in the pew and looked around.

# Chapter 32

# Weezie

Something warm was tickling my ear. Somebody lifted the corner of my quilt, and I became vaguely aware of a body sliding in beside mine.

"Daniel!" I sat straight up in bed. "What do you think you're doing?"

"Getting in bed," he said, yawning. "My plane just landed an hour ago, and I'm beat."

"You can't sleep with me," I protested, giving him a shove.

"Since when?"

"Since we're getting married tomorrow. I'm the bride. You're the groom. You're not even supposed to lay eyes on me, let alone crawl into bed with me."

"Aw, Weezie," Daniel groused, pulling a pillow across his face. "Cut me some slack. I spent the last ten hours trying to get out of LaGuardia. I'm not interested in having sex with you—I just want some sleep."

"Not in my bed you're not," I said, pushing at his bare shoulder. "Come on, out. It's bad luck for you to see me before the wedding."

"That's the stupidest thing I ever heard of. Who came up with that bad luck bullshit? Your mother?"

"My mother has nothing to do with it," I retorted. "It's a well-known custom. Like something old and something new and a sixpence for your shoe."

"I never heard of any of that crap. Just pretend you don't see me. I swear, I won't look at you."

"You certainly won't, because you're not staying here tonight." I knelt on my side of the bed and shoved hard, and he slid right out and onto the floor.

He gave me a wounded look, but with a sigh he stood and pulled on his jeans.

I turned my back to him and pulled the quilt up to my shoulders. "Sweet dreams," I called.

"Bullshit," he muttered, stomping out of the bedroom and slamming the door behind.

# Chapter 33

✦

# BeBe

M s. Loudermilk? This is Petty Officer Brawley with Coast Guard Station Savannah."

"Yes?" I clutched the phone so tightly my knuckles were white. "Do you have news for me?"

"We've had word from our cutter that the vessel they have in tow is the *Jitterbug*."

"Thank God," I breathed. "And Harry?"

"Yes, ma'am, I've been authorized to tell you that Captain Sorrentino and his passenger, a Dr. Templeton, are on the cutter, and there are no medical issues."

"They're fine? No injuries? You're sure?"

"Yes, ma'am. Our communication with the cutter indicates that they will not need medical attention. Is there anything else I can do for you tonight, ma'am?"

"How soon? How soon will they be back?" It was after three now.

"We expect it within the hour," Brawley said. "Good night, ma'am."

Tears were streaming down my face. "Good night, Petty Officer Brawley. I can't thank you enough for calling. And Petty Officer?"

"Ma'am?"

"Merry Christmas."

It was four thirty in the morning when I heard the key turn in the lock. Jeeves and Jethro threw themselves at Harry's ankles as soon as he walked in. I managed a little more restraint, but only because I was too exhausted to do much more than sink my head against his chest.

"Thank God," I murmured. "Thank God."

By the time he got out of the shower and into dry clothes, I'd fixed him a hot toddy of Earl Grey tea, honey, and bourbon. He told me what had happened in between sips of tea.

"Around two this afternoon, we noticed the sky was starting to look a little ugly and the water was getting choppier. But the fish were biting like crazy, and we were having one of those days where it seems like every time you throw out a bait you reel in a keeper. Then the wind changed direction, and the temperature dropped—like twenty degrees in what seemed like just a few minutes. I heard radio chatter about that storm front moving down the coast, and I thought we ought to hightail it for home, but damned if Templeton just kept fishing.

"Finally, about four, I picked up the anchor, and we were heading in, but the seas were pretty high, and we had headwinds of twenty-five or thirty knots, maybe higher, beating us to death. We were three miles out, near the Savannah light. And all my electronics blanked out. They just quit. A wave came over the bow and knocked the engine down to idle speed. I was able to keep the boat pushed into the wind, but nothing more. Then my antenna snapped and the radio went before I could send out a mayday."

I shivered at the mention of the word "mayday."

"I knew something bad had gone wrong," I said quietly. "You promised to be home by dark. I knew you wouldn't deliberately break your promise. Not after last time."

He reached over and gave me a rough kiss, and the scratch of his day-old beard on my face reminded me that he was home. And alive. And all was well.

"I'm so sorry," Harry said. "I feel like such a shit. I should never have let Templeton talk me into taking him out. I'm done with fishing, BeBe. Swear to God, I'm done with it."

"I don't want you to quit fishing, Harry. What I want is for you to quit your day job. You think I don't know how much you hate it? For the past week, you leave here and you look like you're getting ready to go to jail. That's no way to live."

"Risking my life fishing in high seas—that's no way to live either."

"You've been running charters for how many years now?"

He shrugged. "Thirty. Round about."

"And have you ever had to be rescued by the Coast Guard before?"

"This was the first time. I've had close calls before, but this was the first time I ever really wondered if I'd get back to the dock in one piece."

"It was a freak storm, right?"

"Pretty much. I wouldn't have gone out as far as we did if I'd known what kind of weather we were heading into."

I thought about the *Jitterbug*, pitching and bucking in those high seas, seven miles offshore, and it made me shudder. I liked to fish with Harry, but I'd never enjoying deep-sea fishing.

"Is there any way you could change your charter business?" I asked.

He looked puzzled.

"The *Jitterbug* is a deep-sea boat. I get that. But it's so expensive— all the gas it takes to run six or seven miles offshore. Couldn't you just as easily fish inshore?"

"Not in the *Jitterbug*. I'd need a boat to fish the shallows, to get through the narrow creeks. Something smaller."

"Is there money in that?"

"Sure," Harry said. "Guys are getting interested in light tackle, fly-fishing. And it's not as much of a time commitment. There's definitely a market for inshore fishing around here."

"Nobody know these waters like you do," I said, entwining my fingers in his.

"That's true," he acknowledged.

"The inn is making money now," I said. "With the baby coming, it'd be good to have you around a little more—but not too much more. If you were fishing in-shore, I don't think I'd worry as much."

"It's a cheaper business model, that's for sure," Harry said. He raised our entwined hands and kissed the back of mine.

"It's a lot to think about," he said.

"We don't have to figure it all out tonight," I said. "Right now I just want us to enjoy what we have. Each other, the baby, the new house. That's enough for me. Actually, it's all I need."

"Me too," Harry said. He reached down and ruffled Jeeves's fur and scratched Jethro's ears. "I've got everything I need right here."

# Chapter 34

# Weezie

Sunday. My wedding day. I sat up in bed and gazed out at the clear blue sky beyond my third-floor window. The downtown church bells were chiming. Eleven o'clock already.

I could smell the coffee brewing by the time my feet hit the landing downstairs.

Cookie stood in the middle of the kitchen at the island. He was wearing elbow-length rubber gloves and an apron, and he was humming while he smeared polish on the outside of the largest sterling silver punch bowl I'd ever seen. It was the size of a birdbath.

"Good morning," I said, pulling up a stool to the island.

"Precious Weezie!" He planted a kiss on my cheek. "What time did you get in last night? We were starting to wonder if we'd have to start this wedding without the bride."

I helped myself to a mug of coffee and took a sip.

"Late," I said. "My one-hour layover in Atlanta turned into two and three, and then four hours. By the time I finally got on the plane, I could just as easily have rented a car and driven home."

"Poor girl."

"Poor Daniel. He got here around three, and I had to kick him out. He was not a happy camper."

"Bad luck for him to see you before the wedding," Cookie agreed. He paused in his polishing. "What did you think of our little decorating scheme?"

"Wowsers! I hate to come off like a Bridezilla, but I thought we had an agreement. Tasteful? Understated? Does any of that sound familiar to you?"

"Sweetie, we tried. Really we did. We sprinkled those little pathetic flowers around, and put your sad little white tablecloth on the dining room table . . . but it was just all so . . ."

"Appropriate?" I offered.

"Skimpy. Boring. So we added a few little flourishes."

I took another sip of coffee.

"I don't want to seem ungrateful, but I am a little sad about my dining room. That was a hand-blocked de Gournay wallpaper, you know. I saved up for years to buy the stuff."

"Whatever. Your silly period-appropriate wallpaper is just fine, dear girl. The silk is just tacked on top of it, and then I hot-glued gimp as a border. It can all come down in less than an hour, if that's what you really want."

"Thank you." I didn't want to think about all the tack holes he'd in-flicted on my wallpaper.

"Where's Manny this morning?"

He gave me a mysterious smile. "He had an errand to run. But don't you worry, he'll be back in plenty of time for the final fluffing."

More fluffing? How was that possible?

Mama called just as I was about to eat my toast.

"Oh, good. You're home. Did you try on the dress yet? I left it hang-ing in your closet."

"I just got up and I'm having breakfast. I'll try it on as soon as I'm finished."

"Don't eat too much now," Mama warned. "I don't have time to let out any seams today."

I crossed my eyes and shook my head. "Talk to you later."

"I'll be over in an hour or so," she said. "You know your daddy. He has to have his lunch at noon. Wedding or no wedding."

Mama bustled into the kitchen at two. She'd already worked herself into a state, and the wedding was still five hours off.

She set her sewing machine down on the counter without a word, then hurried back outside without another word. Five minutes later, she was back, trying to shoo Daddy through the door.

"Come on, Joe," she coaxed. "It's just Weezie right now. It's her wedding day." She turned to me. "Today, of all days, he's as mulish as I've ever known him. It took me forty minutes to talk him into putting on his suit. I was this close to leaving him at home."

I stepped outside and found Daddy sitting on the wrought-iron bench in my little courtyard garden. He'd picked a red camellia from the shrub by the gate, and he was twirling it by the stem, studying it intently.

"Hey, Daddy," I said, sitting down on the bench beside him. "How was lunch?"

He didn't look up. "Marian burned the grits. Forty years we've been married. Forty years of burned grits on Sundays."

I managed to stifle a giggle. He turned and flashed me a grin. "You won't burn Daniel's grits, will you?"

"No," I promised. "Because usually he cooks the grits. And I do the dishes."

He patted my hand. "Good girl."

He stood slowly, and it pained me to see his stooped shoulders and his shuffling gait as he made his way into the house.

Mama sat him at my pine kitchen table and handed him the Sunday paper. "Your crossword puzzle is inside."

He took a pencil from the breast pocket of his starched white dress shirt and began leafing through the *Savannah Morning News*, the same way he'd done every morning of my life.

"You sure look handsome today," I told him. He was wearing his good navy blue suit, a white shirt, and a red tie with a design of white snowflakes—Mama's doing, of course. He even had a red silk pocket square.

"Don't look at his shoes," Mama said, exasperated.

I did. He was wearing his favorite scuffed brown leather house shoes.

"I like these shoes," Daddy said, scribbling letters with his pencil. His wire-rimmed glasses were perched on the tip of his nose. "They don't pinch my toes like those black lace-ups."

"Those are slippers!" Mama said. "Who wears a navy suit and brown slippers to a wedding?"

"I do," Daddy said. "Nobody but you cares, Marian." He glanced up and gave me a loving smile. "Weezie's the only person anybody's going to look at today."

"And what about me?" Mama pretended to pout. "Don't I matter?"

She'd done her own hair, teasing it into a 1980s bouffant, and she was wearing a pink lace dress with long sleeves that fairly screamed Mother of the Bride. She was wearing her everyday white Keds over her Sunday-best suntan-tinted support hose, but I had no doubt that a pair of dyed pink heels were tucked into the enormous tote bag she'd placed on the counter.

"You look lovely, Mama," I said.

"Pretty as a picture," Daddy added, beaming over at us. "Both my girls."


I sucked in my breath and tugged at the side zipper on my wedding dress. Maybe I'd overdone it a little in New York. Finally I managed to get the balky metal zipper fastened. I tugged at the skirt and walked into the bedroom.

Mama's face fell. "I knew it. I just knew it. BeBe had me hold it up to her to check for the length, but with that big old baby belly of hers poking out, I couldn't really gauge properly." She plucked at the tulle skirt.

"It's miles too long on you."

I fanned out the skirt and looked down. The hem rested right above my ankles. Not exactly tea-length, but not necessarily an earth-shattering development either.

"It'll be fine. I'm wearing four-inch-high heels." I scrabbled in my closet, brought out the shoe box and slipped my feet into the creamy satin Jimmy Choo sandals I'd bought at an Atlanta consignment shop. Even secondhand, they'd cost $125, which I considered a huge splurge, but once I saw that they were my exact size, I had to have them. I laced the narrow satin ties around my ankles and struck a pose.

"See? Perfect."

"No." Mama shook her head. "Still too long. Take it off. It's a good thing I brought my seam ripper and my machine. I'll just have to take that skirt off and cut it down again."

"We don't have time for that," I protested. "It's nearly four o'clock. It's fine just the way it is."

She held out her hand and gave me the look. The warning look that told me that Marian Foley was still the final authority on matters such as this.

"Give me the dress," she ordered.

\* \* \*

Daddy was still in the kitchen, working on his crossword puzzle. Mama set up her sewing machine across from him, and was trying to rethread a bobbin. The back door flew open and two furry torpedoes launched themselves into the room.

Jethro bounded over, jumped up, and planted his muddy paws on my chest to give me an enthusiastic Milkbone-flavored slurp on the chin.

"Hey, Ro-Ro," I laughed, scratching his ears. "Did you miss me?"

"I'll say he did." BeBe leaned against the island. "I wasn't going to mention it—but he ran away twice while he was with me. The cops had to bring him home the other night. It got so bad I didn't dare leave him home alone with Jeeves."

"Ro-Ro!" I admonished. He slunk off to his customary spot under the kitchen table, where Jeeves had already taken up residence.

"Sorry about bringing them both," BeBe said. "But I really do think Jethro is suffering a little from separation anxiety. Jeeves started barking his head off when he saw me loading Jethro in the car. I was afraid my guests would start complaining about the racket. We can put them both out in the garden when the wedding starts."

"A wedding is no place for dogs. And neither is a house," Mama said with a sniff.

"Hi, Joe."

Daddy looked up and gave her a vague smile. I realized he couldn't remember her name. "Hi, Marian," BeBe said. "I love your pink dress. Very festive."

"Thank you. You look very nice too, BeBe. All things considered."

BeBe looked tired. Her blond curls were swept up into a loose topknot, but all the concealer and blusher in the world couldn't hide her pale skin and the dark circles under her eyes. She was wearing a bright turquoise maxi-dress with gold metallic banding at the V neckline and the cuffs and hem.

She made a face. "I think this would have been called a caftan in my mother's day. But I don't care. It meets all my maternity-wear requirements—doesn't bind or chafe, doesn't involve elastic, and best of all, doesn't require me to worry about shaving my legs, panty hose, or fancy shoes."

BeBe lifted the hem of her dress to show off her chic gold sandals.

"Love it!" I said.

"No panty hose? To an evening wedding?" Mama's shrug shouted her disapproval.

"Where's Harry?" I asked, looking toward the kitchen door, expecting to see him stride through at any moment. "Don't tell me he's still fishing."

"No, he finally made it home around four," BeBe said. "He got caught in that awful storm last night, they took a wave across the bow, one of the boat's engines quit, and then all his electronics quit working. I had to send the Coast Guard out looking for him. Worst night of my life. Ever."

"You poor thing," I cried. "You must have been out of your mind with worry."

"Totally crazed," she agreed. "But he's home, without a scratch on him. And that's all I care about. He was still sleeping when I got ready to leave. He'll be along later, after he goes to check on the boat."

\* \* \*

"There!" Mama snipped the thread and held out the wedding dress with a flourish. "Go try it on, Weezie."

"I can't right now. I've got to get my cake out of the freezer and get it frosted so the layers set up in time."

She pressed her lips tightly. "I'll just take it upstairs and hang it up until you do have time to try it on." She looked over at Daddy, who was still laboriously filling in blanks in his crossword puzzle.

"Joe, could you please take my sewing machine and put it out in the car?"

"Mmm-hmm." Daddy nodded pleasantly.

I got my grandmother's big milk-glass cake pedestal from the bottom shelf of the Welsh cupboard, then removed the wedding cake layers from the freezer, setting them on a waxed-paper-covered cookie sheet to thaw.

"Hand me that jar of lemon curd from the fridge, would you?" I asked BeBe.

In the meantime, I took the sticks of softened butter and cream cheese and put them in the KitchenAid's stainless-steel mixing bowl. I dumped in a large bag of confectioner's sugar, some lemon extract, and a dribble of half-and-half. I lowered the beaters and set the bowl whirring.

Daddy put the newspaper down and looked over at me. "What was it your mama asked me to do? Water the tomatoes? I just watered them yesterday."

BeBe shot me a startled glance.

"Never mind, Daddy. I'll put the sewing machine in the car. You just enjoy your paper."

After I got back inside, I handed BeBe an organically grown lemon and a zester. "Grate this peel into a small bowl, will you? And make the shavings as long and curly as you can. Think artistic."

When the icing was the right consistency, I set the largest, bottom cake layer on the pedestal, "gluing" it in place with a dab of frosting applied to the plate. Using a flat spatula, I spread a thin layer of frosting on the first layer, followed by a thicker coat of the lemon curd. Then I carefully placed the middle layer on top of the curd, centering the cake in the middle of the first layer.

The doorbell rang. "That must be Daniel's people from the restaurant, with the food. I'm gonna show them where to put everything in the dining room." BeBe followed right behind. "I'll help."

It took us a good thirty minutes to ferry all the foil-wrapped trays out of the Guale truck and into the house. Julio, Daniel's assistant manager, got busy transferring everything to the silver chafing dishes and trays that Cookie had arranged around the tabletop, while Hayley, one of the waitresses, started bringing the china and wineglasses from the kitchen to the sideboard.

When I got back to the kitchen, Daddy was staring intently down at his crossword puzzle. I picked up my spatula, ready to frost the second layer of my cake. But it was gone.

I looked around the countertop. "Daddy, do you know what happened to my cake?"

"No, shug," he said mildly. "Did you fix me a birthday cake? That's nice."

"Oh no." I bent down until I was at eye level with the two dogs cowering under the kitchen table.

Jethro had telltale smears of white frosting on his brown muzzle. Jeeves was in the process of barfing up what looked like a glob of homemade lemon curd.

"BeBe!" I screamed.


"What do we do now?" she asked. I'd just finished mopping the kitchen floor, after banishing both dogs to the courtyard garden.

"Not sure," I admitted, looking around the kitchen. The dogs had left two cake layers intact, but they were the two smallest top layers, only six and seven inches in diameter—not nearly enough to feed the forty people we were expecting.

"Well, all I can say is, thank goodness we have my groom's cake," Mama said. "Everybody loves chocolate cake."

"Yes, thank goodness," BeBe drawled.

"And I've got a surprise for you," Mama added. She reached into her tote bag and lifted out a small cardboard box. She plucked out the contents and placed it squarely in the middle of the groom's cake. "Ta-da!"

"How sweet," BeBe said.

It was a plastic bride and groom cake topper. The bride with orangish skin and a gown of crimped white crepe paper, the groom with a dark crew cut and a black tux. They stood under a heart-shaped arch fashioned from yellowing pipe cleaners.

"I made that myself in my crafts class when Joe and I got engaged," Mama said proudly.

"Wow."

My strictly unsentimental mother wiped away what looked suspiciously like a tear. She had never saved any of my baby clothes or my childhood toys, but she'd saved this one memento of her own wedding forty-some years ago.

"I love it," I said. And I did.

While Mama was interfering with the restaurant people, I snuck upstairs and put in an SOS call to Uncle James.

"Jonathan and I are on our way over right now," he said. "Is your mother driving you crazy? John's offered to sedate her iced tea with one of his mother's chill pills."

"Yes, she's driving me crazy. But no, I don't guess you should slip her a mickey," I said reluctantly. "But I do have another emergency. Can you run over to the Publix and pick me up some kind of a cake from their bakery?"

"You want a store-bought cake? I thought you baked your own cake."

"Jethro and Jeeves ate most of my cake. Just get me the biggest cake they have. It doesn't matter what it looks like. Yellow would be best, but I can't be picky at this point."

\* \* \*

"Shouldn't you be getting dressed?" BeBe glanced at the kitchen clock. "It's nearly six."

"In a minute," I replied. "You're sure Mama's not coming?"

"The coast is clear. John's mom has got her in the den, and your mama is talking her ear off about her Pinterest boards."

"Good." I opened the cardboard bakery box and quickly sliced the sheet cake into quarters. With my spatula, I proceeded to wipe away the thick blue-tinted commercial frosting, along with the flowery orange "Happy Birthday Bubba" piped writing.

I put the first quarter on the milk glass pedestal, iced the now-nearly naked cake with my own cream cheese frosting, spooned on a thin layer of lemon curd, and placed the second layer on top of that. I followed up with the third and fourth layers.

"Genius!" BeBe said. "Nobody would ever guess you didn't bake that." She glanced over at the groom's cake. "Think your mama will be mad that you out-caked her?"

"Probably," I said.

"What goes on the top?" BeBe asked. "It does look a little naked."

"I know," I said. "I kept looking for just the right vintage topper while I was in New York, but the junking up there was pretty slim pickings."

"You didn't buy a single thing?"

"Just some vintage Christmas ornaments..." A thought popped into my head.

I ran upstairs and was back five minutes later with the pink hatbox.

"What's all that?" BeBe leaned in to look.

I plucked the pastel bottle-brush trees from their tissue wrapping and planted a small grove of them on top of the cake.

"Ohhhh," she breathed.

Digging around in the layers of tissue, I finally found one of the vintage mercury glass Christmas tree decorations. It was the largest of the church ornaments, the only one that still had an intact steeple. I pressed it firmly into place in the frosting, then stepped back to admire the effect.

"Absolutely the perfect thing," BeBe exclaimed. "Are you sure you didn't plan this, Weezie Foley?"

"Trust me. I planned nothing that has happened today." The doorbell rang. She gave me a gentle push. "Go. Get dressed. I think your wedding guests are starting to arrive."

# Chapter 35

✳

# BeBe

"Okay," Weezie said. "I think I'm ready."

But Marian was still fussing, plucking at nonexistent stray threads on the dress, tugging the bodice up, and the hem down.

"Mama," Weezie said sharply. "I love you, and I love the dress. But if you touch me one more time, I cannot be responsible for my actions."

"Honestly," Marian said. "That's the thanks I get for working my fingers to the bone. If I had talked to my mother like that on my wedding day . . ."

"Mama?"

This time Marian got the message. She headed for the doorway of Weezie's bedroom. "I'm going to go downstairs and try one more time to get Joe to put on his good shoes."

When she was gone, Weezie sat down at her dressing table and opened the bottom drawer. She took out a small silver flask and took a long swig.

"Bourbon?" I said longingly. I held out my hand, took the flask, and inhaled sharply.

"God, I miss this stuff."

Weezie took the flask back and took one last swig before capping it and returning it to the drawer. She reapplied her lipstick, then stood up and fluffed her skirt.

"Now I really am ready," she announced.

"You look amazing," I told her. "Like something out of a fairy tale. And I'm not just saying this because you're my best friend, but you truly are the most beautiful bride I've ever seen."

"I can't believe this day is finally here," Weezie said. "But I keep feeling like I'm forgetting something."

"Not the groom. I saw Daniel and Harry pull up in Harry's truck half an hour ago. You've got your something old and something new, right?"

She nodded. "Mama's dress is the old. The borrowed are your pearl drop earrings and the bra and panties set you gave me are the new. Although I can't believe you spent two hundred fifty dollars for two pieces of lace that tiny."

"That's what maids of honor do," I said. "You wouldn't believe the amount of vicarious pleasure I got shopping for sexy lingerie. Not after I had to go buy nursing bras. Ugh!"

"You'll be back to your old size in no time," Weezie said.

"What about your something blue?" I asked.

"That's it!" she said, snapping her fingers. She scrabbled around in her jewelry box, finally bringing out a small blue rhinestone brooch in the shape of a Christmas tree.

"Is this the one you bought the year you and Daniel got engaged?" I asked, pinning it to her satin waistband.

"No," she said quietly. "This was his mom's. Daniel found it with her things after she passed away last year. Paula didn't have a lot, you know, but it really touched him that she'd kept it for all those years after he and his brother saved up to buy it for her the first Christmas after their daddy left."

We heard the sharp tap of high heels from the hall outside. The bedroom door opened, and Marian stuck her head inside. "Weezie! It is ten after seven and we have a house full of people downstairs wondering if you've changed your mind about getting married. For goodness sake, young lady, stop dawdling!"


The first person I saw when I walked into the parlor was Harry. He was standing in front of the fireplace beside Daniel, dressed in his new charcoal suit, with a silver tie that matched Daniel's and a small orange blossom boutonniere. His graying hair curled just the tiniest bit over his collar. His deep fisherman's tan was a sharp contrast to the crisp white dress shirt. He was clean-shaven, and when he looked up and saw me walk slowly into the room, his face broke into a broad smile that I knew was meant for me and me only.

Just a smile, but it literally made my heart flutter.

Cookie Parker was seated at a glossy white baby grand piano, and Manny was standing beside him, with a violin. They were playing Pachelbel's Canon in D. But when Manny caught sight of me standing in the parlor doorway, he gave Cookie a subtle nod, and they segued into "Moon River," which I knew Weezie had chosen because the composer, Johnny Mercer, was from Savannah.

I turned my head ever so slightly, and Weezie nodded. She tucked her arm through her daddy's.

The music swelled, and I made my way slowly toward the makeshift altar, where Daniel and Harry stood to the left of James Foley, decked out in a navy pin-striped suit—but no necktie, not even for his favorite niece.

The room was filled with so many familiar faces, all of them turned to see the radiant bride gliding toward her future.

Finally I reached the altar. I turned. Weezie handed me her bouquet, and I planted a quick, impulsive kiss on her cheek before stepping to the right.

Joe Foley seemed reluctant to release his only daughter's arm. He looked uncertainly at his brother. "Hi, Joe," James whispered. "Good job."

"Daddy?" Weezie whispered. "It's time."

But Joe was not about to be hurried. With a trembling hand, he caressed the bride's face.

"You are every bit as beautiful today as your mama was when she wore this dress."

"Oh, Daddy," Weezie whispered. "Thank you."

"Be happy, baby girl. You hear?"

He turned to Daniel. "You make her happy, son. Every day."

Daniel reached out and shook Joe's hand. "Thank you, sir. I will. I promise."

Joe gave me a wink. "She got it right this time, didn't she?"

"She sure did," I whispered.

Weezie and Daniel stepped under Cookie's not-really-Jewish canopy/chuppah, and I broke tradition and stood beside Harry, twining my fingers between his. He gave my hand a squeeze.


"Who gives this woman in marriage?" James asked.

Joe Foley stared blankly at his brother. Weezie nudged him gently.

"Oh. Oh, I do. Marian does too," Joe blurted.

Laughter rippled from the front seats.

From there, the ceremony proceeded as weddings do. But my attention had wandered. I was busy looking out at the group arrayed around Weezie's parlor.

Joe had seated himself in the front row beside Marian. She was clinging to him and weeping, and he was patting her back. James's partner, Jonathan McDowell, sat at the end of the Foley family row with his mother, Miss Sudie, and Jon was beaming with happiness for his partner's favorite niece.

I glanced toward the back and saw that Manny had joined Cookie on the piano bench and they were holding hands.

My own grandparents, Spencer and Lorena, had announced that they had no intention of missing my best friend's wedding, even though

Granddaddy looked the frailest I'd ever seen him, and was wearing a small oxygen mask. Grandmama sat right beside him on the stiff gilded chair, her hand tucked into his elbow.

My back was killing me, and I was suddenly feeling dizzy. I leaned slightly against Harry, and his arm crept around my waist, his hand resting lightly on top of my belly. Suddenly it all felt so right. Harry and I, standing in this room, two more links in a circle of love that radiated out from Weezie and Daniel.

"Jean Eloise Foley, do you take this man, Daniel Thomas Stipanek, to be your lawfully wedded husband?" James asked.

The baby kicked me hard. Harry pressed his hand against the sensation, and the baby kicked back. "I felt it," he whispered, turning to me.

"I do," Weezie said firmly.

"And Daniel Thomas Stipanek, do you take Jean Eloise to be your wife?"

"I do," Daniel said.

Something came over me. I clamped my hand over Harry's. "I do too."

"Really?" Harry looked astonished.

"Really," I assured him.

"Time to cut the cake," Cookie announced. He handed Weezie a beribboned sterling silver cake knife and led her back to the dining room.

I'd been sitting throughout most of the reception. I was tired and too nauseous to eat anything. I nudged Harry in the side. "Look at that."

"The cake? Do you want some?"

"God no. I mean, look at it. Weezie had to slap it together at the last minute from a bakery cake because Jethro and Jeeves ate her cake. All the stuff on the top, the little church and the Christmas trees, those are vintage Weezie. But that cake topper, that was Marian's. She must have stuck it on top of Weezie's wedding cake."

"What's wrong with the chocolate cake?" Harry asked. He did love chocolate.

"That's Weezie's mom's cake. It's a shame the dogs didn't attack that one."

"Jeeves is pretty particular about his chow," Harry pointed out.

We stood up and joined the crowd about to watch Weezie and Daniel cut the ceremonial first slice of wedding cake.

Harry was snapping pictures of Weezie and Daniel, and Weezie and her parents, and me and Weezie with my cell phone when I gasped and grabbed the back of a dining room chair.

"It's time," I said, feeling my face flush.

"What?" Weezie asked.

"Now," I repeated.

Harry looked from Weezie to me and frowned. "Now? You want to announce our engagement now?"

"Your engagement!" Weezie cried. "You're getting married? When did this happen?"

"Now," I repeated. "Right now."

"Uh, BeBe," Harry said uneasily. "You don't want to steal Weezie's thunder. This is her and Daniel's big day. We can announce our wedding date later."

"Now!" I said it as loud as I could. "Get the car right now and stop arguing with me. I think my water just burst!"

# Epilogue

＊

## BeBe

Five hours after we arrived at the hospital, Michael Garbutt sauntered into the delivery room at St. Joe's/Candler wearing a big blue shower cap and surgical gown and mask. He barely noticed me, instead giving Harry a hearty slap on the back.

"Man, I was just about to sit down to dinner with the whole family when the answering service called to tell me you were on the way here."

"Sorry to interrupt your Christmas Eve," Harry said, glancing down at me.

"Hey, it's all good. I'll take any excuse to get away from the in-laws," Michael said. Finally he looked down at me.

"How you doing, Mama?"

I was limp and sweaty and exhausted. I'd been in hard labor for what felt like an eternity. How did he think I was doing?

"I'm okay," I mumbled.

"The contractions are coming pretty close together," Harry volunteered.

"She's fully dilated," the delivery nurse said.

"All righty then," Michael said, gleefully rubbing his hands together. "Let's go get ourselves a baby!"


"Oh, oh, oh, ohhhh," Michael said softly. He held up the baby for me to see. "Lookie here," he crooned. "Looks like you and Harry got yourself a little cadet."

He was cherry red, with tufts of dark hair plastered to his still-damp scalp, and his face was scrunched into a scowl so like his father's I burst out laughing.

The nurse took him then, and did the things they do with newborn babies, and then they handed our son back to me, and he was wrapped up in what looked like a big red flannel Christmas stocking, with a soft candy-cane striped cap on his head.

Michael shook Harry's hand and offered him a cigar. Then the nurse dimmed the lights in the room, and we were left all alone.

I looked up at Harry, who was perched gingerly on the edge of the bed. He was blinking back tears. "Isn't he beautiful?"

"Boys aren't beautiful," Harry said, trying to sound brusque. He put out his finger, and the baby wrapped a tiny wrinkled hand around it.

"This one is. He's absolutely the most beautiful, perfect baby ever."

"If you say so." Harry dropped a kiss on my forehead, and then one on the baby's. We sat quietly like that for a long time, admiring our son, who quickly dropped off to sleep.

"You want to hold him?" I held the baby out.

"Think it'll be okay? I don't want to wake him up."

"Take him," I said, smiling. "He'll have plenty of time to sleep."

I transferred him into Harry's arms, and the baby stirred for a moment, and then fell right back to sleep.

Harry stood up. "He's a sturdy little fella, " he said, hefting the bundle in his arms.

"At eight pounds, two ounces, he's more than sturdy. He's a chunk," I pointed out. "I don't even want to think about how big he'd have been if I went full term."

"He's long too," Harry observed. "Twenty-two inches? That's about the size of a nice red snapper.."

I yawned. "He's definitely a keeper. Don't you think?"

"You both are." Harry stretched out on the bed beside me, and I transferred the baby into the crook of my arm. "Did you mean what you said, back there at Weezie's?"

"What do you think?" I said teasingly.

"I think we better get married right quick, before you change your mind," Harry said. "What are you doing next Saturday?"

"It might take a little longer than that, just to get the legal stuff with Richard ironed out," I reminded him. "But yes, I want us to get married, and as soon as possible. Maybe James will give us a two-fer—a death certificate and a marriage license."

"That'll work," Harry said. He gazed down at the baby.

"What are we going to call this little guy? We haven't even really talked about it much, have we?"

"We talked about naming him for your father."

"No. Look at him. He doesn't look anything like a Louis."

"You're right. How about my dad?"

"Arthur's a good, strong name," Harry allowed. "I kinda like it."

"But maybe not for a first name." I yawned again and looked at the clock. It was nearly one in the morning. It had been a very, very long couple of days.

"Hey," I said. "You know what? It's Christmas Day!"

"You're right." He kissed me on the lips. "Merry Christmas, BeBe. You just gave me the best gift any man ever got."

I felt just the tiniest bit smug about delivering a Christmas baby after all. And then I had an idea. I looked down at the baby, whose rosebud lips twitched just a little as he hiccupped in his sleep.

"What would you think about calling him Nicholas? Is that too gimmicky?" I crossed my fingers.

Harry grinned. "Nicholas? You mean, like St. Nick? Yeah. Nick! I had an Uncle Nick. He gave me my first Penn fishing reel when I was ten. Nicholas Arthur Sorrentino."

The baby stirred. His eyes opened wide. He made a faint mewing noise, and then, I swear, he smacked his lips.

I pushed down the neckline of my hospital gown and guided him into place, tickling the side of his cheek, the way the nurse had shown me earlier. He latched on to my breast, and a moment later, he was contentedly sucking away.

"He did it," I marveled. "First try. He's a genius!"

"Like his mama." Harry shifted in the bed, then drew a lumpy green-and-white-striped tissue packet from the pocket of his rumpled suit pants. He dropped it into my free hand. "I almost forgot."

"What's this?"

"Christmas present."

"Open it for me, please?"

He tore the tissue away, then held out a narrow filigreed platinum band with a round cushion-cut diamond surrounded by a galaxy of smaller stones.

For once, I was speechless.

"Weezie told me I should tell you it was a push present. You know, for having the baby. But it was never going to be that. In my mind, it was always going to be an engagement ring."

"Harry, it's beautiful!"

"It was my mom's. I could get you something more modern if you don't like this . . ."

"My fingers are kind of swollen," I told him, holding out my left hand. But he slipped the band onto my ring finger and it fit like it had been made for me.

"What made you change your mind? About getting married?" he asked.

"You did," I said simply. "I always loved you. Always. But I'd thought I'd been in love before. Too many times. Last night I knew this was different. We were different. I knew what we had was good and lasting. And then today, watching Weezie and Daniel, and my grandparents, even Joe and Marian Foley, it struck me—we have what they have. And they made it work. They made it last. Their marriages aren't perfect. Ours won't be either. But no matter what happens, I could never walk away from you. No matter what. You can be a fisherman or a farmer, or a, I don't know, a forest ranger. You're stuck with me, Harry Sorrentino. Forever."

"Okay." He offered me his hand. I hooked my little finger around his. "Forever. Pinkie swear."